D1090401

PAPER MOON

Center Point
Large Print

This Large Print Book carries the Seal of Approval of N.A.V.H.

PAPER MOON

LINDA WINDSOR

CENTER POINT PUBLISHING
THORNDIKE, MAINE

This Center Point Large Print edition
is published in the year 2005 by arrangement with
WestBow Press, a division of Thomas Nelson Publishers.

The text of this Large Print edition is unabridged. In other
aspects, this book may vary from the original edition. Printed in
Thailand. Set in 16-point Times New Roman type.

ISBN 1-58547-624-2

Library of Congress Cataloging-in-Publication Data

Windsor, Linda.
Paper moon / Linda Windsor.--Center Point large print ed.
p. cm.
ISBN 1-58547-624-2 (lib. bdg. : alk. paper)
1. Large type books. I. Title.

PS3573.I519P37 2005
813'.54--dc22

2005001272

CHAPTER 1

The high whine of a blow-dryer gnawed at Caroline Spencer's last nerve. Why on earth had she agreed to let Annie have her friend over for the night, when they all had to be at the airport by 5:00 a.m. for check-in? The girls, too wired with excitement to sleep, had giggled up to the sound of the alarm. Now they primped and preened and monopolized the bathroom, while Caroline fidgeted outside the door.

"Annie, honey, please hurry. I have to dry my hair," she called.

"Karen's in there," her daughter replied from behind her.

"Sorry, Miz C. Be right out," Karen called, cutting the dryer off.

"Mom, you don't have to dry your hair. That's the whole point of your new perm." Annie fluffed the wet ringlets of Caroline's red hair with her fingers. "That's why that old salon woman called it wash-and-wear."

"Stylist," Caroline corrected, feeling the ringlets rearrange themselves the moment her daughter let them be. "Old" salon woman indeed. "And Sally is just a few years older than I am."

"Whatever."

"Just what I need, a sixteen-year-old know-it-all at three in the morning. Besides"—Caroline yawned and recovered—"that's what the tag said about this shirt too, but guess who's been ironing while you gals scarfed down your breakfast burritos?"

The bathroom door flew open, revealing Annie's counterpart, her enviably dry shoulder-length hair pulled up in a ponytail with a sparkling band.

All those kilowatts, not to mention precious minutes, just for that?

"Oh, no, Miz C," Karen said, looking at Caroline's crisp safari-print top as though the cheetah on it had bared its teeth. "You've got to wear the T-shirt Señora Marron handed out." She cut her gaze to Annie. "Like, you did give it to her, didn't you?"

Annie smacked her palm to her forehead and spoke, preempting the snap of Caroline's one remaining nerve. "I totally forgot. I'll get it right now."

Lord, lead me not into this melodrama, Caroline thought as she followed the girls into her daughter's bedroom.

"Here ya go, Mom. The bigger one's yours."

Caroline stared at the neon orange garment in her hand.

"Oh my."

On the front was the Edenton Christian High School mascot perched on a banner that said "Go Eagles."

"What's the Spanish word for clash?" she asked.

"Mom, you will be totally cool, trust me . . . and everyone is wearing them."

"Well, we certainly won't lose anyone with these on," Caroline conceded. "Guess I'll pack my safari shirt for—"

The phone rang, launching Annie into overdrive. "I'll get it!"

As Caroline changed her shirt, she heard Karen's voice from the next room.

"What do you mean he's not there? He's gotta be. Gram . . ." she whined, as if she stood on the deck of *Star Trek's Enterprise* and the future of all mankind was hanging in the balance. "I knew something would go wrong. He didn't want to go to start with. All he cares about is work, work, work."

"What is it, Karen?" Caroline called out.

Caroline knew that Karen's trip had been touch-and-go since her grandmother fell and her father volunteered to go in Gram's place. The trip rules, designed to promote family togetherness, required that every child have at least one parent or relative along.

"Dad's not come home yet from Toronto, so Gram is going to take his suitcase to the airport. I'll just die if he doesn't make it."

Look out, William Shatner. The princess of drama is rising. Caroline let out her breath in a mingle of relief and annoyance. She should have known better. Since Karen had enrolled in Edenton several months earlier and become Annie's friend, Caroline had seen the girl become melodramatic over something as simple as cold fries. "Honey, calm down. It's just a change of plans. I'm sure that if your father misses this flight, he can catch up with us in Mexico City."

"But if he doesn't go, then—"

"Honey, he's going . . . bought and paid for." Caroline

had helped Señora Marron coordinate the trip and had personally taken care of the last-minute change in the airline bookings.

"Besides," she said, zipping up her toiletry bag, "you're staying with Annie and me anyway, so if your dad misses the first night in Mexico City, it won't be the end of the world. With all that's going on in airports these days, delays are common."

From what Caroline had gathered in bits and snatches from Karen and chitchat with Karen's grandmother at the women's Bible study, Karen's father was a widower, away a lot on business.

"Hey, at least your dad is more than a support check," Annie consoled her friend. "My dad replaced us with a whole new family."

Caroline said a quick prayer for the hurt and cynicism in her daughter's voice. Frank Spencer had left Caroline for a colleague, claiming that Caroline, who ran a day care at home to put him through law school, was no longer his intellectual match. Annie had been six at the time and never understood why Daddy remarried and moved to the West Coast, much less why he never visited.

But this was no time to dwell on what she might or might not have done to make it easier on them both. Taking up the blow-dryer, Caroline stared in the mirror, bemused by her unaccustomed curls. She'd worn her hair in a single braid for so long that she had no idea how to attack this shorter, wilder, shoulder-length job. In desperation, she snagged a pair of

Annie's barrettes to pull it off her face.

With the jeans and tee, she could almost pass for one of the kids instead of the owner of Little Angels Day Care Center. At least until someone got close enough to see the bags under her eyes. Not enough makeup in the Cover Girl empire to hide those babies—especially at this hour of the morning.

"Mom, are we supposed to be leaving at four?" Annie said, sticking her head in the doorway. " 'Cause it's quarter till."

In disbelief, Caroline glanced at her wristwatch and shifted into high gear.

"Okay, troops. It's time to zip and load," she announced. There was no time to dry her hair now. She'd have to trust in her hairdresser and go as she felt at the moment—washed and worn.

The Philly airport reminded Blaine Madison of an ant colony, hundreds of individuals busily making their way through the network of intersecting corridors. He claimed a generic black piece of luggage from the conveyor belt and checked the ID tag. Not his. With an aggravated grunt, he tossed it back onto the moving platform to snake its way around the bend. Maybe he should have put some ridiculous marker on the handle to make it stand out—like the neon pink pom-poms on the case claimed by the older lady next to him.

"Cute bear," the woman said, referring to the stuffed toy under his arm.

"My daughter collects them," he explained, without

taking his attention from the endless stream of black nylon cases. "I try to bring her one from every place I travel."

It was something he'd done since Karen was old enough to appreciate the toy more than the box it came in. He'd picked up this bear—which sported a T-shirt with a Canadian maple leaf superimposed over crossed hockey sticks—at the Toronto airport during the delay caused by a security check. He'd missed his connecting flight and had to catch a later one. He'd be lucky if his bag even made it.

The lady leaned over and picked up a smaller bag bedecked with matching pom-poms while Blaine checked the tag on another black nylon case. He let it go and shoved frustrated fingers through his dark brown hair. He didn't have time for this.

"Here," the lady said, handing him a pink slip of paper. "Take a look and take a breather."

Blaine glanced at it, but on seeing the header "Psalm 127:1–2," he shoved it into his pocket. Why do these self-appointed evangelists force this stuff on people? If he wanted to get spiritual, he'd go to church. And he'd seen no point in doing that in a very long time.

"Thanks," he said with polite indifference. "I could use a breather."

Not that chaperoning the Edenton Christian High School's class trip to Mexico was his idea of a break. It meant time with his daughter, and he'd begun to wonder if his little girl had been abducted and some moody clone left in her place. No more ribbons and lace. The new clothes she wore looked like rags. She had no concept of time or commitment, except when it came to meeting her friends at the mall. And despite the private schooling that Blaine worked hard to afford, he hadn't heard her complete a sentence in months. Now he was boarding a plane with a whole group of similarly clothed, idly chattering, high-strung, attention-deficient creatures and their holy-roller parents.

He grabbed another likely looking suitcase and flipped the tag. Bingo. And by the time he hoisted it off the conveyor and lifted the pull handle, the tract-passing pom-pom lady was gone. At least she hadn't tried to save him on the spot. Maybe his luck was changing.

With a stab of guilt at the antagonism he felt toward basically good people, he took up the briefcase at his feet. Blaine had no quarrel with religious people, as long as they kept their faith to themselves. He hadn't the time for a God who had ignored his prayers one time too many.

Hurrying to the security checkpoint, he almost ran into his mother, who was hobbling with a cane toward him.

"Thank God you made it," she said. "Karen checked in your bag for the orphanage. Here's your vacation bag."

"Sorry you had to bring it." Blaine leaned over and gave his mom a kiss on the cheek. "Don't know what I'd do without you."

"Karen was in such a stew. She was just positive you

wouldn't make it on time."

His daughter always seemed to be in a stew of some sort. "The flight from Toronto was delayed," he explained. "Then I missed my connection. But I think we won the bridge contract."

"You're just like your father." His mother's observation was framed with concern. "Don't do what he did, son. Take some time out for yourself."

Blaine knew what she was getting at. His dad had burned out by the time his retirement came and he could turn the business over to his children. Blaine's "baby" sister, Jeanne, had become a successful marine archaeologist. His younger brother, Mark, supposedly helped him with the business but spent more time at play than at work. If Blaine wanted the business to succeed, he had to see to it himself.

"How's the ankle?" he asked, changing the subject. Until Neta had twisted her ankle in the garden three days ago, she was supposed to accompany her granddaughter on the trip.

His mother let it go, but her frown spoke volumes. "Never mind me, just give me the bear and get on that plane. Karen won't forgive you if you embarrass her by giving her a teddy bear in front of her friends."

Blaine grimaced. He hadn't thought of that. The idea that his little girl had outgrown teddy bears from her daddy stung somewhere deep inside. He gave his mom a hug and a hasty kiss on the cheek and handed over the stuffed animal.

"Thanks, Mom. You take it easy while we're gone. I

mean it." He put a hand on her shoulder, lightly tanned from early morning hours spent in her garden. With a little help from boxed hair color and a complexion that defied time, she hardly looked her sixty-two years. She'd always been blessed with good health, and he was blessed with her. She had rented out the home she and her late husband had shared in Florida and moved back to Edenton to take care of Karen after Ellie's untimely death.

"Now if that's not the pot calling the kettle black," she snorted, "I don't know what is."

"I don't know what I'd do without you," he repeated in earnest.

"Me neither." Neta gave him a gentle but firm shove. "Now get going. I promised Mark I'd meet him for dinner tonight."

"If he's not there by the end of happy hour, I wouldn't wait for him," Blaine called over his shoulder.

At the gate, Blaine handed the ticket clerk his boarding pass.

"Welcome aboard, Mr. Madison." A bright-eyed miss in uniform flashed a picture-perfect smile.

"Thanks for waiting." Not that it was her decision.

Some of the other travelers were not as tolerant, given the scowls cast in Blaine's direction. Scanning the seats, he spied a block of passengers wearing the orange-and-green colors of Edenton. In their midst, his daughter stood, waving frantically to get his attention.

"I didn't think you were going to make it," she accused.

“I was beginning to wonder myself. My earlier plane was delayed by a security alert. It made me miss my connec—”

“Here’s your shirt.”

“What?”

“We’re all wearing the same T-shirts so we know who is in our group.” Karen enunciated carefully, as if he had the wit of a Neanderthal.

“I’ll put it on later . . . although, you realize, it clashes with my tie,” he said, hoping to lighten the mood.

With a roll of her eyes, she dropped into her seat.

Blaine hesitated a moment. The only seat open in the group was not beside his ponytailed daughter, but behind her.

“I was supposed to sit with you, but when you didn’t get here, I swapped with Miz C so I could sit with Annie,” Karen told him.

“Hi, Mr. Madison,” said a perky blonde-haired clone beside Karen, her braced teeth gleaming through her smile.

So much for father-daughter quality time.

“Annie, good to see you again.” He vaguely recognized her. Karen rarely had friends over, and if she did, they stayed locked up in her room as if adult exposure might be contagious.

“Sir, please take your seat and stow your briefcase.” The flight attendant gave him a tightly fixed smile.

“Sorry.” He slid into his seat.

“I have you checked in, Mr. Madison. Glad you could make it,” a woman with a clipboard and heavy Spanish accent announced from across the aisle. Wearing dark-rimmed wire glasses, and with her equally dark hair knotted in the back and skewered by what looked like short wooden knitting needles, the lady dropped the board into a briefcase and shut it with an authoritative click. Blaine wasn't certain if it was the taut coiffure or heavy eyeliner that gave her coal-dark eyes the illusion of a slant.

"Thank you, Miss—" What was the name on the permission slip he'd signed? He finished with a smooth "Marron."

"Mah-rrrown," the Spanish teacher corrected, rolling her r's with a sharp purr. "Señora Mah-rrrown, *por favor.*"

"Señora Mah-rrrown," Blaine repeated. "Sorry . . . er . . . *lo siento.*"

"We could switch back, if you'd rather sit with your daughter," said a voice to his right.

Distracted from his impromptu Spanish lesson and Karen's not-so-empathetic grin, Blaine turned to the young woman next to him. Clad like the teens in denims and the green-and-orange shirt, she didn't look old enough to have a daughter Annie's age. Blaine searched his memory, wondering if Karen had mentioned in passing that Annie had a big sister.

"Aw," the girls moaned in collective dismay.

"Now, girls, this is a family trip."

No, she was a mother. Moms were masters of that steeled-velvet intonation.

"Thanks," Blaine said, "but I can take a hint. This is

fine." He shoved his briefcase in the floor space in front of his seat. Once he was settled, seat belt fastened, he turned to his neighbor. "Miss . . . um . . . Señora C, I presume?"

"Caroline." She offered him a firm, friendly handshake. "Caroline Spencer."

CHAPTER 2

"Caroline it is." It was an effort not to stare at her as if she were a project to be analyzed. "And I prefer Blaine to Señor or Mr. M."

Now, why hadn't he just introduced himself as he usually did? His left brain had been in overdrive for so long that his less predictable right had obviously seen its chance to trip him up with memories of a happier time—even if he'd been more of an observer than participant. Blaine quickly switched back to his more comfortable, dominant nature, where whimsy had no place.

"Blaine it is." The copper spirals of hair, barely held in check by barrettes, bounced with her nod of agreement. "Karen has told us so much about you. It's wonderful that you were able to juggle your schedule to make the trip. I think it meant a lot to her."

"At least the trip part." *Juggle my schedule?* Jeopardizing a contract he'd been trying to win for months, putting his secretary through the wringer to reschedule airline tickets, and handing over the follow-through to his younger brother was more than a *juggle*. He could almost feel his blood pressure rising, just thinking about it. "And the dad part," Caroline insisted over the dubious note in his voice. "She's quite proud of you."

"I am so ready for Mexico," Karen exclaimed in front of them.

"Totally," Annie chimed in.

A cryptic smile tugged at the corner of Blaine's mouth. "I rest my case."

"Ladies and gentlemen, this is your captain speaking," the speaker crackled. "I'd like to . . ."

"How about case adjourned till we're up and away?"

The stubborn purse of Caroline's lips told Blaine she was digging in for the debate. Fortunately for him, the captain's welcome captured her attention. As the pilot informed them that they were next in line for takeoff and that the weather conditions in Mexico City were clear skies and temperatures in the eighties, dropping to the seventies at night, Caroline's demeanor metamorphosed from playful to strictly business.

The plane taxied to the runway, its overhead monitors dropping down from the bulkhead to play the info video on the flight safety and emergency procedures. Around him unseasoned travelers, including Caroline Spencer, tugged the laminated information sheets from the seat pockets. She oriented herself on the map of the plane with the zeal of a commando prepping for a rescue.

"First time flying?" he asked.

"Gee, ya think?" The wisecrack was more of a nervous laugh, followed promptly by a becoming color creeping to her cheeks. At the high whine of the engines revving up for takeoff, her blush drained.

"Hang on, Mom," Annie called through the crack between the seats in front of them. "It's going to be okay. We prayed, remember?"

Prayer or not, Caroline Spencer left the safety sheet in her lap and hung on to the seat arms with a death grip as the pilot released the brakes, launching them forward with a jerk.

Blaine resorted to distraction to help her along. "Be careful not to hit the window switch on the side there." He nodded at the seat reclining button just shy of the woman's bloodless fingers. "If you open that window during takeoff, the ladies behind us will get a new hairdo."

Caroline stared at him as if he'd grown horns. He watched her slowly process his warning in the liquid green of her gaze. The corners of her mouth twitched with uncertainty. Once . . . twice . . . bull's-eye. As the plane lifted off, pressing the passengers against the upright seat backs, she laughed hysterically, although Blaine imagined it was more of a release of tension than genuine amusement.

By the time they leveled off above a layer of white, sun-dashed clouds, her knuckles were no longer white, nor were her fingers anywhere near the seat release.

"I don't know whether to thank you or smack you," she said, letting out the last breath she'd tried to hold throughout the takeoff. "I—" A loud hiccup cut her off. Startled, Caroline placed a hand over her chest. "Now look what you've—*hic*—oh, rats!"

"Mom," Annie exclaimed in a mortified voice. "They can hear you all over the plane."

"It's not like I can—*hic*—help it."

"I could try to scare you." Blaine pinched his cheeks between his teeth so as not to laugh outright. Each time her breath caught, her curls bounced.

"You scared me *into* them, thank—*hic*—you." She slanted an accusing look at him. "Window switch indeed."

"Sorry." He was trying not to laugh. The realization tripped his train of thought. He couldn't remember the last time he'd even been inclined to laugh. "I had to do something to distract you before you bent the arm rest."

"No you di—*hic*—dn't."

"Mom, puh-leeze."

Karen chimed in with her friend. "Why don't you two act your age?"

Blaine met Caroline's startled, stricken look with one of his own.

"What is—*hic*—wrong with this picture?"

The tension from the rushed contract presentation in Toronto (had he forgotten any details?), worry about his mom, the airport hustle and shuffle from Toronto to Philly, and the less-than-gracious reward for the "juggling of his schedule" unraveled. Blaine dissolved into laughter with his gullible companion. If there was any merit to the *Reader's Digest* claim that laughter is the best medicine, he might actually be able to skip the melatonin his holistic guru of a secretary had given him. Maybe this break from routine *was* just what he needed.

The image of the pink pom-pom lady flashed through his mind—her kind smile and words. *Take a look and take a breather.*

Blaine rifled through his jacket and withdrew the pink slip of paper she'd passed on to him. *Unless the Lord builds the house, its builders labor in vain. Unless the Lord watches over the city, the watchmen stand guard in vain. In vain you rise early and stay up late, toiling for food to eat, for he grants sleep to those he loves. Psalm 127:1–2.*

A mental *whoa* lifted the hair on Blaine's arms and the back of his neck. Not that he believed in this kind of spiritual thing.

Take some time out for yourself. Neta Madison's words echoed in his ear.

Blaine stared, no longer seeing, at the pink slip of paper. The stranger, the verse, and his mom—three strikes were hard to ignore. And spiritual aspect aside, there was some wisdom in the tract. Work consumed most of his waking hours and much of his sleeping ones. Maybe he did need some time off, time with his daughter and in the world outside of projects and contracts.

She was caught in a twin-bladed nightmare of embarrassment and discomfort. Worse, she was seated next to a guy who reminded her of a movie actor. What was that guy's name? With those broad shoulders and narrow hips, he had a body a tailor could love. And his eyes matched the dark nutmeg in the tweed of his jacket. Not that she was shopping, she told herself, but she could admire the window dressing . . . or the *man*-nequin.

Caroline winced as another hiccup stabbed her between the shoulder blades. Evidently the prayer she'd led the group in before boarding the plane about blessing their trip and keeping them safe hadn't been specific enough about first-time-flying nerves or hiccups.

Lord, I don't mean to sound ungrateful, the plane being safe in the air and all, but shouldn't there be atmospheric-pressure control or an oxygen bag dropping down, like on TV, to offer some relief for this?

"Miz C, I saved my coffee stirrer from breakfast if you need it," offered a boy across the aisle from Karen and Annie. "It's a surefire cure for hiccups."

A coffee stirrer? Caroline hesitated. She'd known Kurt Gearhardt since day care; the kid was a perennial prankster.

"I don't know about coffee stirrers, ma'am," a flight attendant said, appearing at her elbow, "but here's a glass of water. There's not much ice, so you can drink it straight down."

Great. Annie wasn't kidding; they *had* heard her all over the plane.

"Thank—*hic*—you." Caroline looked at the water. She took a deep breath, but before she could get the glass to her lips, a hiccup headed it off. Some of the water sloshed on her nose.

Her handsome traveling companion pretended not to notice, but seemed absorbed in reading something on a scrap of paper. As if he could miss a gasping, convulsing, frizzy-haired woman in shock-orange sloshing water at his elbow.

"I'll take that stirrer, Kurt." What did she have to lose? "Now what?" she asked.

"Just hold it between your teeth like a horse's bit and drink the whole glass of water down."

"Oh, no." Annie sank down into her seat, no doubt wanting no part of what she foresaw as humiliation to the nth degree.

Kurt watched from across the aisle. "You go, Miz C." Next to him, his constant companion, Wally Peterman, leaned over to watch, shoving his black glasses up on his pug of a nose.

Caroline knew her daughter and Karen had declared the pair total nerds, but the boys had a special place in Caroline's heart, mischief and all.

"You're really going to go for this?" Blaine Madison remarked under his breath as she positioned the coffee stirrer in her mouth.

She took it back out. "You got a better idea? If I don't do something soon, everyone on the plane will—*hic*—be spazzing with me."

"I heard there was one born every minute," he teased, shoving the paper into a pocket.

With a scrunched-up face, Caroline put the stick back, determined to wash away the hiccups or drown trying.

What water didn't choke her wound up doing the latter—drowning her. Now she was a *wet* gasping, convulsing, frizzy-haired woman in two shades of shock orange.

Unlike the teens, who responded with "Way to go" or non-verbal hysterics, Blaine was polite enough not to say, "I told you so." Mastering the amusement tugging at his square-jawed restraint, he produced a pristine handkerchief from inside his jacket.

"You wouldn't have a Turkish—*hic*—towel in there, would you?" Caroline quipped. She wished a trapdoor would open and she could drop down into the belly of the plane. Taking the handkerchief, she mopped ineffectively at her lap.

"Here, honey," Dana Gearhardt said, offering a fistful of tissues from her seat behind her son. "You ought to know better than to listen to that son of mine."

At that moment the attendant reappeared with a tea towel.

"You need a beach towel, Miz C," Kurt teased from the security of his seat. While safe from Caroline, he wasn't beyond his mother's chiding thump on the head.

"Ow!"

"And *you* should know by now, young man, that we moms stick together."

Having known Dana forever, Caroline knew that the mischief in the Gearhardt clan didn't fall far from the tree.

Dana looked past Caroline at Blaine, and a devil dressed as Cupid practically danced in her eyes.

"That's our Caroline. Like the watch, she takes a licking and keeps on ticking."

Caroline shrugged. "And to think, I—*hic*—got up early to shower for nothing."

"I could just die," Annie groaned amid the ripple of amusement around them.

"Maybe getting up and walking to the back will help," the attendant suggested.

Or at least get her out of the limelight. Caroline excused herself and made her way to the short line by the lavatory, meeting the sympathetic smiles of other passengers as she went.

Just ahead, Christie Butler and Amy Collier stood waiting, heads together.

"My real mom couldn't be bothered to make the trip," Christie was saying, "but I don't care. My stepmom is more fun. It's like—"

"You want to cut ahead of us, Miz C?" Amy asked, upon seeing Caroline.

"I'm fine, thanks," Caroline answered, giving Christie an impromptu hug. "Unless you're afraid I'm going to—*hic*—use up all the air in the cabin."

"I'm more afraid of using the john," Christie confided in a low voice. "Kurt told us about this woman who flushed before she stood up, and the vacuum held her to the seat until the plane landed."

Caroline lifted a skeptical brow. *Oh joy.*

"I heard about it, too," Amy said. "The crew tried to pull her off, but she was just stuck."

"Can you just imagine how embarrassed she was?"

Caroline could come pretty close. She shuddered involuntarily. Kurt could have kept that story—and his coffee stirrer—to himself.

The acoustics in the restroom did little to discredit the story. It sounded as though someone had left a window open somewhere. The only thing more unsettling was the glimpse she caught of the red-haired wild woman in the spattered mirror. No wonder Karen's father kept staring at her. She looked like an aged adolescent who'd lost a water balloon fight.

Not that I care what he thinks, she told herself.

Caroline pushed the button on the faucet to wash her hands. A jet of water came out, propelled by the same force that likely had vacuum-sealed some hapless passenger in the restroom for the duration of the flight. It splattered the tiny sink, the mirror, and the elbow's worth of counter, and soaked Caroline for the second time that morning. There was no room to escape it.

"I hate flying." With patience far short of Job's, Caroline began mopping up the mess. "Face it, babe," she told her double in the mirror, who now looked as if she was on the losing team of the kiddie water balloon league. "Karen's dad must think you are the mother of mayhem. All the primping in the world won't help you now."

With a sigh of resignation, Caroline grabbed the bolt on the door, but it wouldn't budge. Her heart seized for the second it took to realize she was pushing it the wrong way. She tried again, and it slid with ease from the red to green position. Humiliation heating her cheeks, Caroline sidled through the bifold door with a silent *Thank You, Lord, for loving Your imperfect, scatterbrained children.*

Randy Gearhardt, Dana's hubby and president of Edenton's PTA, stepped aside so that she could get by. "Tight squeeze, eh?" he teased.

Randy was one of those civic-minded citizens who were involved in everything. Caroline had served with him and Dana on more than one fund-raising committee for the private school.

"Tell me about it . . . and watch the faucet. It's a shower in disguise."

"Look, I don't know what this is about," he apologized, "but Dana insisted I give you this." He handed her an airline coaster with "Harrison Ford" scribbled on it.

That was who Blaine Madison looked like—a dark-haired Harrison Ford à la *Sabrina.* It was scary how Dana and she were so often on the same wavelength. And so far apart on others, Caroline mused, envisioning her friend loading her quiver with Cupid's arrows. Why was it so hard for married women to accept that singles could lead normal, fulfilling lives?

When she reached her row, Blaine glanced up. "Looks like you've recovered after all."

Caroline looked at him, blank. Was he seeing the mad, wet hen she'd just seen?

"The hiccups," he prompted. "They're gone, aren't they?"

"Told you the coffee stirrer would work," Kurt piped up.

The button that sealed the woman to the potty seat more likely flushed them away, Caroline thought, but she kept her observation to herself. She slid into her seat with a sheepish glance at the man next to her. "The offer still stands."

"What offer is that?" Blaine's clear-eyed appraisal took the cold out of the air-conditioned blast chilling her wet clothing.

"To sit next to your daughter, rather than by a hiccuping, water-soaked lunatic."

"Don't let her fool you, Blaine," Dana warned from across the aisle. "This is just one of Caroline's many facets. She's a wizard with finances, a pied piper of children, and a gem of a friend."

"Thank you, Dana." If her friend was trying to help, it wasn't working. Now Caroline didn't feel the dampness of her clothes at all. Self-consciousness had steamed them dry.

"A little cracked, maybe," Dana added, "but a true gem."

Blaine laughed—a short, manly, and genuine laugh. "Gems are scarce these days, even cracked ones." He leaned over, an incorrigible grin tugging at the corners of his mouth. "I think I'll keep this seat, but . . . would you like my jacket? They've cranked up the air-conditioning, and you're shivering."

Shivering? Who was shivering? Global warming could be blamed on the heat of her embarrassment. And that's all it was.

"A lady doesn't turn Sir Galahad down, Caroline,"

Dana advised, peering over her wire-framed glasses with the authority of Miss Manners and Dr. Ruth combined. "And the flight is five hours."

"That would be nice." At least Caroline's voice was working, if not her brain. It was in a stall, nose-diving all the way.

"I can't believe it!" Karen peeked back at them through the crack in the seats. "My dad is hitting on your mom."

"Your father is being polite," Blaine corrected, wrapping the jacket about Caroline's shoulders. "So mind your own business, miss."

Caroline sank into the embrace of the suit jacket, its silk lining still full of Blaine's warmth. She saw Karen's face disappear from the narrow opening, replaced by Annie's one-eyed appraisal. It was amazing the degree of disbelief that one eye could broadcast.

"Polite," Caroline warned, before further fuss could be made. Her heart was making enough for the lot of them at the moment—drummed alternately by her daughter's incredulity that a man might be attracted to her *old* mother and by the certainty that even if he was, this woman was *not* interested. It was going to be a long five hours.

CHAPTER 3

Despite Señora Marron's machine-gun command of her native language, the helter-skelter passage through the maze of baggage claims and customs reminded Caroline of herding cats. At one point, it seemed as though twenty people were in twenty-five places. Caroline lost both girls once in the gauntlet of duty-free shops and Karen again in the ladies' room.

"Okay. From now on, we are inseparable, right?" Caroline linked her free arm in Annie's. "Annie, you hook onto Karen. And we don't let go of each other, got it?"

"Got it." Karen giggled, pointing toward the newsstand just ahead where Señora Marron was zeroing in on Blaine Madison. "But it looks like it's too late for Daddy."

"Señor Madison, we *will* keep together, did I not explain on the plane?"

Startled from his study of the *Wall Street Journal*, Blaine switched from an initial scowl at the market numbers to surprise at the interruption, then on to mischief with a rakish lift of one eyebrow. "I'm waiting for my daughter, Señora. It's also against the rules for fathers to go into the ladies' rooms, no?"

The señora's huff of irritation deflated through her flame-red painted lips. With a short nod, she clapped her hands over her head and summoned the group to her, clucking Spanish like a mother hen until all her chicks, both big and small, made a straight line through the same turnstile and customs desk to the terminal pick-up area. There, puffing hard in the thin, diesel-laden mountain air, they handed over their bags for the second time that day and boarded a once-silver bus with the Virgin of Guadalupe swinging from the panoramic rearview mirror.

After the driver slammed the gaping side of the bus shut and climbed into the faux tiger-fur-covered seat behind the wheel, a young man stood up in the front of the bus, a microphone in his hand. His black hair was as straight and unruly as it was thick, and his smile spanned the entire width of his face.

"*Buenas tardes, señores y señoras,* and welcome to Mexico," he said into a static-riddled public address system. "Although I am told that I look like the guy that chases the gopher in *Caddyshack*, I am actually just Hector Rodriguez, who will be your tour guide until you leave the country of the cactus and eagle. And this is Guillermo Josef de Aldama."

With a twinkle in his dark eyes, the guide—who did look a little like a Mexican version of Bill Murray—waited for all the syllables of the driver's name to sink in before adding, "But to us, he is just Bill."

Wearing a tropical shirt much like the one Caroline had donned earlier that morning, Bill waved in the mirror. Then, his mustache-crowned grin fading, he eased the bus into the mainstream of through traffic.

"Bill will be driving us from here to the coast and . . ." Hands flying to his hips, Hector swung them in a little circle à la Macarena. ". . . Acapulco."

The teens on the bus erupted in a cheer.

"But we must do our history before we play, no?"

To the collective "Awww" of his audience, Hector shrugged. "*Ni modo.* It can't be helped. All play and no history makes Hector a dumb boy. Besides," he added, "no history, no paycheck for me." He rubbed his fingers together, his expression a mirror of mischief that could not help but elicit the goodwill of the group.

The bus started up and around an overpass, with Hector holding on to the pole behind Bill's seat and swinging with the flow. "But you will see that Mexico City is more than just history. Tonight we go to Banditos, the hottest dance club in town for peoples your age."

Again the youngsters hooted with enthusiasm, feeding the impish light in Hector's gaze. "Don't worry, *mamás y papás,* no alcohol is served from eight till midnight," he assured the parents. "So you will have time to check in and have a look around, exchange currency, if you wish, and get ready to dance the night away . . . at least until the late karaoke show. Then all the *Seen-der-eh-yas* and handsome princes from seventeen years down turns into squash."

"Squash?" Christie's expression mirrored the skepticism in her voice. "You mean pumpkins, right?"

"Squash, pumpkin, whatever you are, don't miss your ride," Hector advised. "Or you will be squashed. *Entiende?* Adults only after midnight."

"Sí."

"We *entiende.*"

"Got it."

By midnight I'll feel like squash, Caroline thought.

"The palms you see lining the highway surrounding our Alameda Park," Hector continued, "are royal palms. The museum to the right houses the mural of the Alameda painted by famous Diego Rivera. It was nearly destroyed by the 1985 earthquake—"

"Looks kind of run-down to me," Kurt observed from a nearby seat.

The way she felt. At the moment, the entertaining tour talk stimulated sleep more than cultural interest.

"But alas, it was saved and put into that museum over there." Hector pointed through the tinted windows.

"Who's Diego Rivera?" Annie asked.

Hector looked as if she'd asked who Santa Claus was. "You don't know Diego Rivera?"

Unaffected by his dramatic censure, Annie shook her head.

The guide broke into a wide grin and shrugged. "Neither do I, but we'll find out on our tour tomorrow."

Grinning, Annie shifted next to Caroline and moved to put her backpack under the seat in front of them.

"Just hold it in your lap, honey," Caroline suggested. "Señora Marron said it's only twenty or so minutes to the hotel. With luck, we can get a nap before dinner."

"But you heard Hector. We need to get some Mexican money and look around," Annie protested. "Besides, you already had a nap." With the finesse of a magician, she brandished a Polaroid shot from the knapsack and waved it in Caroline's face. "See? I have proof."

Caroline cringed. There she was, wrapped in Blaine Madison's jacket, her head pillowed against his shoulder, his head resting on her crown of curly hair. Both were lost in a dream world of their own . . . until someone saw the photo op and grabbed it. She had been awakened by the sudden flash of light to see Kurt fairly glowing with mischief.

"That will look great in the September school newsletter!" he crowed.

"As who?" Caroline couldn't help her yawn, nor the first thing that popped into her mind. "Mr. and Mrs. Van Winkle?"

"As if." Annie and Karen giggled in unison.

Mr. and Mrs. Caroline didn't try to retrieve the words. Chewing them once was enough. Better to fade away in a meltdown of embarrassment.

Which was why, when she corralled Annie away from Karen in the terminal, Caroline had made it clear that the two of them should ride together on the bus.

"But why?" her daughter complained. "I thought you and Mr. Madison were getting along great."

And they had been, despite Caroline's adolescent appearance, her fear of flying, the hiccups, and her verbal faux pas. But when she flung her arm out in a motherly instinct as the plane braked after a bumpy touchdown, she surely must have cracked his rib cage. Blaine had been startled, but gracious.

As for Caroline, she hoped to avoid the man until at least the next millennium.

Karen's stricken voice drew Caroline back to the present. "You can't work tonight, Daddy. This is our vacation."

"Karen, you know I cut my trip short to make this work," Blaine answered, apology in his tone. "I have to finalize the contract details and send them to the office to get things moving."

"But everyone is going."

"Perhaps I might make a suggestion," Señora Marron interjected from somewhere behind Caroline. She raised her voice so that everyone might hear. "Tonight is a free night. Since we have been traveling all day, the trip to the show club is optional. Señor Rodriguez and I will be happy to chaperone the students who wish to sample our nightlife. Although it is my hope that some parents will accompany us."

"Mom will," Annie volunteered. "I mean, we paid for the whole trip. We might as well get our money's worth, right?"

Part of Caroline wanted to go, but at the moment the Sleepy in her dwarfed Happy.

"*And* you'll get to practice your Spanish."

When the value of the dollar and high school Spanish failed to raise a response, Annie resorted to pity. "We all worked so hard to raise the money to go."

The whining echoed up and down the line as youngsters petitioned their parents to go, or at least get permission to attend the club with Señora Marron. The kids had put on car washes and bake sales to raise money for the trip, giving up several Saturdays throughout the spring. While a few parents supervised, the students had done all the work. They had to earn half the money, even though most of their parents could afford to pay their way. It was all part of a plan to make them appreciate the trip. They'd done so well that they'd had repeat customers and tips.

"Hey, you guys, keep the line moving," Hector called to two errant students who'd been so involved in a hand video game that they'd lagged behind. "Let's went." He'd been moving the party along with his unique interpretation of *move out,* since they'd gotten off the bus.

Suddenly he turned to Caroline and grinned. "Love could be waiting but a dance away, *Señora.*"

She didn't even know he'd been listening. "When our Mexican moon shines . . ." he sang in a parody of the old love song, "*ni modo*. It can't be helped."

"Could I go with you, Miz C?" Karen peered over the seat edge as if the hope of mankind now rested on Caroline's shoulders. Caroline's tired shoulders.

"Ni modo," she sighed with a toss of her hands. "I guess it can't be helped."

Later, standing with the girls at the hotel window on the fourteenth floor, Caroline stared at the busy street below. The traffic flowed through vendor-lined streets, tangling at intersections with honks of impatience. The magnificent vista of a city set in a ring of sun-dashed mountains, as seen from the plane, was lost here amid the high-rises, but vestiges of the foreign culture were not. The colorful canopies of the street vendors competed with those of the VW Beetle taxi drivers who shouted *"Viva!"* from the lusterless concrete and asphalt beds. Lime greens, lemonade yellow, fiesta red, sunset orange—one was even painted like a ladybug.

The girls wanted to go shopping, and Caroline had gotten her second wind. There were souvenirs to buy for her staff and friends, plus she was eager to put into practice the A's that she'd earned in high school Spanish.

Caroline dragged herself away from the fascinating hubbub of activity below. It could have looked like Philly, or any other big city, but it wasn't. It was Mexico, land of the cactus, eagle, and serpent. And if the ancient Aztecs had searched a continent looking for such a place, then she could skip a nap.

"First we do a room check. Then I'm going to wash my face and pull this hair off my neck, and I'll be ready to go."

"Room check?" Karen gave Annie a puzzled look.

Annie grimaced. "Yeah, Mom has this thing about checking for bugs . . . especially spiders."

Karen snorted. "No way."

"Yes, way," Caroline told her as she scanned the ceiling for cobwebs. "And if you'd been bitten the day of your first high school dance and wound up in the hospital with an allergic reaction, you'd be looking too."

Annie lifted the cushion of the sofa bed. "Uh-oh."

Caroline stiffened. "What?"

"Put a hold on the bug spray, Mom—"

"She brought bug spray?" Karen marveled.

"No sheets," Annie finished.

Caroline's upshot of adrenaline ebbed. "*No hay problema.* I'll just get my handy dandy Spanish dictionary and order them up. Unless one of you ladies would care to."

"No way." Karen stopped the verbal traffic with an extended hand. "Not with my grades."

"You first, Mom." Annie's dubious look hardly shouted confidence.

"And we need more cups," Caroline observed, undaunted. Next to a mini coffeepot were only two Styrofoam cups. She closed the suitcase on the small can of insect spray she'd brought along, just in case.

A knock sounded on the adjoining door to their room, echoed by Blaine Madison's query. "Everything okay in here?"

"Not a spider in sight," Karen proclaimed.

Caroline groaned. "That's a family secret," she warned the girl. Caroline didn't want the world thinking she was a hysterical arachnophobic. She preferred the word "cautious."

"It's safe with me, Miz C," Karen assured her. After a little finagling with the flush-mounted handle and deadbolt, Karen got the door open.

Blaine's six-foot-plus frame all but filled the entrance.

"It's just great here, Daddy. Did you see the taxi that was painted like a beetle bug?"

"A ladybug," Annie corrected, the subject switched to a more acceptable insect.

"We're doing just fine," Caroline assured him. "How is your room?"

"Just be sure to use the bottled water, even if they do

post that the tap water is safe."

"We're slipping out to get some traveler's checks cashed, grab a bite to eat, and do a little shopping. Care to join us?"

"Take in the sights, absorb the flavors of old and new Mexico." Karen grabbed her father's hand and danced as far as his arms would allow.

"I've been in Mexico on several projects, Kitten," Blaine said. His manner suggested to Caroline that he wasn't all that impressed. "You all enjoy. I'll just order up a sandwich and get to work." He winked at his daughter and peered past her. "Are you sure you're okay with the girls?"

Caroline was poring over the Spanish dictionary, looking for the right word for bedclothes or linens. "*No hay problema* . . . now that my feet are on the ground." Linens. Caroline made out the tiny print. She cast a reassuring smile Blaine's way as she punched the phone for room service.

A woman answered, drawing her full attention. *"Servicio."*

"Yes, have you . . . *Necesitas a los linos . . . para la cama y tambien una vaca en cuarto numero catorce veinte,*" Caroline finished in triumph. *We need linens for the bed and also a water glass in room number fourteen-twenty.* At least that's what she thought she said. But when the woman repeated the request in a mix of uncertainty and incredulity, doubt set in.

"Sheets," Caroline reiterated.

"Sábanas," Blaine prompted. His smile was as unset-

tling as the housekeeper's tone. "You asked for a tablecloth for the bed."

"Oh, *sábanas,* no *linos,*" she said, shaking her head as though the woman on the line could see her.

"And *un vaso para agua,*" Blaine prompted.

"Y un vaso para agua." Caroline glanced at him. "What did I say?" she mouthed silently.

The corner of his mouth tipped upward. "You said you needed a cow . . . I think."

"Mother!" Annie declared in half-giggle, half-horror.

"I'm more checked out on travel Spanish than rural," he admitted, breaking into a full grin.

"What did the operator say?" Karen asked, plopping down on the bed next to Caroline. Her dark eyes, like her father's, danced with delight.

Caroline focused on the floor, head shaking. With a *"Sí, muchas gracias, Señora,"* she hung up the phone. "So much for high school Spanish."

"Hey, all you have to do is brush ten years' or so worth of dust off it, and you'll be fine."

Caroline cut her gaze toward Blaine. "Very gallant, but add a few *or so's worth* to that ten."

"As long as you have both feet planted on the ground, I have complete faith in you."

"And so do we," Annie proclaimed, as she threw herself across the bed.

"Even if I have to sleep on a tablecloth next to a cow," Karen added, grinning.

Caroline ruffled Annie's ponytail. "You two would do anything to be footloose in Mexico."

"Have a good time, troops, and don't drink the water or take anything from anyone on the street to carry back to the States." Blaine closed the door between the rooms, dodging the girls' indignation.

"Like, duh." Karen rolled her eyes towards the ceiling. "Hector already warned us."

"And Señora Marron, and every other adult on the planet," the other girl chimed in. "It's like everyone thinks we missed 9-11."

"Then it's good to know that you remember so well what you were told." Caroline grabbed her shoulder bag from the bed and struck a tour guide pose. "Let's went."

CHAPTER 4

After cashing some travelers' checks into colorful denominations of pesos, Caroline led the girls around the block from the hotel, where, according to the moneychanger, there was a KFC. Annie and Karen were starved, but not enough to try the food from the street vendors. Enchiladas, tacos, and corn on the cob served with chili, mayonnaise, and lime, it looked and smelled delicious. But sanitation didn't appear to be high on many of the owners' lists, so Caroline yielded to the plea to find some American food.

The scent of fresh *pan dulce* and roasting coffee beans from the sidewalk espresso café beside them was making her tummy growl in protest, when Karen pointed to a red-and-white sign that seemed to blend into the line of canopies, marquees, and lights.

"There's the Colonel!"

Inside, the restaurant had the same decor as the one in downtown Edenton. With a minimum of fuss, they purchased their meals and found a table.

The potatoes tasted a little strange, most likely the result of being made with heavily treated water. Caroline advised the girls to skip the spuds and slaw in favor of the biscuits. "The last thing we need is Montezuma's revenge."

"My dad does business here all the time, and he's never had that." Karen twirled her straw inside her can of soda. "But he carries enough milk of magnesia for an army . . . like a gallon or something."

"That was one of the suggestions in the pamphlet that Señora Marron handed out before the trip," Caroline reminded her. She had a travel-size bottle in her own case. "He travels a lot, does he?"

"All over the world, but mostly in the States, Canada, and Mexico." A cloud settled on the girl's face. "You'd think he'd want to show it to me . . . Mexico City. After all, I am his daughter."

"Maybe he's just busy finishing up the business from this last trip so that he'll be free tomorrow," Annie said. She slurped the last of her Coke from the bottom of the can—another precaution. Fountain drinks were not recommended on the tip sheet.

Caroline conveyed her motherly disapproval with a grimace. "You know," she said to Karen, "we parents don't always get to do what we want to do either. There's this little thing called *earning money* to put food on the table, clothes on our backs, and a roof over our heads that comes first."

"That's what Dad and Nana are always saying. I wish Uncle Mark or Aunt Jeanne had come instead. They're more fun."

Caroline packed their trash into the large bag their meals had come in. "Maybe so, but I'd cut him some extra slack. After all, your dad didn't get to plan this trip in advance."

"Yeah, give him a chance," Annie chimed in. "At least he came. My dad didn't even bother to tell me he was too busy. No call, no nothing."

The words squeezed Caroline's heart. As she looked away from the girls, the clock over the soda cooler caught her eye.

"Oh my goodness, it's six-thirty!" Incredulous, she glanced at her wristwatch to confirm it. "We have to be dressed and in the lobby in one hour."

Fortunately, Caroline and the girls weren't the only ones who had lost track of time. An hour and a half later, they squeezed into the backseat of one of the VW taxis. The front passenger seat had been removed to facilitate getting in and out. Outside, Hector worked with the taxi drivers to sort passengers like cattle to squeeze the most bodies into each vehicle.

"Okay, we need one more," Hector said, after peeking into their cab. He held up his hands to indicate the narrow width of space allowed.

"Thank goodness I made it in before he started measuring," Caroline mumbled under her breath, exacting a giggle from Annie.

"You're not *that* big, Mom."

Judging from the jabbing hipbones of the girls on either side of her, Caroline was at least older and rounder.

"Think we can squeeze two more in here?" Hector asked.

Standing outside were Kurt and Wally, looking like lost sheep in their idea of evening attire—clean T-shirts and jeans.

"You know Eddie and Rick are with Amy and Christie," Karen remarked.

"Sure, there's always room for more." Annie moved over as far as she could. "Who wants to be with those snobs anyway?"

"I don't want to be with all of them . . . just Eddie," Karen said, unaffected by the look Caroline shot in her direction. "Or maybe Rick."

"Who needs those guys when you got the best?" Kurt announced.

"Oh, puh-leeze," Karen groaned as he squeezed into the back seat next to Annie.

"Sorry, princess," Wally said as he settled on the nonexistent front seat, which was literally a cushion on the floor.

"What about seat belts?" Caroline protested.

"Yeah, isn't there a law or something?" Kurt chimed in.

Hector simply shrugged. Apparently safety precautions weren't as important in Mexico as in the States. "No worries, Señora. It's a short ride."

But not short enough, Caroline thought when they pulled up in front of the nightclub. There hadn't been room to breathe with four of them wedged across the back, not even to gasp when the driver threaded through the thick traffic so fast that the street signs blended into a continuous neon blur. Poor Wally would need his hands pried from the armrest, and she needed an oxygen tank.

"Are the others behind us?" the spectacled youngster asked.

"Can't tell," Caroline said. "We're packed too tight to turn our heads."

They got out of the car under a flashing marquee that read *Banditos*. The mountain air raised the gooseflesh on Caroline's clammy skin as they made their way into what appeared from the outside to be a movie theater. The lobby had been converted into a soda-fountain bar, while its display cases were still filled with a variety of sweets. The menu behind the counter boasted all manner of nonalcoholic frozen drinks and concoctions aimed at the teen clientele.

Beyond it, three steps down, tables and chairs lined each side of a huge dance floor. While Hector took care of the cover charge, Caroline picked the clingy silk of her tank top away from her skin. Until that cab ride, she'd never suspected she was claustrophobic.

Ushers and waiters clad in tight black trousers, billowing red-and-gold poet's shirts, and an occasional patch over one eye met their party and led them into the purple glow of the dance arena. Black lights. It had been years since Caroline had been in a club with black lights.

"*Para la Señora linda*. For the pretty lady."

Turning, Caroline accepted a fresh long-stemmed rose from one of the gallant *banditos*. "What a lovely idea. Thank you."

Even she felt a hint of the thrill that had obviously infected the girls, who coveted the flowers as if they'd been dipped in 24-carat gold. They returned iridescent white smiles to the dark-eyed charmers. There *was* something about that accent . . . Not only were the ladies escorted to the tables, but their flowers were arranged for them in the glass vases on each one by the ushers.

"Boy, do these Mexican men know how to treat a woman," Annie sighed, watching her escort make his way back to the entrance where more young ladies awaited seating.

"They don't impress me," Kurt snorted under his breath.

Karen gave the young man a derisive look. "Well, I'd *hope* not."

Hector turned back to the students, who by now had settled around a circular table. "There is a karaoke show the first hour. Then there is dancing."

Señora Marron finally arrived with the third taxi load. "Ah, Señora Spencer, I must ask you a favor." She leaned over, dropping her voice for Caroline's ear only. "I am having the most terrible of headaches. *Female problems,*" she mouthed, backing away and crossing her arms so that her black silk tasseled shawl overlapped with them. "May I impose upon you to remain as chaperone with Hector and the students, to allow me to return to the hotel and take medicine?"

Me? *Alone with crazy Hector and eight sixteen-year-olds in a dance club?* Despite her instinctive reservation, Caroline agreed. "By all means, Señora. I—"

The rest of Caroline's sentence was drowned out by a burst of music so loud, she could have sworn the floor beneath her feet shook. God forbid it was an earthquake, she prayed as she glanced around, looking for a sign that it was more than oversized speakers and a DJ a little heavy on the bass dial. They'd passed several places in the city where buildings had been reduced to rubble and laid waste for years due to lack of money to rebuild.

"Just save me one of those headache pills in case I need it," she shouted into the Spanish teacher's ear.

Grinning widely, Señora Marron mouthed, *"Muchas gracias."*

Still a tad warm from the close ride, Caroline ordered a frozen drink at an outrageous price. Now she knew how the place got its name . . . and afforded to serve the younger set. Unlike the host ushers, the *bandito* assigned to their table was built more like Wally Peterman than like the larger boys. Although the server's frame hadn't quite fleshed out yet, when he kissed Annie's hand, Caroline thought her daughter would swoon straight away.

To Caroline's left, Wally expressed his disdain to no one in particular. "I think I'm gonna puke."

"Would it be different if it was one of the *banditas* rolling those limpid dark eyes at you, Wally?" Caroline teased, shoving her shoulder bag under the table.

"Mom!"

Thinking Annie's indignation a bit overdone, Caroline protested. "I think I see a few girls over there at the bar. See, their hair is either short or pulled back."

Annie pulled Caroline closer. "Not that. It's your glowing bra."

"My wha—?" The question died in Caroline's throat. She'd been so distracted by all that was going on that she hadn't noticed the way the black light picked up the dainty white scallop of her new eighteen-hour wonder of support, making it glow fluorescent through the white silk of her blouse.

Annie performed a discreet but dastardly imitation of a grade-B horror actor. "It's alive!"

And, unbeknownst to Caroline, she'd paraded it from the entrance to the table. "Oh, my." Reaching under the table, she retrieved her purse for cover. No wonder the usher and waiter had grinned so widely at her. She felt like the old "living bra" commercial on the nostalgia television network. Annie used to howl every time the Jane Russell–sized undergarment popped out of the washer with a mind and invisible body of its own to demand special detergent from the startled sixties housewife.

But tonight Caroline wanted to hide, not howl. "Does it show too much?" she whispered as the waiter returned with a tray of drinks for their table.

"Just don't let it dance, and you'll be fine."

Caroline gave her smart-alecky daughter a dirty look. With no prospect of help from her offspring, she assessed her present company for a possible solution. No one had a jacket, but the boys who'd come with Señora Marron wore unbuttoned cotton shirts over their tees. While Caroline would pay them good money for either shirt at that moment, she was too embarrassed to ask.

Handing her wallet to Annie to pay for the drinks the waiter brought, Caroline kept her handbag pressed against her chest and slumped against the back of her chair. Okay, so she'd just slink down and pray for a quick end to what promised to be a long evening. It couldn't get any worse.

"Excuse me, is this seat taken?"

Or maybe it could.

Looking as if he'd just stepped off of a page of an L. L. Bean catalog, Blaine Madison stood at the vacant sixth seat of the table, across from Caroline. He'd changed into a pair of jeans and a white polo shirt that flaunted the muscled evidence that he was no stranger to a gym. Eye-catching as he was, Caroline's attention honed in on the jacket he held slung over his shoulder.

"Dad, you came!" Karen practically took Kurt's foot off with her chair as she slid away from the table to greet her father. "What happened?"

"I started thinking about all the fun you would be having without me," he told her, grinning. "Besides, how could I pass up spending the evening with the most beautiful girl in Mexico City . . . especially when she's *my* girl?"

Karen looked as though happiness would lift her off the floor.

"By all means, sit down." Caroline pointed to the chair and raised her voice above the Spanish lyrics of the young man who had taken over the karaoke microphone. "Although I'll warn you, it's chilly in here. Maybe once the dancing starts, it won't seem so cold." She shivered, more from humiliation than temperature. Had he missed the glow-light special, or was he being polite and pretending to ignore it like everyone else?

Regardless, he took the bait—hook, line, and sinker. "I have a jacket, if you'd like."

Thank You, Lord.

"That would be a godsend." A real one. It never ceased to amaze Caroline, the minor details that God saw to.

"Mexico City nights do tend to get chilly." He handed her the jacket and sat down. "We're in a high, dry lake bed surrounded by mountains. Never go out in these parts without a wrap of some kind."

"You are so bad," Annie chided under her breath as Caroline cloaked herself in the jacket

She kicked her daughter beneath the table. She hadn't lied. It *was* chilly in the club—even though she was a smoldering hot pot of embarrassment. Besides, surely God would rather she allowed Blaine to draw the wrong conclusion than have her eighteen-hour wonder exposed in all its fluorescent glory.

CHAPTER 5

The flashing lights behind the karaoke performers gave the show a professional look, although a few of the talent-challenged would put the lights to the test. The students made themselves at home with their Hispanic counterparts, dancing without inhibition, while a young man sang solo by the karaoke setup on the main stage.

"Teen divas, look out," Caroline remarked when girls from their group took over the mikes for a rock-and-roll number.

Blaine didn't reply. He stared at his daughter, his expression a mixture of pride and wounded disbelief. Was that his little girl moving onstage like a Britney Spears wannabe?

Having been there for Annie's first bra and heels, Caroline had eased into the transition, although with no less regret than what she read on Blaine's face. The hardest task for a parent was to encourage them to grow, but not too fast for their own good.

"I didn't know you could sing," Blaine said when

Karen returned to the table, flushed with excitement and the high of the applause.

"There's a lot you don't know about me, Daddy. Can I have money for a drink?"

Caroline flinched for Blaine, who handed over some Mexican currency. With an impassive expression, he watched Karen and Annie head for the soda fountain with Kurt tagging along like a love-struck pup.

At the end of the karaoke hour, the DJ switched to dance numbers. As Karen abandoned her soda for dancing, Blaine caught her arm and said something to her. The music was too loud for Caroline to hear, but clearly Karen was resisting her father's words. Finally Blaine shook his head in resignation and sent her off with a semblance of a smile.

"There was a time that she begged me to dance with her," he told Caroline, slipping into the seat next to her. "She used to stand on my shoes."

The meticulous Blaine Madison let his little girl scuff his shoes? Caroline smiled inwardly. "She's just growing up. At this age, peers trump daddies as dance partners."

Karen and Annie ganged up on Wally, the only one of the students still sitting, and coerced him onto the floor.

Blaine snorted in disbelief as Karen danced a circle around the spectacled youth. "Even the nerd beats good old Dad."

"Be nice," Caroline warned. "Wally's grown up with these kids."

"Hey—" Blaine threw up defensive hands. "I was a nerd. No girls ever dragged me out onto the dance floor."

Try as she might, Caroline could not picture Blaine Madison any way but tall, dark, and collected—everything she was not. Particularly, not collected. Perhaps it was the whiff of some masculine spice in his aftershave, impossible to ignore with his nearness scattering her thoughts.

"So, are you off the clock for the remainder of the trip?" When one's senses take a leave of absence, stick to business.

"What's that?"

The large speakers blasting from the DJ's equipment platform would leave them both voiceless by midnight.

"Did you"—the thunderous drum finale ended—"finish your business?" Caroline's shout ended with a belated taper in volume, her words hanging in the air like a Harrier jet, all roar and attention grabbing. She'd have ducked under the table, but for the spell cast by his dimpled grin.

"In a manner of speaking. I turned the formalities of getting the agreement on paper to my brother and our legal team."

Something about the way he said it gave Caroline the impression that he wasn't sure he'd done the right thing.

"So you're one of those 'if you want it done right, do it yourself' types, eh?"

His humor faded. "You said on the plane that you have a daycare center. Is there any other way to run a business?"

"I've been lucky enough to find reliable help, so that I can get away from time to time."

Blaine smirked. Even so, it was a charming smirk.

"By the time one finds out the help is unreliable, one can be bankrupt."

Her confidence faltered. "Of course I've worked alongside my staff, so I've learned their strengths and weaknesses. And I realize that no one is perfect, including me."

No, she was not perfect, but the God she leaned upon was. She hesitated, succumbing to her old insecurities. Would she downplay His work, His blessings of success? A wave of shame washed over Caroline as she realized her past fears were intimidating her. Frank almost had Caroline believing the day care she'd run from her home was nothing. Even though she'd built it into a successful enterprise, the old hurt and insecurity still raised their ugly heads—especially in the company of professionals like her ex-husband and Blaine Madison.

Blaine wasn't even paying attention to her at the moment. With his gaze narrowed like that of a hawk spotting a mouse, he watched as a fair-haired young man from a nearby table asked Karen to dance.

"Relax, they're just kids," Caroline assured him.

"With raging hormones," Blaine countered. "And the way she dresses and dances—"

"Is normal." There wasn't anything seductive about Karen's dancing. Like Annie's, her movements were somewhere between a bounce, a flail, and a wiggle without the curves to define it. "It's a hard age. She's becoming a woman."

"Not tonight." Blaine's words sounded more like a prayer than a declaration.

"Let her be Cinderella for the night. She's on cloud nine."

"Have you seen Annie's prince?" Blaine nodded to where a tall, lanky young man with red, as in patriotic red, hair talked to her daughter. It looked as if he'd been shot-gunned with studs. They lined his ears, brow, lips—Caroline refused to think beyond that.

"Relax, they're just talking," he said, the square of his jaw softening with his "gotcha" grin. Blaine slung a casual arm over the bentwood back of his chair in an attempt to do just that. "You seem to know all these kids pretty well."

"Most of them since grade school," Caroline answered. Christie had cried on her shoulder when her parents got divorced. Caroline had carried casseroles over to Eddie's house while his mom was treated for cancer. And the number of trips she'd chaperoned couldn't be counted on her combined fingers and toes—the zoos, the camps, the ball games and band competitions, the state and nation's capitals. "They're all my kids."

"Lucky you." He didn't sound envious.

"Yeah," she conceded, "but Scripture says go to all

nations and lead them. These kids are my little nation."

With a thoughtful nod, Blaine looked away, losing himself in his surroundings.

Had she blundered? Some people retreated at the mention of faith as though it were catching.

All she'd done was to say what she felt and why. It wasn't as if she were judging him for not being at ease with the kids, or flaunting her faith in his face.

"You know, their culture is different," he told her without diverting his attention from the young man who had begun a slow dance with his daughter. "I'm afraid he might take the American girls' friendliness for looseness, if you know what I mean."

Caroline observed the couple without reply. Karen wasn't exactly dirty dancing. It was more like chatty dancing. Rigid compared to her partner's ease on the floor, the teen talked nonstop.

At the music's end, Karen led her debonair partner back to the tables and introduced him to her father and Caroline.

"Señor y Señora Madison, el gusto es mío."

"No, silly." Karen's giggle bubbled from the toes up. "This is my dad. Miz C is Annie's mom."

Tall, tan, and fair-featured, the obviously American youth stood out in the nightclub. His impeccable manners, as he introduced himself as John Scott Chandler, made him extraordinary in any setting.

"Where are you from, John?"

There was a guard-dog edge nipping at Blaine's show of cordiality. Or perhaps it was just fatherly instinct.

Caroline's father had passed away before she had reached the age of sixteen.

"Chicago, sir."

"You look older than a high school student," Blaine observed.

"Actually, I was an exchange student in my senior year. Now I'm a senior at the University of California here in Mexico City."

"What part of Chicago are you from? What does your father do? What's your major?" Blaine barely gave the kid the time to reply to one question before he fired another.

Was this overkill, or should she be asking questions too? Her mother radar on full alert, Caroline looked across the room where Annie and a young Mexican boy were going over the DJ's music list.

Karen had reached the end of her endurance. "For heaven's sake, Dad, are you writing a book?"

White smile gleaming, John brushed her protest aside. "Hey, it's okay. He's a parent. It's what good parents do." He extended his hand to Blaine. "Nice meeting you, sir. You too, Miz C."

His undaunted "It's okay" would have done, but "That's what good parents do"? A little too much icing on the proverbial cake.

"Nice meeting you too, John," she answered.

As John led Karen out to the dance floor, her voice wafted back to the table. "*Now* he decides to be a parent!"

"There goes a con artist, if I ever saw one," Blaine

observed in a sawmill whisper.

"So what set off your fatherly red alert?"

"He wouldn't look me in the eye. Tells me he's hiding something."

Where fatherly suspicion had been, a mix of hurt and confusion now ruled his expression. Caroline could almost see the one emotion trying to squeeze the other out of his heart.

"If only I were as adept at reading my daughter as I am others. Talk about mixed signals. One minute I'm the dad of the year; the next, I'm the worst thing that's happened to her since her mom died." He clenched his fists. "I don't pay enough attention to her. Then I'm too intrusive. How's a parent to know?"

Blaine could hardly believe he was asking a stranger advice on his daughter, but a fish out of water is a desperate fish. He had learned to handle diapers and training wheels, bring the anticipated presents when he returned from a trip,. attend the annual Parents' Day at school. He'd been king in his daughter's eyes, and Karen was his little princess. Then things fell apart at the castle.

After Ellie died in a car accident, the drinking that led to it left him with a hovel of cracked walls and a broken rule. His mom said Karen was angry, that time would heal . . . all the right Christian platitudes.

He'd done all he knew to help Karen through the ordeal, but sometimes she acted as if her mother's death was his fault. It wasn't as if he'd abandoned Ellie and her problem. He'd been through many a hellish night helping his wife through withdrawal from alcohol. He'd hired the best doctors and sent her to the best clinics. He'd read so much about dealing with the problem that he could have opened a clinic himself. But in the end, he couldn't fix it. So he'd retreated into his business, where he did have control.

Now Karen obviously found something wrong with him, or something was wrong with her. And once again, he felt powerless to fix it.

"Nothing is tried and true when it comes to raising kids." Caroline made a rueful grimace. "It's a shame babies don't come with instructions."

"Maybe Mark Twain had the answer. Something about putting them in a barrel when they're little and feeding them through the bunghole. And when they become teens, plug the hole."

Although at the moment, he'd prefer to put John Scott Chandler in one.

Blaine reached for his drink and looked at Caroline. As a single mother, she must have had her share of problems, although Annie appeared to be the wholesome girl-next-door type. That was it. The mother was a mature version of the same type—not the kind to catch a man's eye at the first pass, but the kind a guy might confide in. The kind with whom a guy could follow more than one train of thought.

"Actually, I take that back."

He gave himself a mental shake. "Take what back?"

"Babies *do* come with instructions, actually." Her

gaze lit up like the glass ball over the dance floor. "The Bible, silly."

"Oh." Out of politeness, he held back a "Been there, done that." Didn't work then. Didn't work now.

Tonight he'd acted on an urge evoked by the pink tract the lady at the airport had given him. It had fallen out of his pocket when he hung up his sports coat. As he put it on the top of the TV, he'd read it again. *Unless the Lord builds the house, its builders labor in vain. Unless the Lord watches over the city, the watchmen stand guard in vain. In vain you rise early and stay up late, toiling for food to eat, for he grants sleep to those he loves.*

The straw that broke his back was the mental picture of Karen's disappointment when he'd told her that he wasn't going to Banditos with the group. Her initial surprised welcome gave him heart, but the stay was becoming miserable, save present company.

"And in addition to raising kids with the Word, the Bible says we shouldn't provoke our children, and they need to honor us. It's an exchange of respect that has to be earned on both sides."

Blaine didn't want to go there . . . not into a biblical debate. Politics and religion were taboo subjects if one was enjoying the company of others. And he was. A glow of realization emanated from his brain to the rest of him, warm and pleasant.

The music slowed again. He didn't recognize the song, but it gave him an out. "What do you say we show these youngsters a thing or two on the dance floor?"

Her surprise gave way to delight. "I'd love to."

"Want to leave the jacket here? It's probably warmer out there away from that air vent over our table."

With a glance at it, as if she hadn't noticed the air-conditioning outlet before, Caroline drew his coat closer around her. "Now I know why I'm so cold-natured tonight, but I'll keep this, if you don't mind."

"Suit yourself." Blaine took her hand and led her out onto the dance floor.

As he took her into his arms, he doubted that Caroline Spencer had a cold-natured cell in her body. She was sunshine and warmth from the soul out. Distracted by the wildflower scent of her hair, he hardly noticed when she scuffed his freshly shined shoes until she glanced up with a wide-eyed apology.

"Sorry. I . . . I haven't danced in—" She shrugged, her shoulders lost in his jacket. "In I don't know how long."

"Me neither." *Not since Ellie was killed.* Blaine filed the thought in the back of his mind. He was supposed to be relaxing.

"And I have a second left foot," she babbled on nervously. "That's in addition to the right, which has a mind of its own."

Blaine smiled, not his usual polite smile, but one that came straight from his heart. This woman had a way of making him laugh, ready or not.

"And you're so good, it's disconcerting, which puts your toes at even more risk."

He laughed. "My mother was from Atlanta. Every Southern mother worth her magnolias insisted on dance lessons for her children. I hated them at twelve, but they have come in handy later."

He pulled a little closer. There was that heady scent again. It reduced his voice to a throaty whisper. "Just follow my lead."

She stumbled against him, raising her gaze to his face. "It's been a while."

But the determination in her tone and brightness in her gaze told him she was bent on making the best of it. Her eyes reflected the spinning light over the room, telling of a part of Caroline Spencer that remained forever young. Blaine found himself envying it. Not that he'd ever been a fraction as daring as the woman in his arms. Somewhere, deep inside, there was a part of him that longed to let go as well. And it was pleased that he'd heeded its voice to ask the lady to dance. The realization took him by surprise. When he'd found out he was headed for Mexico, this was the last thing he'd imagined on the agenda. When the music changed to a faster number with a beat he'd not learned, Blaine fretted himself into being relieved. He should have stuck to chaperoning, or better yet, remained at the hotel and gone over the contracts that his brother had let slide. But as he started to escort Caroline from the dance floor, she tugged back.

"I thought we were going to show the kids how to do this."

Disconcerted, Blaine looked at the dancers, or rather thrashers around them. "Do what?" he shouted. "Dislocate something?"

Caroline laughed. "It's easy. Just let the music move your feet."

"It's scientifically impossible for music to move feet," he pointed out. But whether he was inclined to dance or not, he was too polite to leave a lady on the dance floor alone. Not wanting to look like a statue, he began to mimic Caroline's movements when he heard Karen squeal from across the room.

"Omigosh, that's my dad. Hey, Daddy!"

Emboldened by his daughter's approval, Blaine loosened his step another notch, feeling like he was caught in Michael Jackson's robotic moves and was about to spin a bearing.

Caroline, on the other hand, had come to life with the unstructured dance. If she thrashed, she did so with a grace the other girls should envy. Blaine couldn't take his eyes off her, even if he wanted to, which he did not.

The Holy Spirit with a piece of pink paper, a free spirit, or just dumb luck . . . whatever the reason, he was glad he had come.

CHAPTER 6

Outside Banditos, patrons dispersed in all directions after the closing hour in a studded denim, tattooed, and sundressed stampede. "Yo!" translated universally to the cabbies hailed over the curbs.

Beneath the Banditos marquee, John Chandler gave Karen Madison a brief kiss on the cheek. He'd have done more, but the girl's father watched him like a ready-to-pounce eagle from the curb, where he and the tour guide were trying to arrange transportation back to their hotel.

"Tomorrow?" he called after her as she pulled away to join her group.

Karen took a deep breath and sighed, her dark-lashed eyes a dancing reflection of the marquee lights overhead. "Tomorrow."

John wondered that she didn't fall, the way she backed away from him, ponytail swinging, blowing kisses until she reached her group. The perfect target—naïve and eager to please. She was cute, but way too young for him. She was more suited for the curly-haired dude in a new Banditos T-shirt, who tugged her around with a reprimand.

"Get a grip or you're gonna fall," Wally said.

"This, from the King of Uncoordinated?" she shot back in derision.

The nerd's involvement with her was obviously one-sided, but he was better for her than the kind of guy that tripped her trigger. *Guys like me.*

"So, *la señorita* is, how do you say, good to went?" Javier Rocha lit up a cigarette at John's elbow.

"You mean good to go?"

"Whatsoever. We have no time to play around," he said, exhaling through wide nostrils.

"I know it." John drilled his metaphor-challenged roommate with an impatient look.

Javier showed more Indian ancestry than the Spanish

his affluent family so proudly claimed. It was all a front for some of the lowest life on the planet—thieves and scoundrels cloaked in mock designer clothes with cushy digs. Cushy for Mexico, that is.

"She took the bait."

John wasn't pleased. He'd rather have chosen someone else, someone who didn't look like his youngest sister, complete with the little gold cross that his grandmother had given her. He had received one too, bigger, more masculine, but he hadn't worn it since he began his studies at the university. Given his activities of late, it would be somehow a sacrilege, an affront to the devout woman who'd given it to him.

"She is very young," Javier observed, picking up on the uncertainty riddling John's mind. "Do you think she can be trusted not to open it . . . or even lose it?"

John, and sometimes Javier, routinely picked the most naïve and gullible of the American students and struck up a friendship. Once they had the person's trust, making her or him feel important, they'd hand over the stolen property for the student to post upon returning to the States. And Javier knew they were both pinched for time, so his question was moot.

"We agreed not to wait for the older crowd because Jorge wanted it out pronto, right?" John couldn't help the anger in his challenge. But it wasn't directed at his friend. It was directed at the situation he'd gotten himself into.

"Sí, that is true. It has three weeks until the summer semester ends."

"So who was left but the kiddies? She took the bait . . . and she's with a Christian group. They're usually a dependable lot. Let it go at that."

"So when will you give her the goods?"

John snuffed the pang of conscience, watching Javier blow two perfect smoke rings. Not only did Javier mix his metaphors, he'd definitely watched too many gangster flicks.

"The *goods,*" John mimicked, "go out tomorrow . . . or on the bus trip at the latest." Most of the Mexico City–Acapulco tours had the same itinerary.

Javier nodded. "*Bueno.* I will tell my uncle that everything is going up as planned."

"That's going *down.*"

Javier shrugged. "Up, down, howsoever. Just so it goes, no?"

John gave a short, less-than-amused laugh. "Yeah. *Howsoever.*"

The package had to go out this week. Javier's uncle was insistent. And no one bucked Jorge Rocha, who had dubbed himself *El Jefe,* and lived to tell about it—unless they got away fast. So John routinely picked the most rebellious or the most naïve and gullible of the American students in the club.

Despite warnings from the authorities about accepting packages from strangers to carry across the border, the teen didn't hesitate to say yes to mailing a card from a fellow American student to his mom upon the group's return to the States. His complaint about the Mexican postal service being so unreliable hadn't been a stretch of the truth, but the card wasn't going to his mom. It was going to Rocha's dealer stateside—all $50,000 worth of it. It wasn't big-time like drug smuggling, but 50K worth of collector's stamps wasn't exactly chump change either.

"You *blondez* do have more fun." Javier patted John on the back. "I'm going back to the bar. You did good, *gringo.*"

"Catch you in a minute, *hermano.*" This blond had had all the fun he could take. The aspirin he continually popped eased his headaches, but there was no balm for his nerves. He glanced back to where Karen's tour guide had two taxis lined up at the curb.

"*Vámonos,* princes and princesses, your coaches are waiting," the guide shouted. "Move now or they will turn into—"

"Squash!" several of the kids chorused.

Their cheer made John feel fifty rather than just six years their senior. He gave Karen one last lingering smile and waved. Maybe he could find someone older who was just as gullible—someone who didn't remind him of his little sister and who wasn't traveling with a church school. Taking a deep brace of cool air, he reentered the club.

The mountain-cooled night air brought some semblance of order to Caroline's bedazzled senses as she waited for the kids to get into the cars. In her mind, she still spun in the laser flashes of light in Blaine's arms. A divine dancer in the slow, measured sense, he'd been one lost puppy when the music passed the old jitterbug. But just being on a dance floor with an awkward but game partner had made Caroline feel footloose and fancy-free for a while. Between molting in the jacket to hide the glow of the living wonder lift and the fact that her partner's last name could be Charming, her heart had done the rumba.

Still is, she amended, fanning herself with the Banditos rose. Since when did hot flashes and schoolgirl giddiness strike at once?

Blaine opened the door to a yellow VW taxi with a flourish. "Ladies, your coach, pulled by horsepower rather than mice."

A man up on his fairy tales. Another layer of Caroline's heart melted away. Blaine continued to play the wry cavalier by taking the cushion on the floor in front of her.

After a swerving, dodging, speeding, braking ride, they made their way into the hotel lobby. Caroline marveled that Blaine could walk straight. He'd reminded her of a clown punching bag, rolling and jerking with the motion of the vehicle. She could still feel the muscular shoulders she'd grasped to steady him.

The fatigue of the day's travel and the night's dancing having caught up with them, the students fished blindly in purses and pockets for keys as they filed into the elevator. Karen hugged her Banditos package to her chest, leaning against the brass rail at the back with a sigh. "This was the most romantic night of my whole life."

From the corner, his dark hair still plastered to his

head with sweat from dancing and socializing with the *señoritas,* Wally agreed. "Definitely cool. I didn't even have time to finish my game."

Next to him, Kurt, who had recovered from Karen's jilting before the next dance ended, leaned against the elevator wall next to a quiet Annie and nodded.

Caroline exchanged a jaded grin with Blaine. The starstruck kids were so young. If they only knew. The moonlight and the long-stemmed roses she and the girls carried from the club would wither by morning. Romantic love was a wonderful start, but it wasn't eternal.

Caroline had wondered for years exactly what had gone wrong with her marriage. All the excuses boiled down to one reason—God was not at the center of their union. At best, He was a part-time boarder. Frank didn't go to church at all. Determined to be the perfect wife and mother, Caroline had gone through the motions of "churchianity" and somehow missed God. It wasn't until she came back to her faith after the divorce that she discovered the difference.

She turned the red rose in her hand, lost in self-study. If she'd had more of a relationship with Jesus instead of the altar ladies . . . The elevator door opened.

"Peso for your thoughts." Blaine's voice drew Caroline back to the present.

She suddenly realized that they were the only two remaining in the elevator.

"At this hour, they're not worth a peso."

Annie had bolted ahead of the others. By the time

Caroline and Karen caught up with her, the room door was open and Annie was exactly where her mother expected—in the bathroom.

Leaving Caroline standing in the hall, Karen tapped at the door with an equal urgency. "Don't take all night!"

Beside Caroline, Blaine shook his head, bemused. "Females!"

And the urgency didn't get any better with age. Caroline waited with him until all the students were in their respective rooms and the click of the deadbolts resounded in the empty hall.

"Well, *Seen-der-eh-ya* . . ." He mimicked Hector's pronunciation to perfection. "I think all our little mice are accounted for." Blaine took her hand in his and lifted it to his lips.

"Who?" Caroline asked, as his sweep-'em-off-the feet smile took out her knees like a smart bomb.

The corner of his mouth quirked. "Cinderella? Mice?" He paused and then added, "Squash?"

"Oh," she laughed, holding up her souvenir flower. "I thought you just wanted to smell my rose." Squirming partly from nerves and partly from the same urgency the girls suffered, she let the flower slip from her fingers.

In a rush to avoid making a further fool of herself, she leaned over to pick it up, only to bang heads with Blaine as he did the same. Before she knew it, she fell back against the doorjamb and slid to the floor with an unceremonious plop.

With one hand on his head where their noggins had collided, and the rose in his other, Blaine knelt down in front of her. "Are you hurt?"

"Only my pride."

"Dad, what *are* you doing?" Karen exclaimed. Behind her, Annie stared at Caroline in dumb wonder.

"Trying to help a klutz," Caroline rallied, before the confusion claiming Blaine's face cleared his response. A picture of what they surely looked like to the girls, she sprawled against the doorjamb, he kneeling between her knees brandishing a rose, gave rise to a slaphappy giggle at the back of Caroline's throat. And one begat another, which begat another until, no matter how Blaine tried to help her up, his efforts were useless.

"Mom?" Annie asked, her expression hovering between amusement and concern.

Karen was no less torn. "Dad?"

At that, Blaine laughed as well as he hooked his arms under Caroline's and lifted her to her feet. "Good thing we have hard heads, eh?" he teased.

"And a well-cushioned tush." Caroline felt her eyes grow wide in shock at her retort. "Me, not you!" Another wave of scarlet rose from her neck and slapped her cheeks. *Lord, I've been around the girls so long I don't even know how to act with a man.*

When Blaine propped her up against the open door and backed away, Caroline could have sworn a part of her went with him. Her breath, at least.

"We'd better call it a night before someone calls security."

Caroline nodded. She could hear it now. There's some guy trying to pick up a laughing hyena in the hall. What was worse, as tired as she was, she still had a buildup of schoolgirl giggles just dying to be released if she so much as opened her mouth. What on earth was wrong with her?

"Don't worry, Dad," Karen said, taking Caroline by the arm. "We'll take care of Miz C."

"Yeah, when Mom gets overtired, she gets kind of doofus."

Stepping inside, Caroline gripped the brass handle of the door latch. "Thank you for being so gallant."

Blaine tipped an imaginary hat. "My pleasure. Good night, ladies . . . and bolt the door."

"We will, Dad."

"See you in the morning, Mr. M," Annie said.

Easing the door shut after Blaine turned to go, Caroline dutifully slipped the bolt into place and then floated into the bathroom, lifted by the clamor of her fairy tale–infected heart's *Good night, sweet prince.* But when she stubbed her toe on the marble threshold, reason had its say. *He was just being the gentleman his Atlanta-born mama raised him to be.* Caroline sat on the toilet lid and rubbed her protesting toe, her lips pulling into a wistful smile. *But thank you, Neta Madison, for bringing me the Cinderella moment à la your son's dance lessons. It might be sensible shoes tomorrow, but for tonight, it was glass slippers all the way.*

The moonlight madness of the night before gave way

to a peek-aboo sun above the surrounding mountains and sleep-deprived, grumpy faces the following morning. It was hard enough for Caroline to get ready, much less ride herd over the girls, who kept hogging the bathroom. Resigned to using the room mirror, Caroline stood before it in her sleep shirt and rubbed makeup remover on her eyes before she realized the tissues were in the bathroom.

"Annie, honey," she called out, padding over to the door in her bare feet, "hand me out some tissues or toilet paper?" Okay, Caroline knew the experts insisted on cotton balls or pads, but the experts couldn't afford to keep her, Annie, and Annie's friends stocked with them.

"What?" Annie called from the other side of the locked door.

"Unlock the door. I need to get some toilet—"

"Hey, Dad," Karen said, throwing open the connecting door behind Caroline. "You ready yet?"

Caroline jerked her head around to see Blaine Madison sitting on the edge of an unmade bed, a telephone pressed to his ear.

"Karen, *I'm* not ready," she cried. Not with a crumpled T-shirt touting a Winnie the Pooh "Tiggertude" and raccoon circles around the eyes. And her hair was as *wild woman* as it gets before a morning brushing.

Blaine, on the other hand, while unshaved and still in a pair of sweatpants, looked fine in the most flattering sense of the word. Mother Nature hadn't played fair to make females so high maintenance. Caroline groaned silently as he crooked his finger at his daughter, bidding her to come in. To Caroline he afforded a crimped smile that held back at least shock, if not outright laughter.

Blaine motioned for his daughter to close the door behind her and resumed taking the messages that his secretary was reading off. Some ground rules obviously needed to be set.

"What?" Karen mouthed.

"Hold on a minute please, Alice." He covered the mouthpiece of the phone. "Don't ever do that again. It was rude."

A picture of innocence, his daughter lifted her shoulders. "Do what? I mean, it's not like anyone was naked or anything."

Blaine's voice took on a hint of Karen's exasperation. "It isn't proper for unmarried adults to see each other—" He groped for the word, the image of Caroline in a rumpled sleep shirt adorned with Tigger now indelibly etched in his mind. She'd reminded him of a wide-eyed raccoon caught in its mischief. Of course, he doubted he appeared any less startled.

"Dad, you're gonna see her in a swimsuit," Karen reminded him, as if she had the monopoly of wit and wisdom in the room. For the moment, she did.

"It's just . . . improper," he stammered. Talk about lame. "And if you do it again, you won't see the light of day till school starts in September."

"I just wanted to see if you were going to breakfast, but I don't want to eat with a grumpy old bear."

Grumpy old bear? He picked up the roll of antacid tablets he slept with and popped one to put out the early morning fire in his stomach.

"And I can see you're working anyway, so I'll just cut out and leave you to the love of your life."

"*You* are the love of my life," Blaine recovered, wishing he had a mate to carry on this argument so that he could deal with reasonable people. "But that won't excuse you from everything you do. Understand?"

With a big sigh and roll of her eyes to the ceiling, Karen put her hands on her hips again. "Got it. Open the door, grounded forever. Now can I go?"

Already zeroing back in on his messages, Blaine waved her off.

"Did Mark say where he was going?"

"No, sir," Alice replied. "He just said he'd be gone for the remainder of the week and that we'd see him Monday."

Tightening his grip on the phone as though it were his younger brother's neck, Blaine's mind whirred with contingencies regarding the contract he'd just e-mailed. Mark had assured him that he'd be on hand to go over the details in case Blaine had missed something important during his whirlwind presentation.

"Do you want me to start calling around, sir?" the secretary asked.

"Have you got Mark's black book?" Blaine asked, then winced. It wasn't Alice's fault. "Sorry, Alice, I don't mean to be cynical, but—"

"I know, sir. It's Mark." She paused. "What about

Eric Stolzman? He worked on the specs with you. He doesn't really need Mark to give a blank approval."

Which was about all his brother did. If only Blaine hadn't had to rush through the presentation, no one would really need to approve it. He was a stickler for detail.

"It's not protocol," he said. "I set up the procedures and expect them to be followed."

Mark always complains that he doesn't have enough responsibility. So I toss something important his way, and he fumbles. If his brother couldn't follow through on the inside sales, how could he handle the outside trips he was so eager to take on?

"Never mind," Blaine decided aloud. "I'll go over it myself."

"That's not protocol either, sir," Alice reminded him good-naturedly. She was always on him to delegate. Blaine had to delegate to Mark, who was family. He didn't have to delegate elsewhere. He wanted, no, *needed* to have a finger in every pie.

"If I do it myself, I know it's done right," he thought aloud. Then, remembering Alice, he added in a more gentle tone, "Unless it's something you're handling. You're the best."

"Then why don't you listen to the best and take a few days away? Eric knows exactly how you came up with the numbers."

"He doesn't have the managerial eye that I have. That's why I want you to tell him to hold the high line on the Haggarty proposal. They won't balk when they hear our guarantee. Knowing they can rely on Madison to deliver the best on time is an intangible asset worth paying for." Blaine took pride in his company's reputation. Their bids might be high, but they were firm, no mandatory add-ons later.

"Eric may not have a managerial eye yet, but he will soon."

Alice's smug assumption caught him off guard. Had Eric been wooed away by a competitor? "What do you mean?" he asked.

"Because you'll be stroked out in the hospital, or worse."

"I'll take that under advisement." The tension-pressed line of his lips relaxed. "In the meantime, keep your Tiggertude to yourself." If he couldn't finish it before the tour left—

"Excuse me," Alice interrupted in a bewildered voice. "Did you say Tiggertude?"

Did he? The cartoon character on Caroline's T-shirt laughed at him from the corner of his mind. Heat seeped up his neck. "I meant attitude."

"I didn't know you were a Pooh fan."

Winnie-the-Pooh. That's where he'd seen that tiger. "My daughter is." The fact that this tiger had nothing to do with Karen and everything to do with a sleep-bedraggled woman with cute little raccoon eyes was none of Alice's business. "Well, that wraps it up for now. I have to get to work."

"Keep up the *Tiggertude*."

"Will do. Bye."

Blaine hung up the phone and stared at the adjoining door to his daughter's room. *Now* he had an answer to her question as to why it mattered that a single guy should see a woman in a freshly bedraggled state. Because he would never shake the image from his mind, and because his secretary would never let him hear the end of this.

The hotel dining room was busy with the breakfast buffet. The efficient Señora Marron had reserved two large tables for the Edenton group.

"Dad read me the riot act on door etiquette," Karen complained to Annie as they stood in the buffet line. "I mean, it's not like anyone wasn't decent."

"Sweetie, decent doesn't necessarily equal presentable." Caroline maintained a gentle voice as opposed to the authoritarian tone she'd overheard earlier, beyond the adjoining door to their room. Her urge to strangle the girl passed when she saw Karen's crestfallen face upon her return. "I don't know any man well enough to let him see me like that."

Karen made a contrite grimace. "At least you didn't threaten to ground me for the rest of my life if I did it again. I just wanted to see if he was going with us today."

"So . . . is he coming?" Annie asked.

"He said he'd be down after breakfast. Guess he ordered in."

"Well, he must not be too mad at you." Caroline hugged her forlorn charge. "And I obviously didn't scare him all the way back to PA."

"Miz C, you couldn't scare a flea," the girl said with a sheepish grin, not unlike her father's. "I don't think I've ever seen you mad."

"I have," Annie volunteered. "It's not a pretty sight."

"Yeah, just remember that, kid." Caroline flicked Karen's pony-tail and, taking up a tray, focused on the long display of hot, lamp-lit, stainless steel.

The hotel offered the traditional breakfast of *huevos rancheros*—fried eggs on a tortilla—with a side of refried beans and chopped fresh tomato salsa laced with jalapeños. After a few wrinkled noses at some of the dishes, Caroline led the way to the reserved tables where some of the tour members waited for them.

"Where's your dad?" Kurt asked as Karen sat down across from him.

"Getting over a bad case of grumpiness."

"But he'll be down in time for the tour," Annie put in.

"Sleep well?" Dana called to Caroline from across the table. Caroline knew from her friend's mischievous wink that she was expecting details of the evening on the town with Blaine Madison.

"Like a dead-tired princess," Caroline answered. Although she concentrated on seasoning her food, she could well imagine the heat in her cheeks rivaled the red glow from the buffet bulbs.

"When Cortés first saw the Indians eating scoops of beans on their tortillas in 1517," Hector informed the group, once the salt, pepper, and ketchup had made the rounds, "he said, 'Sight of sights. Not only do they eat the food, but they eat the plates as well.' "

Caroline preferred using a fork and knife. She had to smile, though, at the heartfelt amens that echoed around the table after Señora Marron asked that the food be blessed by the heavenly Father. Despite their wistful sighs for a pop-tart or a bowl of cereal, most of their party bravely tried their first Mexican breakfast.

"So, did you enjoy dancing the night away with Blaine Madison?" Dana asked later, as the group gathered in the lobby for the morning tour of the Zocalo and historic center.

Caroline kept an eye on Karen and Annie, who'd wandered into the hotel gift shop. "We danced three dances to keep from getting bored, and the club tossed us out."

"And . . . ?" Dana prompted, her voice low.

"And . . . I scuffed his shoes, dropped my rose, and finished the night with a head butt. I almost knocked him off his feet. End of story."

Dana turned a speculative gaze on Caroline. "Sounds promising to me."

"So promising he didn't show up for breakfast this morning." Caroline raised a hand as though to stop Dana's train of thought in its track. "Besides, I don't want promising. I'm happy just the way I am, so don't go reading something into nothing."

And it was nothing . . . right? Because if it was something, Caroline didn't want it to be. The last thing she needed was a man adding to her responsibilities, second-guessing her at every turn, as though she didn't have enough sense to breathe on her own.

"*Excusamé, señoras,* but is this the walking tour?"

Caroline turned to see Blaine standing beside them. She'd been so busy watching the gift-shop door that she hadn't seen his approach. He did for jeans and polo shirt what a cover girl did for makeup.

"Why, Mr. Madison," Dana said, surprised. "Do you speak Spanish?"

"Enough to get around and do a little business down here, no more." He turned to Caroline. "I apologize for Karen this morning. Whenever Ellie and I traveled, we always booked an adjoining room for her and a friend. She still thinks she can bob in and out at will."

"Since you survived the shock, there's no harm done." Caroline glanced at her friend, whose imagination by now was surely off and running at a full gallop. "Oh, look, there's the bus," she said in hopes of distracting Dana. She pointed to the glass lobby front, where a large black-and-silver transport had pulled up to the curb. "I'd better get the girls."

"Today is the walking tour," Dana reminded her.

Which was exactly what Blaine had just said. Where on earth was her mind?

Caroline shrugged, ignoring her friend's smug look. "Just wake me up when we get wherever we are going."

She wasn't sleepy. Every inch of her five-foot-two body was on full alert. But the moment Blaine came within her radar, her wisecracking evasion of Dana's well-meaning interest became scrambled, one thought knocking the other senseless.

"Bueno, vámonos niños," Hector called from the lobby door, waving a red, orange, and gold fan with the tour service's name on it. "Follow the colors of the Aztec and stay close. I promise you, there will be vendors aplenty and time for shopping later."

Great. More distraction. Caroline filed in the line forming behind the tour guide, leaving room for Annie and Karen, who emerged from the gift shop, prodded by Blaine.

Of its own accord, her stomach fluttered as though filled with spooked butterflies. This was absurd, she reasoned. Dana's suggestions were getting to her, in spite of Caroline's logic. The best thing to do, to avoid fueling her friend's overactive imagination, was to avoid Blaine. That would take care of Dana, she decided, digging through her purse. *And a Rolaids will take out the butterflies.* Caroline chewed the chalky mint tablet and swallowed. It was probably the salsa on eggs anyway.

CHAPTER 7

The walk to the Zocalo was short and cool in the early morning air. Robbed of his usual morning workout by business calls before the tour's scheduled departure, Blaine enjoyed the brisk walk through the early bustle of traffic and vendors. Given his way, he'd enjoy a quick scan of the market section of the newspaper, a black cup of Mexican espresso—no latte or flavored frills, and *pan dulce*—still oven hot—in one of the sidewalk bistros. The continental muffin in his room paled in appeal at the tantalizing scent of the sweet rolls that wafted from the restaurants and street stalls along the way.

Ahead of him, Caroline paused unexpectedly in front of a cascading display of woolen blankets and ponchos. "I'm almost tempted to buy one of those. It's the middle of summer, for Pete's sake. When does this place warm up?"

"By noon you'll be sorry you did," Blaine told her.

With a skeptical look she drew away from the vendor, who'd already dropped the price of the poncho he held up for Caroline to examine. "Special price, just for the pretty *señora*."

"Maybe on the way back," she answered, rubbing her bare arms for some friction warmth.

Blaine checked an instinct to draw her under the protection of his arm as some of the other men had done for their chilled companions. But he'd already made a fool of himself last night and sent the poor woman into shock. He must have been caught up in Hector's Cinderella nonsense, to play the gallant, sending her sprawling in disbelief. And she wasn't the only one dumbstruck. Blaine had never kissed a woman's hand, not even Ellie's.

His mom was right about one thing. He had been working too hard. And now that his right brain had been given a little leeway, it wanted the whole playing field.

"Vámonos, peoples, *vámonos,"* Hector shouted from

the street corner, where the light had changed in favor of the pedestrians to cross over.

The historical center of the city was a mix of the Aztec and Spanish past and the present Mestizo evolution of the two. The Plaza of Three Cultures was constructed upon the ruins of an ancient Aztec temple. Blaine had been there without a guide to have a look at the architecture, but Hector's spiel regarding its history gave him a broader perspective.

The building materials the Spanish used to erect the massive Metropolitan Cathedral had come from the pyramids of the conquered Indians. While he didn't approve of the Spanish motivation and unconscionable acts of cruelty, Blaine could find no fault with their practical use of the pyramids. The Indians no longer used them. Now the excavations of their ruins lay open to the public, and the church in turn struggled to remain intact on the unstable foundation of the city originally built upon a lake. The modern design of the adjacent museum brought both worlds into the present.

"Stand in one spot," Caroline told the girls with a hint of conspiracy in her voice, "and slowly turn full circle. Use your imagination. It's like a time machine."

Bemused, Blaine watched as they all three did so, clicking off pictures with their disposable cameras all the way. "You know," he told Caroline, "you can buy postcards with better pictures in the museum."

"But it wouldn't be what I actually experienced, and I want to take it with me." She looked at him, almost breathless. "Can't you just feel it?"

Arms flung wide, she pulled another spin, nearly taking out a camera-blinded Japanese tourist. Blaine caught her in time, pulling her out of the way with an apology to the disconcerted photographer.

"Oh!" Caroline turned to the man. "I'm *so* sorry."

He nodded. She nodded. He backed away, and Caroline turned her bright-eyed attention back to Blaine, her arms folded harmlessly against her chest. "But it is beautiful, isn't it?"

No, the dingy concrete and ruins weren't beautiful, but Mexico with Caroline was an entirely different country. It was as if she had infected him with the wonder and awe on her face. Even the dourest Scrooge couldn't help feeling her kid-at-Christmas excitement.

"The pride, the pain. In the midst of all this concrete and rock is the color of the people," she gushed on, shades of a stage diva. "Look, I have goose bumps."

"Probably the morning air." Yet, as Blaine followed Caroline's gaze, he almost envisioned more than the drab buildings that he actually saw—images of the heart, not logic. And they were breathtaking.

"Hey, you two, come on," Karen called back to them, as the loosely knit group started off behind Hector.

"Omigosh." As if prodded by a sharp stick, Caroline broke away from the still frame that captured them and hurried ahead, leaving Blaine to catch up.

"He'll do a head count before we leave," he called out in assurance, but by now she was power-walking beyond earshot toward the gathering at the cathedral's dark arched doors. Blaine grimaced, certain now that Caroline Spencer was as spooked by his behavior as he was. Even Karen looked at him like he'd grown a third eye. Although, on second thought, his daughter did that on a regular basis. Realizing his feet were still glued to the spot, Blaine shook himself free with an energized pace, as if to outdistance that which he was at a loss to understand.

"Maybe the Indians knew what they were doing when they refused to attend services inside the church, but worshiped with the missionary fathers here in the open plaza," Hector said as Blaine brought up the rear of the group on the opposite side from where Caroline stood. The guide pointed with a cryptic grin to some scaffolding where repairs were being done on the looming stone structure. "Perhaps both would have done well to take the Scripture about building on a rock literally, eh?"

The "amens" that echoed around Blaine sobered him in an instant. The rock he'd leaned on in his past was like the facade of this church, dark and stern, with all the ornate trappings. When Ellie's alcoholism came to light, he'd wondered what he'd overlooked, what he'd done to deserve the lot dealt him. But he'd clung to the faith of his childhood, believing—hoping—that God would make things right. Then his wife died in the accident, and anger set in. Now there was a strained coexistence of spirit. Blaine didn't bother God, if God didn't bother him.

"Now it's time to discover your ancient roots,"

Hector announced, drawing Blaine out of his dark thoughts. "We will separate into the hunters and the gatherers. Meet here at the door of the National Palace in one hour."

The group broke apart very much as Hector, tongue-in-cheek, had predicted. The "hunters and explorers," mostly men, staked out a bench or section of railing, while the "gatherers"—the women—meandered through the rows of tables and blankets displaying Indian crafts and jewelry. The merriment that drifted Blaine's way as Caroline tried a handwoven hat and posed for her young charges contrasted with his shrouded desire to escape.

Maybe he should have remained at the hotel and followed through on the news that his brother hadn't yet read the contract prepared by Blaine's secretary. Mark was out of the office until the following Monday, according to Alice. Heaven forbid his younger sibling work a full week when the fishing was good or the weather perfect for golf.

Instinctively, Blaine reached for his cell phone and realized he'd left it on the nightstand beside the bed. He never went out without it tucked in his jacket, but today he hadn't suited up for business. Nor did he usually start his morning by seeing a sleep-tousled redhead try to shrink inside an oversized nightshirt. Flustered, Blaine leaned on a section of rail overlooking the temple excavation, and was promptly interrupted by a tap on the shoulder.

"Excuse me, would you mind taking a family picture of us with the dancers?" Ron Butler handed Blaine a good digital camera.

Dancers? Blaine turned, surprised to see that a group of brightly feathered and leathered Indians with bells and rattles had managed to sneak up on him. "No problem. I use one like this for work projects." He waited until the trio paid one of the dancers to pose with them. Nothing came free here.

"Christie?" He thought that was the daughter's name. "Can you move closer to your mom?" Finally he had the two blondes in the picture. "Did anyone ever tell you that you two look more like sisters than mother and daughter?" he observed as they came into focus.

"My real mom is in California," Christie said without embarrassment. "This mom got stuck with me when she married my dad."

Her stepmother gave the girl a quick hug and laughed. "Yeah. We've tried everything to get rid of her, but she keeps finding us."

Blaine captured the glowing bond between the stepmother and stepdaughter with the push of a button. Maybe Caroline was right about taking the experience home with her. Postcards didn't have loved ones in them.

"That's a keeper," Ron Butler said, taking the camera back. "Thanks."

"*Now* can Pegeen and I go shopping?" Christie linked her arm with her stepmother.

Ron mimicked Hector with a wave of his hand. "*Vámonos, vámonos*. Me, I'm going to get one of those snow cones before you two break my piggy bank."

"That extra suitcase will come in handy after we empty the goodies at the orphanage," Dana remarked to an equally package-laden Caroline as they approached the bench where Randy and Blaine were engaged in conversation. "Till then, there's Randy."

"Hey, honey," she called to her husband, "will you carry this for me?"

Randy met her halfway, grunting for effect as he took the bag, but his grin belied any real grudge.

"You gals realize those fake straw bags with *Mexico* on them are probably made in China," Blaine pointed out.

Caroline rallied to the wry observation. "Maybe so, but it's where I bought them that counts to me."

"Would you like me to carry yours?" Blaine offered.

"No thanks, I'm used to being the pack mule." Then she mustered a gracious smile. "Although, you could take Karen's." She handed over a bright woolen blanket rolled up in a used plastic supermarket bag, but Blaine looked past her, distracted.

"The girls are over by the snow cone vendor," she said, anticipating his question. "They'll be along in a minute."

"Aren't those some of the kids from the nightclub?" Taking his daughter's purchase under his arm, Blaine bristled with paternal wariness.

Caroline turned. Sure enough, there was the exchange

student whom Karen had introduced to them the night before and his Mexican companions, including the one with the spiked red hair and enough studs to bear a resemblance to a ballroom globe when he moved in the bright sun.

Caroline shuddered as Spike let Annie taste his snow cone. She'd warned her daughter against the water, but not against the natives. From the flirty look Annie gave the young man, germs were the last thing on her innocent mind.

Just as Caroline started forward, the boys were drawn away by an authoritative figure waving a small Mexican flag over his head. The youths fell in with a group of tourists, ranging from babies in strollers to straw-hatted senior citizens, and walked toward a tour bus parked at the end of the square. A few minutes later, Annie and Karen ambled over with bright red snow cones.

"Isn't it too cool?" Karen raved. "The guys we met are taking a bus tour to Acapulco this week too."

Leaving Blaine to his own concerns, Caroline pulled Annie aside. "Sweetie, you don't drink after strangers . . . or anyone, for that matter."

Annie was indignant. "Mom, Manny hadn't taken a bite yet. I just wanted to see if I should get the rainbow flavors or stick with my black cherry standby."

"Hey, isn't it time to head for the National Palace?" Kurt called out, bringing up the rear of the snow cone aficionados.

As they moved en masse toward the designated

meeting place, Blaine reached down and coaxed the straw bag out of Caroline's hand. At her surprised look, he gave her a rakish grin. "My mother would never forgive me if I allowed a pretty lady to carry packages while I had a free hand."

With her heart curling up and purring in her chest, she mumbled a "thank-you" and concentrated on walking straight ahead before she was tempted to brush kittylike against her companion to coax more such attention. Behind them, a diesel engine roared and popped, but Caroline hardly flinched. Siding with logic, she battled to stop the continuous loop of Blaine's smile and the word *pretty* that held the audience of her senses captive.

Gears groaned as the tourist bus nudged its way into the mainstream of traffic.

"I tell you, man, you have brushed that *señorita* off her feet, no?" Javier said with that silly grin on his face.

John Scott Chandler's gaze followed Karen Madison's group across the plaza. He hadn't found another candidate to move the package. He'd tried, but the young women who came in after the club turned to the older clientele weren't interested.

"It does look that way, *amigo*. If anything goes wrong, Jorge will have my hide drying on the wall of his hacienda before the sun sets on the news."

It was like handing candy to a baby. Karen had dropped the card in her bag of souvenirs while they waited in line at the Ice Man vending truck. After a quick look to see if Big Daddy was around—he couldn't shake the feeling that the man was onto him—John gave her another chaste peck on the cheek in front of the twerp with the crush on her.

Javier grinned. "*Mi tío,* he has his ways."

Like a hundred ways to eat beans. And if Javier kept eating pizza with the same enthusiasm, he would soon be just as round as his uncle. Today, he slurped down a grape snow cone. The ice in the cone that John finished before boarding the bus had given him a headache. At least that was how he reasoned this latest one away. Lately, everything upset him. And Javier, with his delusions of being as big as his uncle, now gnawed on John's last frayed nerve.

Reaching into his shirt pocket, John retrieved the aspirin tin he always kept on hand. Popping a pill into his mouth, he chased it down with the warm bottled water he'd brought on the bus that morning. If only he'd known of Javier's gift for understatement before becoming involved with the Rocha family.

"Why so glum, *hermano?*" The young man beside him kicked back the reclining seat and folded his hands behind his head. There was a purple stain on his white polo shirt. "We get an expense-paid trip to Acapulco and the charms of the *señoritas* until they fly off to see our letters posted in the good U.S. of A."

As if Javier could pick up a female American mark. He was a real ladykiller all right, if boring them to death counted. Guys, on the other hand—like John—didn't care about his Pillsbury doughboy face and short, stocky build, giving his good old *chico* personality a chance to make the pitch. That he bought the beer didn't hurt any.

"This is it, man. I have my degree, and I am back home soon as this one is over."

It had all started with the same line John used with this latest wide-eyed dupe. No one could depend on the *Servicio Postal de Mexicano*. It made perfect sense to help a new buddy get a letter to his *Tía* Rosa by carrying the letter-sized packet to the U.S. to mail.

"I will miss you, *hermano*." Javier checked the bag of pizza pretzel treats he'd polished off before leaving the bus, to be certain there were none left. "We have had some good times, eh?"

John nodded in silence. It had been a game at first. He had a way with girls, and it fed a malnourished part of his ego to manipulate them so easily. Sometimes the contraband was rare stamps, sometimes jewels, always small and always costly.

And the quick, easy money enabled him to live a high life in an apartment with Javier off university grounds. It wasn't as though they were dealing drugs or doing something really sinister. What harm was it to steal from some old rich collector, who many times didn't even miss the valuable until well after it had been lifted and sold on the black market? No one got hurt—as long as things went as planned.

Javier clapped his hand on John's arm. "Good times, no?"

"Yeah, good times." John put his fingers to his head

and leaned against the pillow rest. "Too good, especially last night."

"José Cuervo is not so much your amigo today, eh?"

With no prospects to replace Karen Madison as their unwitting courier, tequila proved a temporary salve for his conscience. But today it was back, pounding his brain from all sides.

"My head feels like a piñata about to burst."

John hardly heard Javier's "You need to eat more regular, man."

Conscience and worse—the memory of the one time something had gone wrong. All the front men—students who handed off the goods to the unsuspecting couriers—had been forced to watch Jorge Rocha and his sidekick, Argon, take turns beating a guy who'd tried skipping with some goods and fencing them on his own. After Jorge and company left, John called the attention of some passersby to the victim in the alley, who in turn used their cell phones to summon an ambulance. John had faded into the crowd, letting the callers answer the police questions.

"Candy?"

Jerked from the nightmare in broad daylight, John opened his eyes to see the punk with the red Mohawk and enough studs to outfit a motorcycle gang holding an open box of multicolored treats. Javier helped himself to a handful. John shook his head.

"No thanks, dude."

God help him, this was it for him. Karen Madison was his last mark.

CHAPTER 8

"Weren't those murals incredible?" Caroline speared a forkful of the lime-basted, grilled chicken salad served on a shell at the open-air café. Diego Rivera's sprawling portrayal of Mexican history at the National Palace had so drawn her in that she'd not even noticed it was after noon, but her stomach had. It grumbled the entire walk from the heavily guarded government building to Chapultepec Park, where the group was to lunch and visit the Museum of Anthropology.

"I bought a book on the murals for the school library," she said, catching Blaine the postcard pusher's eye for approval, "but even those pictures don't do them justice."

"Yeah, it was like a painted time machine," Karen piped up after swallowing a mouthful of food. Most of the students had settled for the tried-and-true *la hamburguesa y las papas fritas*—burger and fries.

Across the park, a large group of tourists looked up in the air where an acrobatic troupe in black and red climbed a tall pole with apparent ease. At the top was some sort of metal frame or ring that reminded her of a playground merry-go-round—with no bottom. The waiter called it the *voladores*.

"Who was that blond-haired guy who came to the Aztecs before the Spanish?" Annie's gaze took on a pensive glow, as though she searched an imaginary crystal ball. "I mean, if he didn't look like a snake with a plume."

"It's pronounced *ket-sal-quate-al,*" Caroline read aloud. "Historians have debated many identities for the man the Indians thought to be the incarnation of the plumed serpent god Quetzalcoatl—St. John, St. Thomas, St. Brendan. Some suggest even Jesus of Nazareth, after His resurrection. Whoever he was, he taught them the basics of Christianity centuries before Columbus and the Spanish conquerors."

"The Irish theory would explain a lot of things." All heads turned at Blaine's declaration.

"Like what?" Caroline asked.

"Why no one can say his name." Humor tugged at the corner of his smirk. "The Celts couldn't spell any better than the Aztecs. They just throw a bunch of letters together and every man helps himself to the pronunciation."

Laughing, Caroline dug into her purse to pay for hers and Annie's meal, but Blaine snatched up the check.

"My treat," he said in a tone that stalled her objection. "You get the next one."

As they left the bistro, Annie linked her arm through Blaine's. "Thanks, Mr. M. It's great to have a dad around once in a while."

The girl—her little girl—looked at the man with nothing less than adoration. Caroline's heart took such a tumble, she didn't hear Blaine's reply.

Heavenly Father . . . Caroline dared not pray further, for she had no idea what to ask for. Nor could she identify the emotions spinning around in her mind like the men now being flung away from the pole on long lines. There was nothing to do but emulate the *voladeros,* who now hung from the ring by their knees, spinning like a child's top, pantaloons and puffy sleeves billowing in the overhead breeze. She had to cling to what kept her from free-falling to her end—her faith that God was in control.

After a quick tour of the Museum of Antiquity, Hector herded Edenton High's finest onto a diesel-eating bus for the ride to the north of the city to see the Villa de Guadalupe. Guillermo, aka Bill the driver, eased the bus in, out, and around, darting past honking cars, motorbikes, and an occasional burro-powered cart with an amazing calm, while Hector pointed out sites and statues of interest along the way.

In front of Blaine, Dana and Caroline and the girls tried on the Indian trinkets they purchased in the museum shop.

"Ooh, I didn't see that one," Caroline exclaimed, fingering the medallion Karen wore on a black cord around her neck.

"It's a sundial or something," the girl said.

Kurt spoke up from across the aisle. "It's an Aztec calendar."

"Thank you, Professor Doofus." Karen wrinkled her nose, making a face at the boy. "So what did you get?"

"A little book on Aztec life. I want to show the guys how seriously the Indians took their sports. You know," he added, seeing Karen had no clue what he was talking about. "Remember when Hector said how they killed the losing team?"

"Talk about taking sports too seriously," Wally Peterman snorted. "Though I kind of liked that big doughnut-looking stone where the Aztecs tied their enemies and let 'em fight to the death in honor."

"Oh, yeah, there's real honor in being tied to a rock while a tribe of savages kills you." Annie rolled her eyes toward the tin-paneled ceiling.

"At least you got to—" The bus rolled over a curb and dropped, cutting Kurt off. "To take some of them with you," he finished.

"And when you're dead, that is going help *how?*" Karen's ponytail punctuated her challenge with a bounce.

Next to Blaine, the boy's father looked up from the brochure he'd been reading with a grin. "You might as well learn early, son, there's no arguing with female logic."

"And just what is that supposed to mean, Randy Gearhardt?" Dana peered over the seat at her husband.

"It means that God gave women a logic all their own, and we men are to love you for it, dear."

Unable to find a quarrel with her husband's explanation, Dana slunk down in her seat, a smile of satisfaction on her lips.

"Nice recovery," Blaine said under his breath.

"I'll take fresh over day-old crow any day."

Blaine laughed out loud. He liked these people. For

some reason he'd had this preconceived notion that as churchgoing Christians, they'd be a dull, holier-than-thou bunch, hemmed in by lists of dos and don'ts. Instead, they seemed to be ordinary Joes like him, doing the best they could in a not-so-perfect world.

Eventually the bus pulled out of the mainstream of honking traffic and up to the curb across the street from the two cathedrals—the old in classic Baroque architecture, the new one reminding Blaine of a collapsing circus tent.

After climbing the crosswalk bridging the street, the group was absorbed by a throng of humanity inching past carts and booths selling cold drinks, fresh fruit, and all manner of garish skeletons and religious relics as they made their way toward the holy shrines. Scattered in between them were beggars, disfigured and gaunt, their hands outstretched for coins. Children in rags plied the same trade, working their way through the tour groups.

Giving a coin to one of the snaggle-toothed waifs with dark eyes large enough to lose oneself in was like tossing food to gulls at the beach. Hector said as much before they disembarked, but by the time the group assembled in the line to enter the cathedral, Caroline looked like the Pied Piper, surrounded by urchins.

"No más." Not only her change, but every mint and stick of gum she carried in her sack purse had run out.

As Blaine moved forward to intervene, he felt someone nudge him.

"Dad, have you got any change? I want to give something to that old lady on the step." Instead of waiting for his answer, Karen dug into his pocket.

"Hold it, whoa, whoa." Blaine clamped a hand on his daughter's wrist. "Honey, this is their profession. Keep your purse closed and tight against you, just as Hector cautioned us."

Shock grazed the teen's face. "You mean they aren't really handicapped and starving?"

"Some may be," Blaine conceded. "But for others it's a sham. There are some people who can't be helped."

He should have just let her go with the pocket change. Now he felt as if he'd just told his little girl there was no Santa.

"Blaine, do you have change for a dollar, or whatever this is?" Caroline held up a colorful piece of Mexican currency.

"Dad thinks these beggars are faking it," Karen told her.

"Oh, no, that can't be."

One disillusioned female was bad enough.

"All I was saying is that some people earn their living begging and will never move up as long as it works."

Caroline pointed to an elderly woman with a disfigured face and hands. "I can't believe anyone would live like this, if she had a choice."

"No, not the invalids," he said, compelled to at least try to pull himself out of the cynical pothole he'd inadvertently stepped into. "But a lot of them won't be helped. I know, because I was part of a project to build safe high-rise housing after the '85 quake for the commuting workforce. To this day, very few actually live in the city. Haven't you noticed the traffic jams in the morning and evening?"

Blaine felt compelled to explain himself—how the first time he was in Mexico working on the project estimate, he too had been moved toward pity. He could have gotten more for the contract than he'd bid, but all he could see were the families sleeping under street canopies and those brown-eyed, dark-haired waifs who'd begged him for coins.

"Then later, I saw the same kids with a CD player like the one I bought Karen for Christmas. It wasn't cheap."

Caroline's gaze brewed with thought for a moment. "Then you've adopted the same mentality as the workers who won't move into your buildings."

"Excuse me?"

"There are charlatans in every profession, yours included. The workers don't trust you as a legitimate engineer because a few unscrupulous ones cut corners at the expense of human lives. You don't trust that these people are in need because a few are shams."

The simple illustration tripped a switch somewhere within, flooding Blaine's grudging mind with the light of conviction.

"In heaven's eye," she said, "it's the heart of the giver, not of the receiver that earns God's favor. If the gift is misused, that is between the receiver and God."

Stung pride demanded a defense, but Blaine could think of none. "Uncle." He held up his hands in surrender. "I won't argue with a pretty woman, especially when she's right."

Blaine entered the vestibule of the new cathedral with a humbler heart than the one with which he'd approached it.

Hector told the story of how the Virgin of Guadalupe chose the Indian peasant Juan Diego to implore the church on her behalf to build a shrine on this site five hundred years ago. When the church leaders would not believe that the peasant was telling the truth, the apparition gave him proof that the order was divine. She directed him to pick some white roses, which he wrapped in his cloak to present to the church fathers. The priests were dumbstruck by the sight of roses, for it was December, but it was the mantle itself that brought them to their knees in awe and reverence. There, etched on the humble cloth, was the image of the Virgin Mary. The shrine was built without further question.

"Will we see it?" Karen whispered, slipping her hand into his.

The face she turned up to him was that of the little girl Blaine remembered, filled with wonder and innocence. He nodded, letting her indulge in the legend of the miracle to her romantic heart's content. Like most religious relics, the cloth could neither be proved nor disproved. It was all a matter of faith.

A hush enveloped them as they stepped into the church. Overhead, chandeliers—lighted clusters of glass tubes designed by Vázquez to represent the white rose blossoms—cast an ethereal glow, steadfast compared to the dancing shadows cast by the thousands of candles representing the prayers of the parishioners. Surrounded by fellow tourists, pilgrims, and local worshippers, Blaine pointed out the large, gilded-glass frame at the center of the modernistic, three-dimensional, gilded-metal backdrop of the sanctuary. Beneath the glass was the cloth with the image of the Virgin like a painted canvas, as fresh and bright as the day Juan Diego presented it.

Caroline's breathless whisper sounded at his elbow as she gathered her daughter in an embrace. "It's just like Hector said, not even faded."

Others echoed her amazement at the phenomenon. Familiar with the research, Blaine knew exactly what they were thinking, even though he'd only heard partial statements.

Should have decayed in twenty years . . . the cactus cloth on which the Virgin was painted . . . Her eyes contain the image of Juan Diego presenting the roses to the bishop . . .

Scientists had done a microscopic study revealing the image reflected in the painting's eyes as it might have appeared nearly half a century before—something impossible for the human hand to replicate.

He'd read it all, but the most forceful argument for the framed relic was the faith it inspired. The air was thick with it . . . or was it incense? He inhaled deeply, as though to fill the painful void that opened to him in the wee hours of the night when there was no distraction to spare him. For some reason, Blaine couldn't draw his gaze from the legendary cloak long enough to seek out the source of the scent. Only the sudden release of his hand by his daughter managed to penetrate the spell.

Giving himself a mental shake, he turned to see where she'd gone. With stinging eyes, he searched the crowd for Karen and caught a glimpse of Caroline looking frantically over the sea of heads between them. Suddenly she caught his eye, and relief flooded her face. With a dramatic gesture, she pointed toward the entrance.

What was going on?

CHAPTER 9

Feeling akin to a salmon swimming upstream, Blaine pushed as politely as possible through the crowd until he caught up with Caroline at the white stone entrance outside. She pointed to where Annie cradled Karen in her arms near a statue of some saint.

"Is she sick?" he asked.

Caroline took the lead. "Don't know," she called over her shoulder. "She just bolted past us, crying. I couldn't keep up, but Annie was on her heels."

Crying? What was wrong now? Once again all that he felt was helplessness.

He caught up with the girls and found Karen sobbing on Annie's shoulder, her face buried. Her friend looked from Caroline to Blaine, her expression a plea for help.

"Kitten, what is it?" Blaine pulled Karen away from Annie and turned his daughter with a firm but gentle hand. "Are you sick?"

Karen shook her head, her gaze fixed on her sneakers.

"Karen, we can't help you if you won't tell us what is wrong," Caroline coaxed.

"G . . . God made me leave."

"What do you mean, honey?"

"Did someone say something to you?" Blaine chimed in. He hadn't heard anything above the reverence in the cathedral. He'd been so caught up in . . . what?

Karen shook her head. "It h . . . hurt, Daddy." Beating her chest with fisted hands, the girl hiccuped. "I . . . *hic* . . . I c . . . couldn't b . . . breathe."

"Should I get medical help?" Blaine looked from his distraught daughter to Caroline. He didn't want to entertain the idea that it was Karen's heart, or something worse, but—

"I'm n . . . not sick!" Karen threw herself against him. "Just h . . . hold me, Daddy."

Hold me, Daddy. How he'd missed those three words. But what once made him feel so big and capable, now rendered him small and helpless. He swallowed hard, tensing his muscles against the tremble rolling through his body.

God. The directionless prayer of frustration emerged, stemming more from basic need than conscious faith. The Holy Spirit's past record with such petitions for Ellie was hardly rock solid.

Wrapping his arms tightly around her, Blaine bent his head over his child. “Okay, Kitten. It’s okay.”

He felt her tears soak his shirt, absorbed her anguished sobs against his chest, just as he had in days gone by when she’d brought a favorite broken toy to him. Except this time, she was broken. And he was at a loss to fix her.

“Maybe we should go,” Caroline told her daughter softly.

“N . . . no, Miz C.” Karen reached out from the cocoon of Blaine’s embrace. She seemed as stricken by the notion of losing Caroline’s comforting presence as Blaine’s.

“Please stay,” he said softly.

Caroline wasn’t certain if Blaine voiced the plea or if she’d heard his desperate spirit seek her own. All she knew was that she was needed, here and now, by father and daughter. *God, give me the right words of wisdom and assurance.*

“Annie,” she said, “please catch up with the group and tell Hector that the crowded church made Karen queasy and that we’ll meet him at the bus on time.”

“Sure, Mom.” Before leaving, Annie squeezed Karen’s arm. “Catch you later. It’s going to be okay. Mom’s here.”

The words hung like a gold medallion around Caroline’s heart, but there was no time to bask in her daughter’s spontaneous accolade. As she turned from Annie’s retreat to the Madisons, two rambunctious boys raced by, knocking Caroline's handbag off her shoulder and stepping on Karen's heel in the process.

"Ow!" Karen pushed against her father even more.

Blaine shouted *"Calmate!"* after the boys, but they disappeared without any evidence of "calming down."

Hauling her purse strap back into place, Caroline glanced around the paved area. There had to be somewhere they could talk without being run down by the inflowing tide of sightseers and worshippers. A few yards away, a senior-citizens group mustered under a cypress tree, emptying the seating next to its gnarled, twisted trunk.

"Why don't we get out of this beating sun and go over to that bench God just cleared for us?"

"What?"

At Blaine's blank expression, she pointed to the bench.

Taking measured steps, Blaine ushered the girl to the shaded spot, as though to rush might tip the frail balance of his daughter's distress. When Karen sat down, Caroline dug out a bottle of water from her handbag and handed it to her.

"Here. You've leaked so much water, I think we need to replace it before you dehydrate."

The girl grinned from the crook of her father's arm and took the water with a shaky "Thanks."

"Just take some deep breaths," Blaine advised as she handed the water back to Caroline. "Is your chest still hurting?"

Karen shook her head. "It felt like God was squishing

my heart with His hands," she said in a rush. "L . . . like, if I didn't leave right then, He was going to kill me in front of all those people."

"Honey, what makes you think God would do such a thing?"

An overwhelming empathy seized Caroline as she pieced together what the child was talking about. Yes, she knew. After Frank left, rebellion and anger had had their way with her. She'd returned to church, ready to give them to God. It had felt as though someone were ripping her soul out with bare hands, ready to dash it on the floor of the church, expose it for all its shame to the people surrounding her. Caroline had wanted to run, to escape the disgust God surely felt for her.

Except that now, she knew it hadn't been God shoving her away, but trying to take her guilt from her beleaguered heart. But Karen was just a baby—

"B . . . because I hate Him," Karen blurted out. "He can grow roses in December and paint cloths for Indians. He did all kinds of miracle stuff for everyone but Mom." She sniffed in defiance, but the tremor of her chin betrayed her pained, fragile state. "Why did He let her die?"

The age-old question echoed in Caroline's mind as she glanced over Karen's head at Blaine. She didn't know the circumstances, and even if she did—

"Wh . . . why couldn't we m . . . make her stop drinking?" Karen sniffed. "I begged her to. I . . . I emptied her bottles when I could f . . . find them."

"We tried counseling, rehabilitation centers . . ."

Blaine trailed off, lost in the hopelessness of the past—a past that clearly still haunted him.

"She d . . . died in a car crash." Karen punctuated her memory with a shaky breath.

"I'm so sorry," Caroline said.

"It was so stupid!" Vehemence stilled the tremor in the girl's voice.

Heavenly Father, what can I say to ease this child's pain, to open her eyes to Your love?

"Kitten, there are a lot of things we see as stupid that we won't understand until we get to ask God ourselves." Blaine's reply was strained, as though the steel cord binding his feelings might give way, should one thread unravel. Or did his heart echo Karen's disillusionment?

"But I need to know *now*."

Caroline's mind raced, prayer and thought running nip and tuck as she spoke. "God loves us so much, Karen, that He gives us the choice to do what is right or wrong. And when we make bad choices, we have to face the consequences of those choices in one way or another."

"So He killed her?"

Now two anguished gazes waited, expectant, hungry for relief.

"God didn't kill your mother, little one, any more than He made my husband leave me for someone brighter and prettier and younger than I. God doesn't do bad things to us. We do them to ourselves and to each other when we don't know or listen to His Word."

God, I'm sounding too much like a preacher, when she needs a comforter.

"But no matter what happens as a result of our human weakness and mistakes, God will take the bad and turn it into something good." Caroline hesitated, reluctant to share the pain of Frank's rejection in front of Blaine.

But what if others hadn't shared their disappointments in life with her, and told her how God turned them into blessings? She'd have been lost, that's what. Misery loves company, needs empathy.

"And we'll be stronger for it, so that we can reach out and help others who know the same pain and disappointment. I lost the man I loved, but had that not happened, I'd never have gotten my degree or built my school. I wouldn't be able to share God's love with you today. All we have to do is give God time to shine His light on our darkness and disappointment."

"But He let her die." The plea in the girl's voice told Caroline that Karen wanted to believe her.

"He let His Son die too, and Jesus had made no bad choices at all. But His death and sacrifice saved all of us. That's how much God loves us." Caroline licked her lips, biding time until she could sort the sudden rush of words springing to her mind. "Sometimes God looks away, just as He did when His Son suffered so on the cross, so that others might be saved."

"*You* could have been in the car with her." Blaine pressed his lips to a bloodless line and swallowed. Tucking Karen's head under his chin, he closed tortured eyes. "I don't know what I'd do without you, Kitten."

Caroline wanted to hug them both, to draw them to her bosom as the Father would. Instead, she prayed they'd feel His arms encircling them in the midst of their despair.

Karen tightened her thin arms around Blaine. "I miss her, Daddy. Why wouldn't she stop? D . . . didn't she love us?"

"She loved us very much, Kitten," Blaine whispered against the dark crown of his daughter's head. "Maybe God knew Mommy was too sick to quit on her own and took her home to keep her from hurting herself and others anymore."

From one Father's lips to another's. Letting go and letting God take over, Caroline focused on a pigeon that had landed in front of them. It walked first this way, then that, head bobbing in search of food. Like the three of them, she thought, searching for answers—food for the soul.

"I'm going to get some cotton candy," she announced, upon spotting a vendor selling the sticky rainbow-colored clouds of sugar. "Can I get either of you something? A soda, maybe?"

"Thanks, but I'm fine," Blaine said. "You've already given us more than I can ever thank you for." The glow of his dark gaze blessed Caroline from toe tip to behatted top. "We'll hold your seat."

Leaving the father and daughter to feed their spirits in God's presence, Caroline made her way toward the cotton candy maker's cart with a heart spun as light and bright as his tempting wares. She made the purchase and started back. Karen saw her coming and jumped up to run toward her, but Blaine remained seated, looking drained.

"Guess what, Miz C?"

Caroline extended the paper cone to her. "What?"

"You know the pain I had in my chest?"

"Yes." Caroline couldn't help the slightly ironic tone in her voice. They'd just agonized over it for what felt like hours, and now Karen was back to her bouncy self, as though nothing had happened. Her eyes were still a little red, but the splotches on her face had already faded.

Ah, the resilience of youth, Caroline mused with no small envy.

"Well, I figured out what it was." She pinched off a piece of candy and popped it into her mouth. "It *was* God squeezing me," Karen told her, "but He wasn't doing it to hurt me. He was digging out my anger."

Just as He'd dug out Caroline's shame and countless other concerns that caused His children pain.

"Like a splinter," the girl explained, mistaking no reply for ignorance. "You gotta take it out before it heals. Get it?"

"Got it." Caroline smiled from the inside out. *From the mouths of babes.* Linking her arm with her charge, she started to take a celebration bite of cotton candy when something splattered right in front of her face.

If Karen's appalled "Ee-eww!" wasn't enough to confirm Caroline's suspicion, Blaine's outright laugh was. There was no point in trying to identify the perpetrator.

There were pigeons all over the place.

"Ya think somebody is trying to tell me something?" she wisecracked, depositing the spoiled candy in the trash bin next to the bench. "I mean, for most people, birds sing."

CHAPTER 10

"You look lovely."

The three simple words had sent Caroline's heart aflutter during the elevator ride to the lobby, as if *it* knew something she didn't. They were to have a dinner of traditional Mexican food, then walk across the Alameda to the evening show of the Ballet Folklórico. Seated at an elegant table in the Mesón del Azul, her heart still beat like a flamenco dancer's fan each time she caught Blaine observing her.

He wasn't flirtatious. It was his unaffected sincerity that got to her and turned her to mush. After all, they'd shared some pretty heavy stuff that afternoon in an outpouring of heart and soul. Not even Frank had shared such private ground with her.

"If you'd like, I can help you with the menu," Blaine said. "When I was working on the postquake housing, my staff and I ate here often."

Caroline closed the menu that was overrun with words that ended in *adas, itos, itas,* and *oles*. "That would be lovely. I'm afraid fajitas, tacos, and burritos are the extent of my knowledge of Mexican food—

unless you count salsa and Fritos."

"Fritos?" he teased. Golden laugh lights flecked the rich brown of his gaze.

"Yeah, they hold the sauce better than the tortillas—not as messy," she confessed. There was no point in pretending to be worldly—unless a trip to Disney World or Busch Gardens Old Country counted. She was born and raised in Pennsylvania farm country-turned-suburbia.

"Very practical."

"How about this one, Dad?" Karen asked, pointing out a dish with a picture next to it.

Blaine shook his head. "If you see the word *habañero,* run the other way."

"How about this one?" Annie chimed in from his other side.

Blaine studied it a moment. "That's grilled tuna with fried plantain and a fruit sauce."

Annie closed her menu. "That's what I want. Thanks."

"De nada," he replied with a courtly nod of his head that turned Caroline to mush, salsa style. She didn't mind at all that he slid so easily into the role she usually played.

While Blaine's recommendation was exotic by Caroline's standards, it was delicious. The shrimp cocktail—*cóctel de camarones*—arrived in delicate tulip glasses, while her lime-marinated scallop salad arrived on a tortilla. Caroline not only ate the food, but most of the "plate" as well. When the waiter displayed a wagon wheel–sized tray loaded with sinfully tempting desserts, she opted for the lightest, a small dip of ice cream served with a *churro,* or fried sugar twist.

Later, filled to the brim with the fine native cuisine, Caroline and company walked over to the Palacio de Bellas Artes. Not even the delicious scents emanating from the sidewalk food carts tempted them now.

"I can't believe they passed the snow cone vendor," Caroline told Blaine as they climbed up the long run of smog-grayed steps.

"Wow, no wonder they call it *Palacio,*" Annie marveled as they followed Hector and an usher through the pink marble lobby.

Karen pointed to a softly lit mural on one of the walls. "What is that, a fairy stuck on a fan?"

"It's another Rivera work," Blaine answered. Dressed in black coat and tie, her father could give James Bond—any one of them—a run for his money in looks and culture. "It's a slam against the industrial machine sucking up the earth's resources, I think. Like a fan."

His acknowledging smile was aimed at Karen, but Caroline's toes curled as if it were for her alone. She hardly noticed she'd tripped until Blaine caught her by the arm.

"Watch your step."

"Thanks." A flush of heat warming her face, Caroline looked down at the smooth marble flooring to see what had nearly sent her sprawling. It was as shiny and smooth as polished glass.

"Slippery, isn't it?"

Okay, it was an excuse. He didn't have to know she put rubber stick-on patches on all her dress shoes just to avoid her ingrained clumsiness. Worse, that swoon-scrunched toes digging in were the real cause.

"Can we change tickets so Karen and I can sit together?" Annie looked from Caroline to Blaine as Karen did a little bounce, her expression seconding the plea.

"It's fine with me. Caroline?"

"Um . . ." Like she really had an objection. "Su . . . sure."

Walking on Blaine's arm as if she actually wore glass slippers, Caroline followed the Gearhardts to a row a section removed from the orchestra. Beyond it was the stage, its breathtaking Tiffany-like glass curtain emulating a view of volcanic mountains through latticed arches. As Caroline sank into the plush upholstered seat, she glanced around at the international mix gradually filling the seats around her. Behind Señora Marron's company, a tour group from Germany filed in. In front of Caroline and Blaine were a Japanese couple and their two children of grade-school age.

"Señor Madison?" A Hispanic gentleman taking a seat two down from the Japanese family addressed Blaine.

It took Blaine a moment to recognize the man in the dim light, but when he did, he rose and extended his hand. "Señor Aquino, it's good to see you again."

"Perhaps you and your friend would like to join us after the show for a late dessert?" Señor Aquino suggested, after introductions to the Asian family were made.

He and Blaine had worked together on a high-rise project in the city. Although the Mexican investor had seen the show many times, he explained that he always brought out-of-town friends to see the culture of Mexico portrayed in dance, just as he had Blaine a few years earlier. Considering the cost of the tickets, even discounted as the tour group's had been, Caroline thought he must be successful in his field.

"That's very gracious of you, but this tour has been merciless where rest is concerned. That's what I get for traveling with teenagers," Blaine kidded, settling down beside Caroline once more. "I'm afraid I must decline this time."

"If you change your mind or wish to contact me while you are in our country . . ." Aquino dug a business card from the inside pocket of his linen coat and handed it to Blaine. "Here is my card."

"Thanks, I appreciate that." Blaine tucked the card inside his jacket, wondering if he'd done the right thing in declining the invitation. He'd won a good amount of business at the social invitation of Carlos Aquino, business that might otherwise have wound up elsewhere. The Japanese had made considerable investments in the country after the last quake.

The theater lights flashed, signaling that the show was about to begin. Señor Aquino gave Blaine a silent salute of understanding and turned to his guests. Up and down the row filled by Señora Marron's group, Edenton's young adults squirmed in their Sunday best. Some strained to see the orchestra that had been tuning in the background of the audience's preshow murmur. Others stared up at the gilded box seats lining the side walls with the same fascination that Caroline felt sitting next to Blaine.

The orchestra struck up the overture. The music was the kind that would allow room for nothing short of festive emotions. It left neither the feet nor the heart alone, raising anticipation so that when the mercurial curtain finally went up, the applause was thunderous. To say that the presentation was panoramic was to understate the lavish scenery, the intricate choreography, and the exquisite costumes. Just when Caroline thought one historical or regional performance could not be outdone, another outdid it. She forgot about Blaine and her surroundings, and was drawn into the colorful drama, her blood pumping with the passion of the Mexicano music and dance.

When they emerged from the theater, Caroline was still breathless with enchantment. In the after-show shopping frenzy for souvenirs, the women and students lost track of the men, most of whom walked ahead to the bus to wait. Caroline bought an official program while the girls tried to decide between jewelry and costumed dolls of assorted prices.

On rendezvousing at the bus, the girls slid into twin seats in front of her with their purchases, leaving the empty one next to Blaine for Caroline. Ignoring the light punch Dana gave her elbow, Caroline tucked her flounced skirt aside and sat down.

"I've just never seen anything like it."

Blaine grinned. "So you said."

Of course she had. If she'd said it once, she'd said it a hundred times . . . or at least once for each dance. Caroline heaved a resigned sigh. "I guess you can take the country gal out of the city, but you can't take the country out of the gal."

"Who would want to?"

There was no point in telling her heart to be still. It was deaf where Blaine was concerned. And she, miracle of miracles, was dumb. All she could do was dip her eyelashes like a love-struck schoolgirl.

"How about a nightcap?" Blaine suggested when they returned to the hotel. "A soothing chamomile tea or decaf latte?"

"Not me," Karen declared. "I'm beat."

"Me too," Annie chimed in.

"I wasn't asking you two. I was asking *Miz C,*" he said, imitating his daughter's name for the lovely woman beside him. Funny. He'd heard Karen talk about a Miz C, but the matronly picture the name evoked was far from the real thing.

"Well, I—"

"Randy and I will see that the girls are safely locked in their room," Dana offered from behind them. She put her hand on Caroline's shoulder. "Go ahead and unwind a little. I don't see a hint of *sleepy* in those eyes."

Just light, Blaine agreed, noting how Caroline's gaze was as multifaceted as the crystal prisms on the chandelier overhead. A man could lose himself trying to discover the nature of that light, for it definitely shone from the inside out. He'd watched it more than the show. And he'd seen it brimming that afternoon when she'd spoken from the heart to Karen . . . when she'd somehow assuaged his guilt, allowing him to breathe again for the first time in ages without its constriction. And it wasn't just her words. Words alone he'd heard before. It was the spiritual depth behind them that touched him. It made him want to know more, not just of her, but of what made her able to bridge the gap between him and Karen, when his love alone could not.

"I shouldn't need anything to relax after the long day we've had, but I have to admit, I'm not the least bit tired."

"Anyone else care to join us?" Blaine held his breath, hoping no one would accept his invitation.

No one did. After letting the others off at their respective floors, the elevator they commandeered continued to the top-floor restaurant. It was one of those rotating affairs, high enough above the city that it afforded a picturesque view of the surrounding mountains from its wide windows. While it wasn't full, it was still busy with the after-theater crowd and those enjoying the late old-world dining tradition. The hostess sat them at a table for four, clearing away the extra settings.

Blaine ordered two decaffeinated lattes, one with hazelnut flavoring for the lady.

"That way I can do without sugar," Caroline explained after the waiter left.

"Not that you need to worry about weight," he stipulated, having been around women long enough to know he should make that clear, "but what about the fat content?"

"Oh, shush."

The petulant purse of her lips was riveting, but not in a sultry lipstick commercial way. He didn't think she even wore lipstick.

"I prefer to look at the positive side. Like whipped cream is 50 percent air—half the calories."

It was her impish side that sparkled over the glow of the candlelight, yet its effect on Blaine was profound. Senses scrambled into an uncharacteristic giddiness, he focused on his purpose. Rattling the plastic bag he'd discreetly carried at his side since leaving the theater, he put it on the table.

"This is for you."

The panorama of emotions unfolding on his companion's face as she peeked inside the bag was as varied as the dances in the Ballet Folklórico. There was shock that he'd bought her a gift, curiosity as to what it might be, surprise to see what it was, and finally what he'd hoped for—delight.

"Blaine, you shouldn't have." Caroline withdrew the boxed doll wearing a replica of the bright dresses with the full circle skirts that she'd oohed and aahed over during the show, marveling how they reminded her of giant, graceful butterflies. "These were too expensive."

He'd seen her examining the doll and putting it back when she saw the sticker price. After she'd moved on, he'd asked Dana to buy it for him.

"It's for your school," he explained, as if that justified the cost. No, that wasn't why he'd bought it . . . and cost was not an issue. "It's the least I could do after what you did for Karen—"

Distracted by his own uncharacteristic babbling, Blaine hastily regrouped his thoughts. "It's for what you did for my daughter today . . . and for me."

He watched mild admonition melt to a glaze of emotion that seemed to erode another layer of the grief and disillusionment constricting his chest. He took a breath.

"I knew Karen grieved," he went on. "But I thought her anger was directed at me . . . because I couldn't make things right with Ellie."

"The Holy Spirit orchestrated all that." Genuine modesty colored his companion's face, camouflaging the freckles sprinkled around her nose. "I just played a part in the script." Were she any more wholesome, she'd have *Made in the U.S.A.* stamped on her forehead and smell like apple pie.

Was that what had moved inside him, before Karen bolted out? The Holy Spirit? Or was he merely infected by the collective sense of reverence surrounding him? "Whatever it was, I'm grateful that you had the heart and courage to speak to a stranger on its behalf. I'm glad you were there."

"So were the pigeons."

Blaine chuckled. "You're not very comfortable with

compliments, are you?"

She averted her sheepish gaze to the window where, beyond the city skyline, a dappled-gold moon hung so close to the mountains that it almost touched.

"I guess they're like woolen underwear," she said with a little laugh. "They're warm, but the itch takes some getting used to."

"We'll have to work on that. Someone like you deserves every compliment that comes your way," he said, backing away as the waiter placed two lattes topped with whipped cream on the table. Was it his comment or the waiter's sudden appearance that caused the lady's brief startled look? Regardless, it was charming . . . charming as the little mustache her first sip of the concoction left on her lip.

CHAPTER 11

"Woolen underwear?" Dana looked at Caroline as if she'd lost her the last brain cell. "He compliments you, and you compare it to wearing woolen underwear?"

Just as mortified by her idiotic response the night before, Caroline focused on the heavy quartz wares spread on a faded woolen blanket in the morning sun. Beyond the thrown-together market of plywood on sawhorse tables and spread blankets on the ground sprawled the remains of Teotihuacan, the ancient city of the Aztec Empire that attracted both sellers and tourists. The moment the Edenton group disembarked from the bus, they'd been surrounded by Mexicanos of all ages hawking their wares—jewelry, dishes, simple musical instruments, woven items.

"You like *thees?*" Smiling from under the brim of her straw hat, a woman with leathery skin and graying black hair pointed to a dish about ten inches square, made of the pink marble similar to that of the Bellas Artes theater. "Or *thees* one?" Her eyes were as dark as the obsidian ash she pointed to.

"Honey, he is definitely interested. He can't take his eyes off you." Dana reached past Caroline. "I like the first dish better." Picking up a similar one, she examined it. "I just can't fathom what I'd use it for."

"I'm thinking a jewelry dish. It'd go perfectly with my bedroom."

"So would a husband."

"*Thees* one," the vendor decided, taking up the one Caroline originally admired. "I will wrap it for you, no?"

"How much?" she asked.

"Twenty dollars."

"Offer her fifteen," Dana whispered aside. "They always start high."

Caroline glanced at the ragged-clothed children playing behind the woman. *Okay, so I'm a sucker,* she thought, digging into her hip purse. But this lady looked like she needed every penny to feed and clothe her family. Caroline would skip dessert tonight to make up for the extra five bucks she was probably overpaying.

“Do you have a bag?” Caroline asked, handing her a twenty-dollar bill.

“Muchas gracias, señora,” the vendor replied as a doll-like little girl peeked out at them from the folds of her mother’s voluminous skirt. *“Uno momento, niña.”*

“I don’t blame you,” Dana said, sighing in resignation as the woman produced a used plastic grocery bag from a stash under the table. “But that reinforces my point.”

“What point?”

“Your heart is too big to ignore that poor man,” Dana told her. “God knows he needs a wife and Karen needs a mom. She adores you. Everyone is saying how you four would make an ideal family. Maybe his mom’s accident was no accident. Maybe God has His hand in this.”

“Everyone?” Great, now it was more than her friend looking for cartoon hearts fluttering out from under her eyelashes. It was *everyone.* “What, do I look that needy? As for God, a man hasn’t been on my prayer list for years.”

Although yesterday at the cathedral, Caroline had felt father and daughter’s pain, guilt, and frustration. They’d been drawn into the oneness of the Spirit, closer than she’d ever been with Frank. Could it be—?

Nah. Caroline took the bag with her newspaper-wrapped dish. Its weight took her by surprise.

“Whoa! I should have waited until I was on my way out to get this.” The thought of hauling her purchase to the top of the Pyramid of the Sun made her arm ache.

"Maybe someone else was praying . . . like your daughter."

Caroline cut a sharp glance at her friend. "Ooh, that was a low blow. Just for that, you can hold my two-ton jewelry dish while I climb the Pyramid of the Sun."

"I'll bet Blaine will hold it for you."

Caroline rolled her eyes heavenward in exasperation. "Give it a rest, Dana." Easier said than done, Caroline realized as she tried to dismiss the idea of Annie wanting a father. It was easier for Caroline to ignore her own wants or needs than those of her daughter.

"Okay, *amigos y amigas,*" Hector called from his perch on a large flat stone nearby. "Let's went!"

Gradually the group reassembled around the fan-waving tour guide. Ahead of them the ruins reminded Caroline of a monumental ghost town of stone and dust, maybe a high-altitude Egypt with mountains surrounding it instead of great sand dunes. Cutting a north-south swath between the pyramids of assorted size was a wide road that Hector identified as the Avenue of the Dead.

"It's dead all right," Wally quipped, wrinkling his nose to raise his glasses as he studied the giant pyramid dwarfing the others. "Not a car in sight. Just old stone."

Kurt gave his buddy the elbow. "You're a real riot, Einstein."

Unfazed, Wally pointed at the largest structure in sight. "That the sun pyramid?"

Hector nodded. "And I promise, all of you kiddies will have plenty of time to climb it, if you wish. But first, we must do our homework."

"All the kiddies and one slightly romance-impaired adult," Dana mumbled in Caroline's ear.

"You going to climb?" Blaine asked, coming up on Caroline's blind side.

"Why not?" Caroline wished the sand would open up and one of those giant worms from the sci-fi channel would put an end to her misery. Or maybe Blaine hadn't heard Dana's comment.

Dana peered around her. "I guess when you work with kids all day, you never grow up."

Caroline wanted the worm to take Dana too.

"Once a kid, always a kid, eh?"

Blaine's wink knocked the temperature of the sun on her face up a few degrees. Or maybe she'd just melt away from humiliation.

"Come on, I want to hear what Hector's saying," Caroline announced, taking off as though someone had fired a starting pistol.

"Over two millenia ago, the Toltec peoples reigned supreme. Around AD 750 the city was ravaged by fire in some sort of rebellion," Hector informed his energy-overdosed audience. "It continued to be used for ceremonial purposes as the alleged birthplace of the gods."

"I thought you called the ancient Indians Aztecs," Randy said.

"The Aztecs were made up of many ethnic groups. Among them all were healers and artists, kind of like the professionals of today—doctors, lawyers . . ."

“Like Indian druids, Dad,” Kurt ventured. “Right, Hector?”

Hector’s forehead knitted, his dark eyebrows almost touching. “I don’t know much about your druids. All I know is that the Indian peoples were divided around AD 750 in a clash of good and evil. The good went south, following the Path of Freedom, while the others migrated north toward Tula, today’s Hidalgo area. They were thought to have black magic.”

“Now, *that* is interesting,” Ron Butler spoke up. “The coming of Christianity to Ireland divided the druids in a similar way.” He glanced at Randy. “You suppose there is something to the idea of Irish monks like St. Brendan making it over here with the Word?”

“Faith and begorra,” Randy teased in his best Irish brogue. “Next thing you know, you Irish will be wantin’ to paint the pyramids green.”

“It’s still amazing,” Caroline mused aloud as they moved on through the ancient ruins.

“What’s that?” Blaine asked.

The man didn’t have ears. He had radar. And Dana had somehow disappeared—not an accident, if Caroline knew her matchmaking friend. “How ancient man could build something so complex . . . so huge.”

“I went to school for years to learn the formulas and physics behind such projects, and some still mystify me. It all originated from the study of the preexisting earth and stars.”

“God isn’t called the Great Architect for nothing.” Caroline stopped with the group to study an early painting of a jungle cat recessed in the rock of some catacombs.

"I don't know that I'd confuse science with religion," Blaine cautioned.

"Oh, no," Annie broke in, groaning as she stared at the wall painting—another mural. "Don't tell me that Diego guy was here, too!"

The atmosphere of awe and wonder Hector had created with his dialogue regarding the Aztec past dissolved in laughter throughout the group. It did seem as if wherever one turned, there was a Rivera painting.

"Someone has her mother's sense of humor," Blaine whispered to Caroline.

"No, Annie," their good-natured guide assured the teen. "Diego Rivera painted everywhere else, but he did not make it to Teotihuacan." Hector went on to explain how the durable dyes the Indians used in the paint on the ancient picture became a major industry after the obsidian gave out.

While he was talking, Blaine took the heavy bag off Caroline's arm, where the handles had cut a little red ridge on her wrist. "You didn't buy one of those pyramids, did you?"

"Thanks, it's a jewelry dish." She gave him a rueful smile. "I should have bought it on the way out. You really don't have to play the pack mule. I'm used to the role."

"Not while I'm around."

She picked up the conversation they'd been having when Annie interrupted. "I'm not confusing science with religion," she said. "I think they complement each other."

Blaine cut her a sideways glance. "Oh?"

What on earth do you think you are doing, debating someone like Blaine Madison? a voice demanded from within. He was a big wheel in an engineering firm, and she was a big wheel in alphabet and diapers. Caroline could champion her faith, but could she defend it on his level?

Well, Lord, I've jumped in, so I guess I have to swim. Feel free to toss me a life jacket anytime.

"The way I see it, God created heaven and earth. That's faith," she said with confidence. "And man has spent his lifetime trying to figure out how creation works. That's science."

"I never thought of it in quite that way," Blaine said, as though he considered her words to at least merit thought.

Maybe she should just shut up while she was still ahead and fall in behind the others. But she hadn't quite reached the shore of her conviction.

"Just think—" Caroline spread lifted hands up as if to envelop the heavens. "When He created the heavens and hung the stars, He gave ignorant man the first calendar-clock to measure time and know when food would grow and when to put food away to survive winter." She tapped the bag her companion held in his arms. "So what is the first thing ancient man did? He copied the layout and made a physical calendar-almanac combination. Then one thing led to another and another, and soon"—Caroline pointed to the giant pyramid towering over the rest—"man was making those. Now he uses a Palm Pilot!"

Blaine stopped, his head cocked as he dug into her gaze with his own.

There was no retreating from whatever he had in mind to say, nor could she if she wanted to. Where better to stand than on the foundation of her faith? It wouldn't fail, although her knees might if he didn't say something soon. What on earth was he looking for, visible signs of lunacy?

With her package tucked under one arm, Blaine leaned against the rock wall behind Caroline with his free hand. "You have the most remarkable way of taking the complex issues and simplifying them so that even a left brain like me can understand them."

That was good, right? This close to Blaine, she couldn't think.

"John, what brings you here?" Karen's hail broke the bubble of awareness surrounding them, letting in the rest of the world.

Blaine straightened as though he'd been jabbed from behind with the spear carved on one of the stone reliefs, as Annie and Karen bolted away from Kurt and Wally's company toward a couple of young men waving from the Avenue of the Dead.

"Well, if it isn't the Bandito kid and his Mexican sidekick," Blaine drawled. "What, are they following us?"

The chance for Caroline to separate her fact from Dana's Romance fiction was as welcome to her as the sight of the Banditos boys to the girls . . . until one of her scrambled senses reported that she was leaning against a centuries-old wall that might house creepy crawlies. Doing a hasty sidestep, she gave the wall that had been at her back a quick once-over. No telltale webs.

"Oh, joy, it's the college boys." As thrilled as Blaine, Kurt jammed a disposable camera into the pocket of his oversized shirt, kicking the dust as he passed by.

Seizing the moment, Caroline excused herself. "Uh-oh, Cupid alert. Maybe I'd better check this out."

"I'm right with you," Blaine said, speeding his step to catch up.

The irony of her situation was not lost on her as she scurried after her daughter. *Lord, I came to chaperone the kids, so why do I feel as if I'm the one who needs watching?*

An hour later, Blaine waited at the bottom of the Pyramid of the Sun with most of the adults in the group and snapped pictures of his daughter as she waved from its summit.

He couldn't shake the spell. He wasn't certain he wanted to. Enigmas fascinated him, and Caroline was a cross between teacher and philosopher, nurturing mom, and the freckled pixie who'd scrambled up the side of the pyramid behind her daughter like one of the kids. He admired her ability to take the complexities of her faith and sift them into common-sense applications. For all his studies, he'd never looked at man's accomplishments as learned from divine design. But then, he'd had problems seeing much divine, especially after his late wife's problems and death. God knew he wanted to.

So what is holding you back?

"Dad!" Karen waved her hands over her head, drawing his attention to where Annie and the boy from Banditos stood on either side of Caroline a few steps from the top of the Pyramid of the Sun. "Dad, we need your help!"

At that moment, the threesome moved down two steps. Caroline sank sideways, her hip propped on the narrow edge, and put her head down. Something was wrong with Caroline, very wrong. Leaving the heavy package with Randy Gearhardt, Blaine started up the steps, his mind accelerating to access the situation. With her fair complexion, it could be sunstroke, although she wore a cute little straw hat.

Above him, Caroline rallied, and the threesome moved down a few more steps. Once again they stopped, with Caroline leaning against the pyramid. By the time Blaine reached them, they'd made it a third of the way down.

"What's the problem?" Blaine stopped to wipe the perspiration from his forehead. His racing heart reminded him that the fifteen-inch risers weren't built to be scaled in haste, but in reverence—sideways, and one narrow step at a time.

Caroline groaned, burying her face in her hands. "I feel like such a dolt."

"You're not a dolt, Miz C," John assured her. "You

feel how steep this thing is going up, but coming down, you *see* it."

"When I started down, one look and I thought I was going to toss up my breakfast or faint," Caroline said, venturing a glance in Blaine's direction. "I'm so embarrassed."

Fear obliterated her characteristic blush of embarrassment with a ghostly pallor. Blaine put a hand on her arm. Despite the sun burning down on them, she was cold and clammy.

"You still feel like you're going to faint?" he asked.

"Only when I look down," she mumbled.

"We tried backing down, but the steps are too tall and the foot part is too short," Annie told him. "Mom skinned her leg and almost fell down the pyramid face-first."

"Why did I ever want to see the view?" Caroline chastised herself. "Those Indians didn't sacrifice people up there. The victims cut their own throats to keep from having to come down."

Blaine had to chuckle. Even in the midst of her terror, Caroline's sense of humor refused to remain submerged for long. And it was a long, steep drop, enough to give him second thoughts about the trip down.

"You are one cool lady, Miz C." John gave Caroline a playful pinch on the cheek. "Now just look into my eyes like before. Annie is behind you, I'm in front of you, and Mr. Madison is on the open side. He won't let you fall."

"I thank God for all of you. I don't know what I'd

have done if John hadn't calmed me down up there. I . . . I felt like I was being drawn over the edge." She shuddered. "I can't explain it, but it was horrible."

"Don't think about it," the young man warned her. "Just keep on doing what we were doing and don't take your eyes off mine, okay?"

"Okay." Caroline allowed John to draw her into an upright position, her feet one in front of the other on the same five-inch ledge. "None of us is getting any younger, and the only thing worse than having four people baby me down would be being airlifted off this thing."

"You got that right," John chuckled. "Now, ready? Take one step down. We've got you covered."

Blaine had to admit, the young man was good. Caroline moved one foot down on his *One* and the other down on *Two and rest*. "Have you done any climbing or training, John?"

"I was a counselor at a mountain camp for a couple of summers," he answered, not taking his gaze from Caroline's desperate one. "Ready? And one . . ." He paused. "And two and rest."

With his one hand on Caroline's shoulder and the other on her arm, Blaine stepped back accordingly, finding the ledge below with the ball of his foot. It wasn't unlike rock climbing, except that the footholds were regular, if shallow.

It was a slow process. Occasionally Caroline spared him a darting glance filled with apology, but for the most part, John talked her down, answering her questions about his summer jobs and aspirations to keep her mind off the prospect of falling.

When Caroline touched down at ground level, the Edenton group, which by now had gathered in its entirety at the foot of the pyramid, burst into applause. Blaine was relieved to see the creep of color come back to her face as they were surrounded.

"Boy, some people will do anything to get attention." Dana gave her friend a big hug.

Caroline reached back and pulled John and Annie into the spotlight. "My heroes . . . and Blaine, of course," she added.

The smile she gave him was sheepish, a mixture of appreciation and something else—something that triggered a quickening in his chest.

"Hey, what about me?" Karen protested.

"And Karen," Caroline added, "for having a mouth big enough to summon help from below to the heavens."

Karen grinned from ear to ear as Caroline tugged her ponytail. It was a joy to watch them together. Caroline Spencer was just what Karen needed.

"Where's my package?"

It took a moment for Blaine to register that he was staring at the subject of his thoughts and that she was speaking to him.

"I've got it," Randy said.

Rattled, Blaine intercepted the package. He'd forgotten what he'd done with it in the hurry to reach Caroline and the girls. "Thanks."

"No more pyramids for you, young lady," Hector teased Caroline as he raised his fan banner to muster attention. "Okay, folks. You have twenty minutes for last-minute shopping, then we need to get to the bus. In thirty minutes, it will be on its way to the mission at Mexicalli."

"Oh man." John Chandler ran his hand through his sun-bleached hair.

"What is it, honey?" Caroline asked, taking another chick under her wing, despite the challenge of John's height.

The young man looked in the direction of the parking lot. "I believe I've missed my bus."

"What was the number?" Hector inquired.

"Fourteen-twenty, I think. It's headed for Cuernavaca, then Taxco tonight."

"I'll call them and tell them we have you, but we are staying two nights at the Mexicalli mission." Hector took out a cell phone and punched in some numbers. "You maybe can hire a taxi from there to Taxco, but it will be costly."

John winced. "I hope they have an ATM at the mission."

"Can't he just catch up with his group in Taxco?" Caroline asked. "We've been kind of running in tandem with his bus anyway."

"Yes," Hector said, "but remember, your group opted to exchange one of the free days in Acapulco for one at the mission. John's group will be in Acapulco the day we arrive in Taxco. Then we will catch up with them the following day."

"I'll pay for his cab. It's the least we can do," Blaine offered.

He wasn't keen on John Chandler joining Caroline's flock. There was something about him that didn't sit well, and it wasn't just the way Karen practically swooned at his feet. But in spite of that, the boy had done them a good turn. They couldn't just walk away from him now.

CHAPTER 12

"Dad, do you mind if John takes the extra bed in your room?" Karen asked as the bus pulled into Mexicalli a few hours later.

John Scott Chandler had no worries at all, save having to wear the same expensive clothes three days in a row. Caroline had insisted on buying his lunch at the roadside restaurant and souvenir shop, which was built around a picturesque courtyard where a jolly trio of mariachis and an Indian family entertained with native song and dance. And in case the lad should grow faint with weakness between stops, the girls shared their stash of gummy candy, making a game of tossing them into his mouth. *Now the fair Caesar is moving in with me,* thought Blaine.

Blaine gritted his teeth, but nodded. "Sure, no problem." At least he could keep an eye on the kid this way.

Once Hector checked the group into the Casa Jacaranda, a quaint little mountain inn shaded by the misty blue trees for which it was named, Blaine and the men in the group helped the driver unload the suitcases that were to remain with the tourists. Cavalier to his Rockport sneakers, John immediately stepped up to take Karen's and Annie's bags. Like groupies, they followed, their wrists and ankles rattling in his wake with their souvenir *agoyotas*—anklets with small gourds strung on them.

Blaine fumed in silence. He'd spent good money on this trip, put his business at risk—heaven knew what Mark was doing back home—and this kid was reaping the reward. The low growl in Blaine's throat died as he was hit with the realization: John reminded Blaine of his younger brother—all flash, smooth talk, and no substance. Spoiled by their mother, Mark had no ambition.

"That is that, *señores,*" the driver announced, reaching for the handle of the raised baggage compartment door. "All the other bags there are for the orphanage. *Muchas gracias* for your help."

At least someone had the forethought to keep the baggage for the orphanage separate, so that they wouldn't have to keep loading and unloading it.

Grabbing his own suitcase, Blaine started up the steep embankment toward the stuccoed row of numbered arched doors to the rooms. As usual, he was next to Caroline and the girls, whose door was open. From inside, Blaine could hear chatter and giggling. Again, he fought down a rise of annoyance as John appeared in the opening, an Edenton T-shirt slung over his arm.

"Need some help, sir?"

And now they were clothing him.

"No, thanks."

Even though the bag with Caroline's heavy ash tray, dresser dish, or whatever was cutting into his wrists, Blaine would give himself a hernia before he admitted to needing a hand from the new apple of his daughter's eye.

Hogar de Niños was located at the edge of Mexicalli, a picturesque village located on a mountain lake. Like nearby Taxco, it was built over a silver mine, which Diego Ortiz, Mexicalli's first mayor, and his wife, Lucinda, had owned. Unlike its world-renowned neighbor, it had not become a main stop on the tourist route between Mexico City and Acapulco. Instead, it absorbed the overflow of artisans who sold their wares in the other town, but chose to live off the beaten path. Lucinda's granddaughter and namesake donated the land between their hacienda and the small stone church in the village for the orphanage.

"The last Señora Lucinda had no children of her own and enjoyed helping at the orphanage," Father Juan Menasco told the Edenton visitors as they sat down in a long cafeteria to await the special meal the resident children had prepared.

On the tour the priest had given them upon their arrival, Caroline had a chance to see how the monies collected from various churches over the years had been put to use. The old stucco building that once housed the administrative offices, in addition to the eating and sleeping quarters for a handful of orphans, now served the faculty only. A building with sleeping quarters in one end and the mess hall in the other now provided food and shelter for over ten times as many little ones.

The problem was that it was too small. There was no room for the older children who served the meal to sit with the guests, even though the younger ones had already eaten in an earlier shift. As it was, the tables and benches were pint-sized. Caroline felt as if the tabletop rested on her knees.

"Where do the children play when they aren't at the village school?" one of the parents asked the priest.

"In good weather, they play on the grounds. In bad, we move the tables against the wall in here and make do as best we can. And with the new plastic toddler equipment we just received, we can bring some of it in when the weather is bad." Dressed in a casual, collarless shirt and trousers, Menasco gave a hapless shrug. "We need a gymnasium, but we need living facilities more."

"Looks like you have plenty of land to build on," Randy observed.

"Yes, that's true," Father Menasco agreed. "I only wish we could afford to purchase the old Ortiz hacienda. It is, how do you say, a fixer-upper? After Señora Lucinda died, the house was sold for taxes and passed from one hand to another with rumors of Señora

Lucinda's spirit haunting the place. It is in much need of repair, but it is more than we have now . . . and we would fill it with the Holy Spirit."

"Cool! I want to go there," Wally spoke up. His proposal was seconded by most of the students, who until now had had little interest in the Villa Mexicalli or Casa Jacaranda.

"Well, I don't," Christie declared.

While the youngsters took sides on the issue, Randy addressed the priest. "So who owns it now?" In addition to being president of Edenton's PTA, Randy was also head of the missions ministry at Edenton Memorial Church.

"A businessman from Mexico City by the name of Aquino, I think. Or at least he is handling the property."

"Carlos Aquino?" Blaine spoke up at Caroline's elbow.

Menasco looked surprised. "You know him, Señor Madison?"

"I've worked with him on several projects in the city. We just saw him last night at the theater."

"Maybe you could find out how much he or his client is asking for the property," Randy said. "If it's in need of repair, it might be a doable project for the church cluster ministry."

"A cluster?" Menasco repeated.

"It's a group of churches located in the same community," Randy explained. "Sort of like a minidiocese, within a diocese. We do various projects together. This one might be bigger than we can chew, but it can't hurt to ask."

Father Menasco opened his hands heavenward. "With God, all things are possible."

At that moment, a young girl tapped the priest on the arm and whispered something in his ear. Grinning, he clasped his hands together.

"And now, *señoras y señores,* the children of Hogar de Los Niños will serve our meal, prepared by their own hands. But first, let us bow our heads."

Above the priest's thanksgiving for the blessings of the day, the visitors, their wonderful gift of shoes, and the food, there was a childlike shuffle in the door behind Caroline, filled with excited staccato whispers.

At his "Amen," the pent-up commotion broke free. Children ranging in ages from six to their teens entered the room in a procession. Dressed in T-shirts with the familiar Edenton orange and green from a previous donation, they deposited trays of food on the tables: sandwich wraps, made with tortillas rather than bread, salsa and fresh tortilla chips, beans, rice, and more tortillas.

"I make *thees,*" announced a young man not much taller than the table as he wedged between Caroline and Blaine to deposit his plate of wraps in front of them.

"You did?" Caroline exclaimed in her most impressed tone. "What are they?"

The little boy smiled, presenting a mini jack o' lantern display of pearly white teeth. "I make *thees,*" he said again, reaching for the pile of sandwich wraps. Placing one each on Caroline's and Blaine's paper plates, he giggled. "I make *thees.*"

Caroline picked hers up and peeked in the open end. There was something dark inside—and squishy soft. She looked expectantly to see if Blaine could tell any more than she could.

He challenged her with a twinkling gaze. "You first."

The boy watched her with large, beautiful, dark eyes as she took a tentative bite. It was sweet, a grape jam of some type, and nutty.

"It's peanut butter and jelly!"

"I make *thees,*" the little one said brightly.

It was the first time Caroline had ever had peanut butter and jelly in a tortilla. *"Muy delicioso,"* she told him. *"Cómo te llamas?"*

"Berto."

Berto was just the right size to cuddle in her lap, but she resisted the urge to gather him up in her arms and nuzzle the shiny black hair that looked as though it had been cut around a bowl. Heaven forbid she rob him of his masculine pride by treating him like the baby he was.

"I could just pack him in my extra suitcase and take him home," Caroline confided to Blaine.

"Berto doesn't speak English," Father Menasco informed them, "but he insisted our guests would like his favorite dish. And ten cases of peanut butter were just donated, so we make the best of what we have, no?" The priest pointed at the other end of the table. "The others have turkey and ham."

“Cool,” Kurt exclaimed, piling two of each kind on his plate.

Wally followed suit. “Yeah, food we recognize for a change.”

“So this was why Hector insisted we have such a big lunch today,” Blaine chuckled to himself. “He said dinner would be potluck, but peanut butter and jelly tortillas?”

“You kidding?” Caroline gave him a game grin. “I’m right at home—nursery school heaven.”

“Once a kid, always a kid,” he said with a wink.

“I’m taking that as a compliment.” Caroline flushed under his teasing appraisal.

At least she hoped it was a compliment. If she’d been with Frank, he would have chided her to kingdom come about acting like a kid. She’d never hear the end of her charging up the steps of the Pyramid of the Sun without thought of what it would be like coming down.

“I meant it as one.” A smidgeon of jam wedged in the crack of his smile.

Teacher to the core, Caroline zeroed in on it with a napkin without thinking until he jerked backward, taken by surprise.

“Jelly.” The heat on Caroline’s cheeks accelerated from warm to hot as she dabbed off the confection. The napkin snagged on a day’s worth of stubble around Blaine’s mouth, and she couldn’t hold back a giggle. At the questioning rise of his brow, she explained. “I’m not used to wiping jelly off a five o’clock shadow.”

With a look of sheer devilment, Blaine leaned over

and whispered in her ear. “Maybe we ought to work on that.”

Caroline stared at him, slack-jawed as a kid watching a highwire act—and her heart was on the line. Had she heard what she thought she heard? She supposed she must have looked as dizzy as she felt, for he rushed to elaborate.

“Don’t panic. I’m just pulling your leg.” His color deepened beneath his tan.

That had to go down as the fastest retraction in history.

“You do know that charming gullibility of yours makes you a perfect natural target.”

Caroline pulled a childish face at him in retaliation, but behind it, she was torn between disappointment and relief.

While the children sang “Jesus Loves Me” and the Edenton students joined the orphans for some games afterward, Caroline’s thoughts ping-ponged from heaven to earth and back again. What on earth had he meant by that? He *said* he was teasing. But if he had meant it, why in heaven would he mean anything by it? And if it did mean anything, why on earth would she be interested? Her thoughts seemingly stuck in a spin-dry cycle, Caroline resisted the urge to hold her head, lest it lift off.

Heaven and earth notwithstanding, the contrary voices in Caroline’s head finally agreed upon one staggering fact. She’d invited Blaine to flirt with her when she instinctively wiped his chin, and he had responded in kind. If he was half as befuddled by his actions as she was by hers, they'd both be stark-raving mad by the time this week ended.

Caroline hoped the downhill walk back to the hotel through the meandering streets of the quaint village would clear the fact from fancy in her head. Instead, the moon threw in its two pesos. Never had she seen it so large and golden, so close. Had they been headed uphill, rather than down, they'd surely be able to touch it just over the next rise. As it was, it bathed the street in its soft glow, casting its spell over the entire company.

The teens meandered ahead of the adults in little clusters, whispering as though the enchantment had robbed them of their boisterous nature. Likewise, their elders followed, divided into couples by an unseen matchmaking hand. Even Hector and Señora Marron's rapid exchange of Spanish mellowed in the moonlight. Although Caroline caught bits and snatches of plans for tomorrow's tour of Cuernavaca, their soft-spoken Spanish sounded romantic.

"That Mexicalli moon is something else, isn't it? It looks like it's resting in the nest of treetops just over the next rise there." Blaine pointed to the golden globe that hung low, seemingly over the next rise.

"It's too perfect to be real. Like the one in my high school prom picture."

He couldn't miss the edge in her voice.

"Did you marry your high school sweetheart?"

Caroline sighed outwardly while the inner voices squared off. *Way to go, Caroline. Talking about your ex-husband really ices the Valentine moment.* Although that was what she wanted, wasn't it?

"Yes. He's remarried and living in California now."

"He must have had a screw loose to leave someone like you."

Caroline seized on humor to escape. "You know, that's *exactly* what I thought." And now she was lying.

Sorry, Lord. I can't say I'm myself at the moment.

With a chuckle, Blaine stopped Caroline, turning her toward him. "Well, that moon is the real thing . . . and almost close enough to touch." He ran warm hands down her sleeveless arms and scowled. "You're cold."

Before she could siphon an answer through the thoughts scrambling her brain, he shrugged off his jacket and wrapped her in it—and consequently, in his arms.

Oh, God, I'm thinking You chose the wrong "me" to bail out. I'm going down with this ship fast. "Thanks," she managed, taking her panicked heart into her own hands and moving away with it before it was lost to the allure of a very real perfect moon with a perfect man. Of course, she knew that there was no such thing as a perfect man, even if her other willy-nilly self didn't.

"And don't be in such a hurry. I don't bite," he called after her.

No, but in her state of mind, she might. Caroline gave herself a mental smack, slowing her gait. "It's the downhill factor, I think." Not the fact that his coat was filled with his warmth and scent, both delicious. No matter how steep the mountain was, she couldn't outrun the woman within. The fatigue she'd started to feel after the meal was consumed by the acute awareness of him . . . and a lovely floral scent that enveloped them as if Cupid carried a can of it just for the occasion.

"What is that smell?"

The moment the question was out, Caroline wanted to swallow it, but it was too late. "Some kind of flower?" she added, hoping to head off any insinuation that she referred to him.

"Laurel, roses, bougainvillaea . . ." He guided her to where a flowering vine spilled over a stucco wall. "We're surrounded by exotic flowers," he said, plucking a small blossom and placing it under her nose.

In the periphery of her vision, she could see that the others had moved down the street ahead of them, meandering to the beat of their own drums. And here she was, a romantic schizophrenic alone with this man in a setting where the senses ruled.

The flower smelled sweet. Her companion was warm. His gaze caressed her face. Her pulse thundered in her ear. The lips she moistened with her tongue held traces of the sugared confections she'd had for dessert.

"Hey, Mom!" Annie shouted from somewhere beyond Neverland. "Ya want me to take a picture of you two?"

Caroline looked away from the flower Blaine held to see her daughter running back up the hill, the little red dot on her camera shining like Rudolph's nose in the dark.

"It would probably take better in the daylight," Caroline managed, her logical self pulling her moonstruck side out of the spell. "Although the moon is doing its best."

Annie backed away, focusing the camera lens on them. "Almost like a cloudy day. Now smile."

Blaine moved closer to Caroline. Or did she move against him? Senses scrimmaged with reason in Caroline's divided mind. *Smile.* She repeated the order as a mental command. Her mouth responded obediently and froze as Blaine's words tickled her ear.

"There's definitely a lot to be said for waiting awhile after marriage for kids."

In that one sentence, Caroline's worst fear and brightest hope were confirmed. The moonstruck madness that had addled her had infected Blaine too. She hoped a good night's sleep and a healthy dose of daylight would cure them both.

CHAPTER 13

Nothing went to waste at Hogar de los Niños. While the men assembled the brightly colored playground equipment, the ladies cut the cardboard boxes into sheets to be used for future projects. After the women's work was done, Caroline entertained the children with the help of one of the aides. Songs accompanied with hand and foot motions were a big hit, even when they didn't translate well. The favorite was the "Hokey Pokey."

With each step, Berto was right under Caroline's feet, shaking for all his little body was worth. At one point, Caroline thought the boy's drawstring trousers were going to drop off his non-existent hips. He cackled in delight at her Spanish, although she wasn't certain the words he tried to teach her were not corrupted by a childish lisp.

By lunchtime most of the equipment was up and ready for use. Too excited to eat, the children played, the ones too big to use the new acquisitions keeping watch on the zealous little ones. The adults enjoyed a simple but delicious meal of beans and rice tortillas prepared by the cook, while savoring the fruit of the men's labor—the ecstatic squeals and laughter of the beautiful brown-eyed children.

"So what do we do this afternoon?" John Chandler asked Blaine, after the tables had been cleared to drag in the youngsters from their new toys.

Seemingly indebted to the group for taking him in, the young man spent the entire morning with the men, either helping with the assembly or acting as a gopher. Yet, eager as he was to please, he seemed to bring out the wary, just short of irritable, side of Blaine Madison. In Caroline's mind, there was more to Blaine's reaction to the boy than fatherly protectiveness, although what it was, she couldn't imagine.

"Some of us are going to try to shore up the old jungle

gym," Blaine replied. "Father Menasco ordered the hardware but doesn't have the hands and know-how to do the job. Then I'm going to walk up to the hacienda with Randy Gearhardt and have a look a the possibilities regarding the mission."

Couldn't Blaine see the boy was anxious for male company? Caroline wondered what John's relationship with his father was like. Distant, she'd guess, based on the young man's efforts to please the adults, especially Blaine.

"Maybe you'd like to join us?" She couldn't help herself. If Blaine couldn't see the boy's need, then maybe she could open his eyes.

They were open, she realized, and drilling her. "Us?" he repeated.

"I've always wanted to see a haunted hacienda." Caroline grinned, squirming inwardly. She never thought of herself as manipulative, but her impish answer disarmed the loaded gun in Blaine's gaze.

His hackles fell with a sigh of resignation. "I guess the more the merrier."

By the time lunch was over, Blaine surely regretted his glib remark. Aside from him, Father Menasco, Randy, Caroline, and John, most of the kids wanted to go as well. With a distinguished leather-bound notebook, complete with calculator, Blaine looked as ready for work as the students were ready for adventure. He quizzed the priest on the way up, taking notes all along the naturally terraced, grassy slope, dotted here and there by clusters of trees. The closer they came to the hacienda, the thicker the trees and bushes became, obscuring all but an arched wall that towered overhead, housing a large bell.

"While the Señora Ortiz's passion was for children, her husband's was for raising Andalusian horses," Father Menasco informed them. "At one time, this was a working ranch, but much of the land has been sold off over the years."

Caroline imagined how it would feel to race one of those beautiful horses up and down the slopes now occupied by goats, chickens, and little patches of garden. She could almost see their manes and tails flying in the wind the way her hair would—if it would grow past her shoulders without developing a mind of its own. And if she could ride more than a carousel horse. There was just something about this place that sparked the fanciful side of her.

"That is what remains of an arbor that led to the stables from the *casa principal.*"

It looked more like an overgrown hedge of vine and weed, affording an occasional glimpse of what remained of the wooden skeleton. Extending from the cluster of high growth around the hacienda, it led to nothing. Still, Caroline could envision it in pristine condition—a high, grilled arbor with flowering vines weaving their way through it—thick enough to ward off rain from those walking to the barn . . . or hide sweethearts long enough to steal a kiss.

"The barn was destroyed in a fire ten years ago," the

priest told them. "Since then I have kept a set of keys to the hacienda for the last two owners, and now, for the realtors . . . in case the authorities or someone needs access," he explained.

With an energy reserved for youth, the students raced ahead and waited outside the arched entrance to the walled courtyard of Villa Mexicalli for the adults to catch up. Maybe the exertion would curtail Annie and Karen's chatter sessions at midnight. It was one thing if the girls kept the conversation to themselves, but they kept dragging Caroline out of her exhausted stupor for comment. Dana said she should be honored they even wanted her opinion on anything, and Caroline was. She just dreaded getting up the next morning.

Unlike some fanatics who got up at the crack of dawn to jog up and down the mountainside. Maybe that's why it was hard to tell that Blaine had a desk job. He didn't have quite the spread that she had in the rearview mirror. On her, a jogging suit added ten pounds. Blaine, on the other hand, looked good in one.

"All right, listen up," Blaine announced, oblivious to Caroline's observation.

"We are looking at the hacienda for business purposes," Blaine went on with a no-nonsense authority that quelled the teen frolic in front of the heavy, iron-hinged gate. "This is not a romp. I expect you kids to behave as if you were on a tour of private property. No touching, just looking. Walk, don't run. Are we understood?"

"Unless we see a ghost," Wally Peterman proposed.

“Then we can run, right?”

Blaine gave a sharp look. “Are we understood?” he repeated, military sergeant at the core. “You act up, you wait out here for the rest of us.”

After an inventory of somber nods, he gave the go-ahead to Father Menasco. The priest opened one of the huge arched oak doors with a nail-on-a-chalkboard creak that all but shouted “Beware” to the active imagination. Beyond lay a stone-paved courtyard surrounded by a beamed, arched portico, reminiscent of an overgrown, rectangular Stonehenge of the tropics. A collective intake of breath resulted at the sight of a voluptuous water nymph, as weathered and cracked as the fountain into which she’d emptied the last drop of water from her vase years earlier.

“Your ghost, Wally,” Blaine said, laconic.

Christie rubbed her arms as she stepped into the cool interior yard of the sprawling mountain villa. The boys had cajoled her into going. “She gives me the creeps.”

“Nothing a ton of face cream won’t fix,” Wally quipped.

“Or a bucket of plaster,” Kurt added.

“Don’t be too hard on her, boys. Clean her up and she’d be one classy lady . . . like Miz C.”

Caroline winced as John clapped her on the back. “Thank you, John.” She cast a dubious look at the green stuff growing under the half-dressed statue’s armpits. “I think.”

“Don’t be too hard on her, boys,” Kurt mimicked under his breath as John draped a protective arm over

Karen's shoulder, moving in ahead of the others. "Like bein' a couple of years older makes him the authority on women or somethin'."

The house was built in an L-shape around the courtyard with a veranda running its full length. Wide granite steps with detailed iron railing led up to the front door at the juncture of the two-story wings.

"There is a dancing room or, how do you say—" Father Menasco broke off.

"Great room, or ballroom?" Blaine suggested.

"Yes, a ballroom behind the front entrance. It would make a good gymnasium with its high ceiling. The living quarters are to one side of it and the sleeping quarters to the other. All the rooms, of course, open onto the veranda as the many doors show." The priest's gaze was aglow at the potential, as though he could envision the many quarters for his homeless, parentless charges.

"Definitely a fixer-upper," Blaine said to no one in particular.

Randy clapped him on the back. "What say we see just how much fixer-uppin' it needs."

Whether the water nymph or Blaine's stern warning had robbed the teens of their rambunctious mood, they were far more subdued when Menasco opened the oak-paneled double doors to the foyer of the house. A two-pronged stairwell rose gracefully from either side around its perimeter to the second-floor balcony, forming a ceiling over a first-floor frescoed archway with intricately carved dust-laden doors.

"The ballroom is through there."

It was elegant enough, even in its state of disrepair, to make a day care owner feel like a Spanish Cinderella. The same effect had the girls ogling the faded, peeling mural climbing the stairs and continuing around the balcony above. Overhead was a large chandelier, draped with white cloth, the same kind that covered what appeared to be built-in upholstered seating in the curve of the stairwell to either side of the ballroom doors.

"The orchestra played up there"—the priest pointed to glass doors at the head of the steps—"on the mezzanine overlooking the room below. There were grand parties with millionaires and movie stars from your Hollywood throughout the last century until it left the hands of the Ortiz family."

The house seemed to go on and on. Some rooms still had sheet-draped furniture. The ballroom came with an out-of-tune baby grand. Even in ruin, it would surely take at least a million dollars, Caroline thought, just to purchase it. Then there was the fix-up. Chunks of plaster were missing in the walls. Tiled floors needed repair and showed evidence of leaks in the roof. The kitchen and baths hadn't been updated since the first indoor plumbing.

Blaine had filled at least three sheets of legal paper with notes by the time they reassembled in the hall later. "The plus side is that there is no substantial amount of land with the place. Plus for the mission," he said to Father Menasco, "as no land limits the villa's potential to support itself . . . unless someone has *beaucoups* bucks to fix it up as a hotel."

"It's so sad that it was let go like this," Caroline lamented. "I can close my eyes and imagine just how beautiful this must have been at one time."

Blaine smiled at her. "If only it could be restored as easily."

"It would take some major money and effort to pull something like this together, even if we could swing the purchase," Randy agreed. "The labor could be volunteer, but there's still the material cost . . . if it's even worth trying to rebuild."

"Actually, it seems structurally—"

A bloodcurdling scream echoed from the balcony overlooking the ballroom, where the girls had climbed to envision the swirling dancers in trim suits and lavish gowns. As the females stampeded down the steps in both directions, Caroline made a quick surveillance of the students below. Everyone but Annie, Karen, and Christie was accounted for.

"What in the world—" Blaine started.

"It's a ghost! We saw the ghost!" Karen gasped, materializing on the upstairs landing with the other girls.

"No," Annie contradicted, just as wide-eyed as her friend. "We heard it. It was playing the piano."

Blaine was skeptical. "I didn't hear anything."

"It wasn't loud," said Christie. "I want to go *now*."

Unruffled, Blaine walked to the closed ballroom doors with Father Menasco and Randy on his heels.

"You all can wait outside in the courtyard if you want."

Instantly, the others fell in behind them, Caroline included. To her astonishment, when the men opened the double doors into the room, she heard the distinct *plink, plink, plink* of the cloth-draped piano.

"Omigosh, it's moving," she managed in a strangled voice at the sight of the cloth being tugged toward the keyboard.

"All right, if you're a ghost, show yourself." Blaine's challenge stopped the music.

"Maybe she only speaks Spanish." Wally was not nearly as gung-ho to see a spirit as he'd been earlier.

"Quíen va? " Father Menasco called out.

A tiny, nonghostly voice bunched up the girls against the boys, who, for all their machismo, were not that far removed from the adults.

"Soy yo, padre."

The drop cloth moved again, pulling away from the piano until it struggled on its own with the alleged *spirit.* Or sprite, Caroline thought.

"Berto, *eres tú?*"

The yard-high height of the spirit dropped with a plop, its billowing cloth cover following it. Father Menasco hurried over and pulled the tangled sheet off its possessor, revealing the bright-eyed munchkin from the orphanage.

"Buenos dias," Berto exclaimed with a grin, dissolving the former wariness and subsequent astonishment into laughter.

"You can let go of my arm now," Blaine whispered to

Caroline. "I think our ghost is harmless."

Caroline jerked her hand away in embarrassment. She hadn't realized she'd latched on to Blaine in all the excitement. Not that she really expected a ghost.

Father Menasco spoke with Berto in Spanish.

"He must have followed us up here." Heart turning to mush, Caroline gathered the happy child up in her arms and nuzzled his forehead, provoking a giggle in both, until Father Menasco's grim expression sobered her.

"I am afraid he thought that his new mama was leaving."

New mama? Caroline felt the blood drain from her face.

"He seems to have taken a liking to you, Señora. For some reason, he thinks you came to take him with you."

"Cool. I always wanted a little brother," Annie piped up.

Caroline reeled at the thought. "Father, you have to explain that I already am someone else's mother . . . and too old to raise a baby."

Father Menasco nodded. "Of course. And you will leave in the morning after church . . . while Berto is in Sunday school. Perhaps it's best if I tell him then. Otherwise, the little scoundrel may stow away on the bus."

Caught in a whirlpool of conflicting emotions, only one thing was absolute. The little boy in her arms had already stowed away in Caroline's heart.

Blaine wanted to round up Caroline and the boy in his arms—Caroline, because she looked as if she foundered in a sea of despair, and the boy, because he'd managed to get under Blaine's skin from the moment he'd drawn up his arm to show off his muscles and then cajoled Blaine into flexing his biceps in return. And when he wasn't playing games with Caroline, he had shadowed Blaine, asking a question a minute about what the adult was doing and why.

Cómo se llama esto? It would have annoyed Blaine, except that when Berto handed him something a second time, he knew its name—in Spanish and English. A man could get used to a shadow like Berto. Karen was his little girl, but she had no more interest in engineering or any of Blaine's business than he had in shopping. This bright little squirt was interested in everything.

"Up you go, kid." John relieved Caroline of her small burden and gave a delighted Berto a horsey ride back to Hogar de los Niños.

Upon seeing Caroline still visibly torn, Blaine covered her hand with his and fell in behind the students. "I'm not trying to influence you, but women your age have children every day."

"It's so heart-wrenching." She sighed, following the bubbly tyke with her gaze. "I'd take them all if I could."

"I believe you would." He didn't mean it as criticism, and her attempt at a smile told him that she didn't take it as such. "You've got a heart as big as the all outdoors."

And he wanted his share of it. Blaine looked west at the blaze of color settling over the time-wrinkled mountains. He didn't think the scar Ellie left would ever heal, but being around Caroline made it fade, escapade by escapade. Maybe it wasn't an accident that had caused him to make a trip he'd never have gone on under normal conditions. Maybe it was ordained by the same hand that painted that skyscape and made the first timepiece in the world. As an engineer, he could appreciate that kind of perfection. As a man, he could appreciate this second chance for his heart.

But was he ready to give God a second chance? Something told him that where Caroline was concerned, God was part and parcel of the deal.

CHAPTER 14

"So you think there's any chance Hogar de los Niños can buy that old place?" Wearing a pair of boxer shorts dotted with sombrero-wearing chile peppers that one of the women purchased for her foundling that afternoon, John Chandler spat a mouthful of Blaine's toothpaste into the hotel sink. The toothbrush was courtesy of the hotel.

"It's a long shot." Blaine stared from his bed at the swirls in the plaster ceiling, hands folded behind his head. "But as the priest said, all things are possible." Since meeting Caroline, Blaine was beginning to believe it.

He stifled a yawn behind the back of his hand. It had been an exhausting day, and everyone, the students included, opted to turn in early. Where his mother got the idea that he'd be relaxing was beyond him. Going night and day like this, keeping up with teens, was harder than his most taxing week of travel. At least he didn't have to entertain clients twenty-four/seven.

"You really believe that?"

"What?"

Upon wiping off his face with a towel, the young man tossed it in a heap on the counter.

Blaine's clenched jaw checked a reprimand to hang it next to the one that he'd meticulously refolded and hung to dry earlier, as the youth walked over to the other double bed.

"That all things are possible," he said, dropping down on the mattress.

John Chandler not only acted like Mark; he looked like Blaine's younger brother at the same age. With sandy blond hair cut to perfection and blue eyes with naturally dark lashes to set them off, he was a female magnet. Once they heard his smooth lines, girls competed over him, while their mothers fawned. Not that Blaine, with his father's darker features, had ever had trouble garnering feminine attention when he sought it. He simply didn't make a game of it like Mark. But then, life was a game to his brother, just as it was for this kid. And the game was called *Let's see what I can get out of this*.

"You got a new toothbrush, shorts, T-shirt, food, shelter, and transportation for two days without putting out a cent, didn't you?"

Strike one. Guilt grazed Blaine's consciousness the minute the cynicism escaped. The boy looked sincere. Or was he just buttering up a babe's old man?

John winced, a painful look flickering across his face. "Okay, I'm talking God's grace, certainly not yours."

The shot hit its mark. Blaine had shown little grace where John, or Mark, for that matter, was concerned. Put John's way, it didn't sound nearly as righteous. "Sorry, I asked for that one."

Apology accepted in silence, the young man shifted on the other bed, mimicking Blaine's position. "My mom *was* religious," he said, "and I was brought up in church. Then Dad died and she remarried. Everything changed."

Blaine took it that the change was not for the good. Strike two with the guilt bat.

"I went from being part of a family to being 'the kid.' I mean, nothing I could do made my stepdad like me. I wasn't as smart as his son. I wasn't as ambitious as his son. It was like there was some undeclared competition, and I was the loser from the get-go." John scratched his nose with the back of his wrist.

"By the time I was in high school, I gave up trying to please. If I was going to go anywhere, it wasn't going to be with help from home. So I got good grades, joined the right clubs and teams, and got out of town." The boy's lip curled with resentment. "He didn't even give me a pat on the back for the honors and awards. Just one when I walked out the door, like he was as eager to see me go as I was to leave."

"To Mexico?"

John snorted. "I wasn't going to UC or anywhere near home."

Blaine did a mental check. "I thought you said you were from Chicago."

"I am. My stepbrother went to UC Berkeley. Not only is he a snitch; he's as bad as his dad when it comes to downing *the kid*."

"Oh." He thought he'd caught John in a lie. Mark was a polished liar, which meant he told the truth. But it was simply shaded in the wrong light.

Silence enveloped them. John turned off the light and settled back on the creaky bed.

Blaine didn't know which pricked his conscience more, the pain in John's voice or his actual words. Did Mark think of him in the same way as John did his stepfather?

"You know, sometimes dads—" *and brothers,* he added to himself—"ride the younger kid because they want him to succeed." He spoke in his own defense. "Because they love him and don't want to see him make a mistake that can ruin his life. The easiest way isn't always the best way, if you get my drift."

"I guess." John didn't sound as if he wanted to agree, but he did. Mark would have danced his way around the issue with what-ifs. "Thanks for being straight with me."

"Anytime." Blaine closed his eyes, waiting, wondering if this odd-couple heart-to-heart was over. Maybe he'd been too harsh with this boy.

Maybe John and Mark weren't the oddballs, but he was. Blaine had had to grow up faster, take over the business and family responsibilities after his dad's first heart attack, and see his siblings educated and established in their careers. It was a thankless job. Perhaps it was the resulting resentment of all work and no play that made him so hard on Mark, more than his concern for his brother's welfare.

It was totally different with their younger sister. The baby of the family was a child prodigy, gullible in her genius, but always walking in family favor and faith. Mark was the antithesis of Jeanne and Blaine.

God, I just don't know. If that is the case, if I am too hard on my brother, open my eyes. I don't want to be like the men who made this kid's life miserable. I just want to see Mark stop disappointing Mom. That's the hardest—

"By the way . . ." John interrupted the spontaneous prayer.

And it was a prayer, Blaine realized in wonder. He hadn't spoken to God since Ellie died. Traveling around with a band of believers must be rubbing off on him. Unlike the world Blaine circulated in, where spiritual issues were taboo, these people talked about praying for this and that as if it were as natural as eating. There seemed to be room for formal meals, like the prayer said each morning before the bus pulled out, and take-outs along the way of "Thank the Lord" when things went well or they found the good concealed in layers within the bad.

“Yes?” Blaine tore himself from his introspection.

“Mind if I borrow one of your shirts for tomorrow? The T-shirt I wore today smells like something died in it, and there’s no Laundromat nearby.”

“Did it occur to you that you might wash it out by hand?” Blaine grated out, impatience banishing the wonder of his spiritual introspection. After all, there was a lot in the Scripture about discipline too.

A moment of charged silence eventually led to the kind of enlightenment Edison must have known when the idea of the lightbulb came to him. “Oh, yeah!” There went the mental click of the switch. “Thanks, dude.”

With that, the bedside light came on, assaulting Blaine’s eyes and testing the restraint of every muscle in his body, including his tongue. *This dude needs shut-eye.*

“I never thought of that. You got any soap?”

Blaine took a deep breath. “Use the bar the hotel provided. It has a lovely scent.” Seizing his pillow, he tossed on his side, away from the additional blaze of lights from the bathroom vanity. “And wash your socks, while you’re at it,” he added, getting a whiff of the sneakers parked next to him by the nightstand. Pulling his pillow over his head, he mumbled into it. “They’ve a pungent bouquet all their own.”

The passing sun-splashed hillsides of roses looked like God-sized bouquets of pink, white, and red as the bus struggled up, down, and around the curving highway leading from Mexicalli to Cuernavaca. Cameras clicked all around Caroline, but she was too wrapped in thought to bother. All she could see in her mind was the face of the little boy she'd tucked into bed the night before. Berto couldn't read, write, or even speak her language, but he'd read her heart.

"Go *mañana?*" he asked, dark eyes peering over the edge of the blanket he'd played peekaboo with earlier.

Caroline couldn't lie. *"Sí, niñito, tengo que ir con los otros,"* she said, sad to be leaving.

He said no more. As she gave him a kiss, he disentangled his arms from the blanket and hugged her tightly. She held the child until he tired and let go. His acceptance without question led her to believe this wasn't the first time the boy had been disappointed. When she rose to leave, wet cheeks were the only sign of his despair. And hers.

Caroline fished a tissue from her purse and blew her nose. This was ridiculous. She'd only known the child forty-eight hours. He probably did that with all the mission people who stopped by the orphanage to help out. She couldn't imagine them having the least trouble finding a loving home for such a darling child, but Father Menasco pointed out to her, when she said as much after church that morning, that there were so many beautiful children and very few homes that did not already have more mouths than could be adequately fed.

Beside her, Blaine covered the fist in which she compressed the tissue with his hand. A quiet understanding met her gaze as she lifted it to his. At the first quiver of her chin, she turned back to the window where a wall of solid brown rock rose higher than she could see from inside the bus. He must think her a silly goose, but he was at least gentleman enough to keep his derision to himself. At his reassuring squeeze of her hand, she forced a smile and leaned her head against the seat.

Closing her eyes, Caroline listened to the groan and growl of shifting gears as the bus climbed higher yet into the wrinkled gray-green mountain range before them. Maybe she was just overtired from the relentless pace of the tour. Maybe it was the paper-perfect moon that filled her heart with fanciful ideas of love and taking a little boy home with her. Maybe . . .

What seemed no more than moments later, the blast of a horn startled Caroline from her nap as the bus lurched off a railed stone bridge and plunged like a whale into a fishbowl of narrow streets designed for carriages—or at the most, the beetle-bug cars so prevalent on the highways and city streets.

Hector tapped on his microphone. "*Señores, señoras, y señoritas,* we are now entering the town of eternal spring . . . Cuernavaca." He leaned to the side as driver Bill made a tight turn. "Because we are behind the others in our tour, we will stop only for lunch. And, of course, shopping," he added with a look that all but conjured dollar signs in his eyes. "Okay?"

"H'okay!" the group answered, mimicking his enunciation.

"To the left," Hector pointed out, "is the Palacio de

Cortéz. He liked Cuernavaca's year-round pleasant weather so well, he says, 'Those Indians don't need that pyramid,' and he takes the pyramid apart and builds this medieval fortress with its stones right on its base."

It was a beautiful town, cobbled streets filled with Spanish colonial architecture. Sidewalk cafés added the mouthwatering appeal of baking breads and sweets, strong coffees, and mesquite meats cooking on grills. An "in your face" Walgreen's and a few other international chain restaurants broke the ambience here and there, but it was short-lived, overpowered by the history preserved in stone that had seen Aztec rule give way to Spanish and French, and then return to independence. The bus eventually squeezed into a parking place among other buses alongside the high-walled compound of the Cathedral de la Asunción, built, according to their guide, like a fortress to protect its Franciscan founders from the hostile natives, as well as to intimidate the latter.

"Now, *mis amigos,*" Hector said over the bus intercom. "There are several cafés and shops in this area, as well as tours of the church and gardens. But," he emphasized, "we only have two hours, because we spent all our time at the orphanage. At 1:30 sharp, the bus leaves. *Entienden?*"

With a chorus of *"Entienden,"* the passengers scrambled to get off the bus.

"Dónde está el servicio de postal?" Kurt asked Hector in his best high school Spanish on the way out

of the vehicle. "I got some postcards to mail and need to get stamps."

Hector pointed down the street. "One block *a la izquierda,* on the left."

"Would you mind mailing mine?" Caroline asked, tugging out the cards she'd written the night before. Hector had warned the travelers that they'd most likely be back in Pennsylvania before the cards got there, but the thought and foreign stamps made them special—at least it was when she received foreign mail.

"Wanna go with us?" Kurt asked Karen, with a hopeful expression.

"Why would I want to do that?" she answered, shooting it down.

"Beats me," the boy recovered, shrugging. "I mean, why would anyone want to give up my charm and Wally's brains for the bubble-wit champs?" Kurt nodded to where the other kids were trying to outdo each other in a bubble gum–blowing contest.

"*Ahora,* no gum in school, no gum on the trip," Señora Marron snapped a few feet away. Producing tissues from her purse, she proceeded to collect the pink goo from the bubble-blowing recalcitrants. "We do not need someone *losing*"—she drew out the word with a pointed lift of one pencil-black eyebrow—"his gum in the museums or shops, no?"

Kurt grinned at Karen. "Need I say more?"

Always a sucker for the underdog, Caroline suppressed a little *Go Kurt* as, pony-express style sans the pony, Kurt and Wally headed for the post office with a backpack of mail from the group. After a lunch of roast beef sandwiches, Sanborn's chain specialty, some of the group headed for the shops, but Caroline opted to spend the remaining time at the Cathedral de la Asunción de María.

Painted in earth colors of red and tan, it fit right in with the other colonial buildings she'd seen, although the walls beyond the facade were aged and weathered stone. The main sanctuary was stark in comparison, with frescoes on the wall depicting someone's martyrdom.

"I'm glad I didn't live in those times," she confided to Blaine. "I don't know that I'd be that committed under the threat of torture, much less be able to endure it. Makes me feel like a spiritual wimp."

"Being around this group makes me feel like a spiritual wimp."

Caroline looked at her companion, startled. "Why would you say that?"

He shrugged. "I haven't paid all that much attention to my"—he paused, searching for the right word—"to developing the kind of relationship with a higher power I see in you and some of these people."

"With God?"

"Whatever you want to call it . . . or Him." His voice filled with disbelief. "I think I envy it."

"Well, for what it's worth, it comes and goes in all of us. What I mean," she added, seeing a flicker of surprise prick at his forehead, "is that it rises and ebbs in all of us. When things are good, that peace is great. But when questions or life assails one's faith . . . well, let's just say forging by fire isn't a walk in the park. Yet, it's by that testing or fire that we get rid of our impurities and grow stronger. I have no doubt that I am stronger and wiser because of some of the hardships in my life. And I've been rewarded many times over for holding on to my faith and persevering when a task intimidated me."

Like the thought of raising a small child in your early forties?

Caroline silently argued against the nagging voice. *Lord, if that's You, You know that's not fair. I've raised Annie. I take care of everyone else's kids now.*

"Picture me as a cat clinging to the window of faith." She held up her hands like claws, exacting a toe-curling grin from the man next to her.

Caroline had hoped to find some peace of mind in the sanctuary, not stir up her feelings even more. She was a professional now. Her schedule wouldn't allow her to take on another child, even though the motherly feelings Berto had stirred in her heart would. Besides, she knew nothing about raising a boy. What kind of role model could she provide him? *It wouldn't be fair to him,* she argued with herself as she and Blaine made their way out of the building into the *recinto,* or walled-in compound. Scribed into the stones of the old church were the names of those who'd died during its construction.

"This trip, being with you and the others, has caused me to re-examine my thoughts on many things . . ."

Blaine said, interrupting her internal argument. "About faith and family." He shoved his hands into his trouser pockets. "I've been trying to maintain the status quo, even when I wasn't happy with it. Maybe because I didn't want it to get any worse. Or maybe it's because I was comfortable, if not thrilled, with what I knew. I preferred discontent of the known to the possible promise of the unknown." He exhaled a breath though his lips with a half whistle. "I guess that boils down to lack of faith, huh?"

"Was it Mark Twain who said only wet babies like change?" Caroline smiled, but Blaine's admission struck a chord in her mind. Is that what she was doing in her life—holding on to the status quo so tightly that she was squeezing out the potential for further happiness or fulfillment? Was she like the guy in Ecclesiastes whose heart rejoiced in all his labor only to find it was all vanity and grasping at the wind? *The wind instead of the joy she'd felt holding little Berto in her arms?*

"I'll bet you keep God in stitches," Blaine teased. He slipped his arm about her waist and gave her a playful hug.

For such an innocent gesture, its effect on Caroline was profound. In addition to a little boy in her arms, she imagined herself in Blaine's embrace. And there was Annie, entering the group hug, and Karen. Great. Now the voices in her head were drawing pictures.

God, is this the result of hormones and emotions running amok, or a preview of what could be—if I were willing to leave my current comfort zone and take a chance on love and faith?

"Time to get back to the bus." Blaine didn't remove his arm. Instead, he used it to usher her through the ancient tombstones toward the gated entrance. It felt so right there, being this close to him . . . and safe within the protective circle of his arm.

"Mom, look what I got for the bathroom," Annie called out to them as they approached the bus. Digging into a plastic bag, she produced a ceramic dish. "It's a soap dish with the same blue as our bathroom, and it says *Cuernavaca* on it." Having resolved to buy a small but practical souvenir from every place they visited, Annie was thrilled.

"It'll be perfect."

"Annie," Karen called out from inside the baggage bay. "Toss it to me, and I'll stow it with my stuff for now. I can't find your backpack."

"Kurt and Wally helped load the luggage this morning while Karen and John and I were at the hotel gift shop." Annie rolled her blue eyes heavenward. "Males! *Everything* is mixed up."

Caroline smiled. Boy, could she relate. Between Blaine and Berto, her heart, mind, and spirit were as mixed up as they could get. Or maybe Hector was right about that moon.

CHAPTER 15

Taxco was nestled into the foothills of the Sierra Madres like a precious child cradled in its mother's arms. Caroline tried to capture the vista from Santa Prica Church with a panoramic disposable camera. It was a fairy-tale setting, the kind that appears only once in a hundred years. Red-tiled roofs and narrow, winding streets added the dimensions of stark ups, downs, and arounds to the standard four map directions. With the passages barely wide enough for two cars to pass without running pedestrians into the shops along the way, there was no point to traditional highway dividing lines. Instead, the road rambled like the flowering vines painted down its center.

With beauty, charm, and very steep inclines, the town literally took Caroline's breath away. And she'd barely regained it from unloading the bus and settling in at the picturesque Posada de la Misión. The fresh slacks and cotton sweater she'd changed into were now damp with perspiration, but the spiral climb through the streets of the vertical city had been worth it.

"Thank God the authorities had the foresight to preserve this," she said to Dana, handing over a dollar to a beautiful little girl for a postcard.

"They're cheaper in the souvenir shop at the hotel," Blaine reminded her.

"But this young lady is such a good salesperson."

The child, of grade-school age judging by her size, beamed. All she'd said was "Cards for the church," but Caroline had overheard one of the nuns nearby explaining to another tourist how the monies were used to help the children of the village.

"I can't argue with the heart."

Blaine's expression of wonder and admiration nearly took what starch the climb had spared out of her knees.

Caroline tried to ignore the sharp elbow jab Dana gave her on the sly.

"Are you okay?" he asked.

Evidently she had failed. "When I signed on to go to Mexico, I didn't know mountain climbing was on the agenda."

Lord, I know the "Thou shalt not kill" rule, but Dana is pushing the envelope.

"At least the return walk will be downhill," her friend consoled her. The madonna innocence on her face switched to a grin of devilment. "And there are all those shops to check out along the way."

"Don't forget," Blaine reminded them. "Dinner is at seven at the hotel. You have four hours. I'm going to head back and make some phone calls."

"Business?" Caroline could have bitten off her tongue. As if it were her business what kind of calls he had to make.

"Always." He turned to where the girls were examining the assortment of postcards. "You two stay with the adults. No running off on your own."

Karen made a face. "Aw, man, we've got a map . . .

and John's with us."

Blaine dug in deeper. "You heard me. It's promise to stay with Caroline or come back to the hotel with me now."

"Uncle Mark lets us go anywhere we want on the boardwalk at the beach."

"I wouldn't turn you loose in Mexico with Uncle Mark." Blaine snorted. "I wouldn't turn Uncle Mark loose in Mexico, for that matter."

"It's not like we have anyplace special to go," Annie pointed out to her friend.

John walked over from where he'd been taking in the view above the town. "Don't worry, Mr. B. I'll take care of *all* the girls."

The flirtatious wink he gave her and Dana tickled Caroline. What a charmer.

"Besides, I can show them the art of bartering. The storekeepers love to haggle over prices."

"My dad is *so* out of touch," Karen complained to the world at large.

Blaine took it in stride, patient but persistent. "So, what's it going to be? Staying with Caroline or going back with me?"

"Miz C." From her tone, Karen might be choosing between hemlock and arsenic.

"We'll have a grand time." Caroline's assurance was directed both ways. "You kids can keep Dana and me from getting lost."

"You bet," her friend threw in. "Heaven only knows where my son and husband are."

Blaine gave a smile of relief. "Great." Before Caroline realized what he was doing, he leaned over and gave her an impulsive kiss on the cheek. "Thanks, and good luck."

As he walked away, Caroline, Dana, and the girls stared after him in stunned silence.

Annie thawed first. "Did you see that?"

"Yeah," Karen answered, no less affected. "I haven't seen him act like this since I was a kid." She snorted in disbelief. "If he asks me if I want to ride horsey, I'll die."

"It's gotta be a moon hangover," John said. "Makes people romantic for days, no matter how old they are."

"But this is my *dad,*" Karen reminded him. She turned to inspect a rack of beaded jewelry on display behind them. "Like, he's too old to be acting like that."

"He's not *that* old," Annie protested.

From somewhere in the flutter of reaction beating about in Caroline's brain, she blessed her very wise child.

Karen turned with all the authority of a self-appointed Miss Manners. "But not *in public*."

Still stuck next to Caroline at the same spot on the cobbled street where Blaine had left them, Dana snickered. "Seems like you bring out the boy in someone," she whispered to Caroline behind the cover of her hand.

Caroline, stuck somewhere between the kiss and being relegated as too old for a public display of affection, remained silent.

"What in Cupid's name are you going to do about

that, girlfriend?" Dana challenged.

"Yeah, Mom, what *are* you going to do?" Annie chimed in, the selective hearing that chronically managed to miss parental instruction now on full alert.

Amid a scramble of positives and negatives seeking order in her mind, one sentiment surfaced. "I think I'll just take it one kiss . . . er . . ." What on earth was she saying? "I mean, one *day* at a time."

Or one prayer at a time was more like it, she thought, ignoring Dana's *Told you so* grin. Prayer that this is God's will. Prayer that Blaine will continue his journey back to the only One who could make this work between them. And prayer that whatever transpired between them would not be *in public*.

Even Karen's rebellion couldn't dampen Blaine's mood as he descended the pebbled incline to the cluster of stuccoed, tiled guest houses the group was sharing. Whistling, he took the steps to his suite two at a time and unlocked the heavy, arched oak door.

While the exteriors of the guest quarters, hotel office, and restaurant were reminiscent of an old Spanish mission, the interiors were modernized and luxurious. His rubber-soled shoes silent on the leather-colored tile floor, he crossed a small living area replete with stone fireplace and mission furniture arranged in a cozy circle. Stopping in the long dressing corridor with tiled sinks separated from the shower and john area by a row of closets, he washed some of the travel grime from his face and hands before heading into the sleeping area at the far end of the suite.

It would be a good time to try Carlos Aquino—before the end of siesta. Tugging out his wallet, he sat on the edge of his bed and searched for the business card Aquino had given him at the Ballet Folklórica. The hacienda was likely to be a steal, given its run-down condition. As a home, Blaine could turn it around into a hefty profit. As an orphanage, it was going to take some creative design. The only asset of the latter was the large ballroom and the proximity to the orphanage itself.

Blaine's business mind tugged at his resolve to turn a golden goose into a turkey as he read the instructions for using the old-time Ma Bell black phone. The fact was, the turkey was needed more, he decided, ending the mind game. But upon dialing the number, he got an answering machine.

"Yes, Carlos, this is Blaine Madison. I came across some property in Mexicalli that I heard you are handling, and want to find out more about it for my daughter's . . . for my church group. They are talking about expanding the orphanage. The place is a ruin, but maybe we can work something out. My cell number is—"

A loud creak coming from the adjoining room drew Blaine's attention. He hastily rattled off his cell phone number and hung up.

"Girls?" He walked over to the connecting door. Stopping, he knocked before turning the old iron knob. "Anybody home?"

No one should be. But someone—or something—was in there.

As he eased the door open, he heard a closing click of yet another door. Tossing caution aside, Blaine hurried into the room. There was no sign that anyone but some women in a hurry to change clothes had been there. Racing to the outside exit, he pulled the door open and stepped through to the stone landing opposite the one to his room.

There were guests and staff in the compound, each moving about with the solitary purpose of work or play. No one seemed hurried or looked as if they'd been in a rush. If it had been room service, he'd heard no knock. Shaking his head at his tourist paranoia, he glanced around, telling himself that nothing was wrong, there was nothing to worry about.

To his left another set of steps wound their way to the roof through a small arched entrance. More out of curiosity than suspicion, Blaine climbed the steep rise to find a lovely courtyard on the roof that overlooked a green slope of mountain dotted with white houses like a pasture with sheep. One didn't have to be a scholar in architecture to appreciate the beauty.

Just as he didn't need a degree in psychology to know that Caroline was the best thing that had happened to him in a long time. Through her eyes, everything was suddenly new and exciting. She gave him new energy, uncovered hope in the ashes of what had been. Blaine wanted to do something special for her. He wanted to be her hero . . . and he'd not felt like hero material in years. His mind churning with possibilities, he tripped down the steps like a kid and went back to his room.

A siesta later, Blaine was showered, shaved, and on the phone with Señor Aquino before a rustle of packages and laughter heralded the approach of the ladies next door. Aquino *was* handling the Ortiz property and promised to get the information to Blaine's office within the week.

As Blaine made the notation on his electronic organizer, John came in with a bag.

"Something new?" Blaine asked.

"Miz C bought it for me." The boy dumped a black silk shirt out on the bed. With *Taxco* embroidered neatly on the pocket, it was a souvenir special, but the material made it costlier than most. "I saved the ladies a bundle, and—"

"They spent the savings on you."

"Guess so. Never thought of it like that," he said, heading for the shower.

Blaine grabbed a tie from his garment bag. He didn't doubt that much was true. Mark never saw his exploitation for what it was either.

John was back in such a short time that, but for his dripping hair, Blaine would have questioned that he'd even gotten wet.

"So, was that the dude who owns the hacienda in Mexicalli?" the youth asked from under the towel as he dried his hair.

"Yes. It is for sale and it may go cheap, since the owner is in some financial straits."

"Cool. It's like . . . like the lady I saw was psychic or something."

Blaine's curiosity was piqued. "Caroline?"

"No man, this lady in front of the church . . . a tourist, I think." He rubbed some sort of styling gel that he'd borrowed from Karen through his short locks. "Out of the blue, she turns to me and says, 'All things are possible. Remember, God loves you.' Like, I didn't know her from beans." He made a little snorting noise and paused, as though replaying the words in his mind. "But after you and I talked about it last night and then this . . ." He shrugged his shoulders. "Weird, man."

"Speaking of weird," Blaine said, "I could have sworn someone was in the room next door when I came back to the hotel."

John stopped pulling his hair up in little peaks and stared at Blaine in the mirror. "Did you see anyone?"

"I was on the phone when I heard someone moving around, but by the time I went in there, whoever it was had left." Blaine dismissed the topic. "Probably maid service or someone in the rooms adjoining the back of ours."

"Yeah, probably." John didn't sound quite convinced.

Blaine watched him wipe his hands free of the lotion. "Weird, huh?"

The youth folded the towel and hung it on the rack. "This whole trip's been weird for me."

But then, John was a kid, even if he was in college, and kids tended to be melodramatic.

A while later, Blaine waited on the roof of the villa for

the others to join him. The same team of anxiety and excitement that he'd known while waiting for Ellie during their dating years skipped around and tripped over male logic and maturity. At the sound of footfalls on the steps, Blaine turned to where Karen emerged on John's arm.

Fancy fled, replaced by a mix of alarm and awe. His daughter was so . . . so beautiful. Instead of a ponytail, Karen wore her hair down, curled slightly toward her face, which was a blend of Ellie's high cheekbones and Blaine's dimpled chin. With makeup accentuating her dark eyes and the fullness of her lips, she looked like a woman, not his little girl. And the colorfully embroidered red dress that exposed her white shoulders underscored her feminine appeal just a little too much for his fatherly taste.

"You look beautiful," he said, getting up and crossing to where Karen turned to show off her new purchase. The full skirt swirled around her legs, brushing just above her knees.

"Real fine," John agreed.

"But this won't do." Blaine pulled the ruffled elastic top of the dress up onto her shoulders. "It makes you look like a . . ."

"Like a what?" Caroline asked from the stairwell.

Blaine took a mental spill. Clad in the same dress, but in black, she joined them. It was souvenir shop fashion, but on Caroline it could have been Dior. She was the most gorgeous *señora* he'd ever seen. And he'd painted himself into an uncomfortable corner with his quick comment.

"A what, Blaine?"

Caroline not only knew what he'd been about to say; she was having fun with him over it.

The heat of resentment cleared his mind for recovery. He gave his daughter a peck on the nose and tugged up her ruffled bodice again from where she'd rearranged it. "You are not a woman . . . yet."

He nodded at Caroline. "She is."

"But—" Karen started.

"Hey, you look hot, no matter how you wear it," John told her.

Blaine drilled the boy with a "hands off" glance. The last thing he needed was the wolf's help with his little lamb.

"Baby," he said to his daughter, "you look as good in the passenger seat as you do in the driver's seat, but you aren't ready to drive yet." The hasty illustration earned him a collective expression of "What?" on the faces turning his way.

"I wouldn't think of letting you drive a car if you were . . . ten," he said, realizing that his little girl was just a month away from getting her driver's permit. "Because even though you might know how to put it in gear and steer it, you wouldn't be ready physically to reach the pedals or mature enough to handle it in a responsible fashion on the highway. Understand?"

Karen lifted her lip in a curl of doubt. "Wearing a dress is like driving a car?"

His failed analogy burned rubber up Blaine's neck. If

he'd only kept his mouth shut to start with. "Some dresses are."

He readjusted the ruffle halfway between Karen's idea of decency and his, balanced at the shoulder joint, favoring the neck. "How about we compromise?"

Between the disgusted look in his daughter's gaze and the mischievous one in Caroline's, he was drowning anyway, so he might as well say what he meant. He braced himself with a deep breath.

"It's just that when I first saw you come up here, you were so beautiful that the daddy in me didn't like it. He's afraid someone is going to pick his little rose and take her away . . . and I can't bear the thought of losing you."

Karen's grudging look melted. She threw her arms about Blaine's neck. "Oh, Daddy, you will never lose me." She gave him a hard squeeze. "You may annoy me, but you will never, ever lose me."

She turned with a bounce and linked arms with John. "Come on, let's go see if Annie's made up her mind which dress she's going to wear."

As they disappeared, Caroline slipped her arm through his. "I think you handled that wonderfully, *Daddy*. You almost made me cry in front of the kids." The reflection of the setting sunlight swimming in her eyes confirmed her words. "Wanna come with me to check out *my* little girl?"

"Sure." He would go anywhere with Caroline the way she looked at him right then. Letting reservation fly with the evening breeze, he leaned down to do what had been on his mind from the moment he'd seen her emerge from the stairwell in that dress, but checked himself just short of the kiss he'd intended to plant upon her shoulder. Her shock from this afternoon's impetuous peck on the cheek told him slow was the better course, if not the most desirable. Instead, he inhaled the clean scent of her perfume, his voice taut from his restraint.

CHAPTER 16

"Pretty in pink," Blaine said as Annie came out on the stoop in front of her villa room.

"Thanks."

He could imagine Annie's freckles fading in a blush the way her mother's did.

"I was going to save this for Banditos in Acapulco, but I changed my mind at the last minute, so I sent John and Karen ahead. I mean, why not go like rainbow triplets?" she finished in one breath.

Annie sported the same dress as the other ladies, but the pastel shade was more suited to her fairer complexion. Although she also wore hers off the shoulder, Blaine had learned his lesson and kept his mouth shut. Besides, with her hair pulled back in a cluster of matching ribbon, she still looked girlish. If John was as affected by Karen as Blaine was by Caroline, he'd wring the boy's neck.

Caroline tugged her daughter's ruffled neckline up to

the same level as Karen's. "Just to avoid embarrassing Blaine any more," she explained at Annie's disconcerted look.

Her playful wink dissolved any resulting miff on Blaine's part.

He held up his hands in surrender, but turnabout *was* fair play. "Okay, I admit it. I don't want our daughters leading some innocent young man into temptation the way your mom is doing with me."

Annie dissolved into a sigh. "That is so sweet." She rose on tiptoe and gave him a big hug. "Karen doesn't know how lucky she is to have a dad like you."

"Thank you, Annie," he stammered in surprise. What he wouldn't give for his own daughter to feel that way one more time.

"And as for you," the teen said, turning to Caroline. "Shame on you." With a grin she adjusted Caroline's ruffle just a little. "Just one notch above red hot chili pepper ought to snag you a husband instead of a . . ." She searched for a word. "A fling."

"Annie—" Caroline broke off, speechless.

Delighted, not just by the exchange but by Annie's implication of acceptance, Blaine gathered the precocious Annie under one arm and her mom under the other. "All I can say is, like mother, like daughter."

Electric lanterns styled in the Spanish mission period softly lit the way to the hotel lobby and restaurant complex. Since both ladies wore heels, Blaine kept them from slipping or stumbling over the stones in the walk that ranged in size from jelly bean to baseball. On the left—and downhill—was a glow from the pool area where the students planned to meet after the meal.

Passing through a glass-enclosed walkway with lavish floral arrangements in handmade pottery, they entered the lobby, where an open pair of iron-strapped oak doors invited guests into the open-air restaurant.

"There you are," Karen called from a table next to a magnificent unobstructed view of the mountainside settlement. "We'd begun to think you'd gotten lost."

Next to her, John rose and pulled out a chair for Annie with a flourish. "Miss Pretty in Pink."

The boy was even using Blaine's lines, and this time Blaine could see Annie's smattering of freckles fade into her blush.

"How gallant, sir." Totally taken, Annie spread her skirt in dainty fashion as she settled next to him.

"Your shirt looks great, John," Caroline observed. "Has Dana seen it?" She glanced around the room.

"Yes, ma'am. The Gearhardts are over there." He pointed to the back of the restaurant.

With a territorial grip on Caroline's chair, Blaine followed her gaze to Dana Gearhardt, who at that moment shook her shoulders like a salsa dancer, giving Caroline a devilish grin.

The moment Dana realized she'd been caught, she gave him a sheepish wave.

"What was that all about?" he whispered into Caroline's ear as he tucked her chair in.

"I have *no* idea what that crazy woman is up to." Caroline enunciated each syllable with precision. "You stick around her long enough, you'll learn to expect anything."

"Kind of like hanging out around you, huh?" he teased.

Her blush was as comely as her daughter's. Blaine wanted to kiss her, but hesitated, lest he give John any ideas. That would have to wait until later, when the time was right.

A white-jacketed waiter presented them with a special menu of Mexican dishes priced especially for the Edenton tour. In the spirit of tasting the culture, each of them ordered a different dish from the limited menu with a promise to share. Blaine tried the *carne asada,* thin fillets of beef served in a chile sauce. Caroline opted for *mole de guajolote,* which the waiter pronounced the most ancient of Mexican dishes on record—turkey with mole sauce. Karen chose a compatriot, poached chicken with mole sauce called *pollo en mole poblano.*

"Hey, how can we go wrong with mole?" she quipped, handing over the menu to the waiter. "They can only mess chocolate, nuts, chiles, and onions up so much."

"I think the heartburn has started already," Caroline confided behind her hand to Blaine.

"I want my chocolate in dessert, not my main course." Annie chose the Mexican version of stuffed peppers, dipped in an egg batter and fried.

"Where is your sense of adventure, girl?" her mother teased.

"In my heart, not my stomach," Annie shot back.

"I like mole sauce, but I love peppers stuffed with farmer's cheese." John ordered a variation of Annie's *chiles rellenos.*

While some of the dishes were hotter than others, the sharing and teasing that ensued as the company exchanged portions of their minismorgasbord proved fun and entertaining. Dessert was not quite as exotic, but no less delicious. The flan, Mexican bread pudding, and Mexican cookies with a dip of vanilla ice cream helped offset any remaining heat from the chiles.

In a courtyard below the window, a mariachi band played a mix of dance music and fun songs to involve the audience. John rose as they struck up a slow song and invited Karen to dance. On seeing Annie's deflated look, Blaine spoke up.

"Annie, would you consider cutting the rug with an old codger like me while your mom finishes her dessert?"

"Doing what to the what?"

"Sweetie, that's old-codger lingo for 'do you wanna dance?' " Caroline translated.

The sunrise of delight on the teen's face made the risk of an embarrassing denial well worth it. "That would be lovely," she said, offering her hand like a princess to her courtier.

Blaine escorted Annie down the steps to the dance patio. Although nervous and awkward at first, after Blaine counted off a few steps with direction, she quickly advanced from her previous experience of rocking from one foot to the other to a two-step.

"You're good," Annie marveled after Blaine walked and talked her through a turn. "I think this kind of dancing is so beautiful. I mean, there's something to it."

"My mother made me take lessons, but I appreciate it now."

"Me too." Annie was a miniversion of Caroline, except that her shyness tended to cloak her sense of humor and romantic nature.

"Annie, I have a question to ask you."

"Sure."

"I . . ." Blaine had it all worked out, exactly what he was going to say, but her expectant look combined with wide-eyed innocence tripped his thoughts. *What if she says no?* "I've really enjoyed meeting you and your mom."

"I think Mom's enjoyed meeting you, too . . . and I know I have. This trip has been such a blast."

"It surely has." Blaine smiled and looked at the trumpet player now taking a solo. If this were a business proposition, he'd have laid it out by now, fast and to the point.

"So," Annie said, drawing his attention back to her, "you think we might be doing this more often?" The little devil brandished the same playful look her mother had earlier as he'd squirmed with the neckline issue.

"Would you like to?"

"What's not to like? If we handle this right."

The warning in her addendum gave Blaine a mental check. "What do you mean?"

"I mean, Mom doesn't make up her mind quickly about anything when it comes to me and her business. She's got this *If it ain't broke, don't fix it* thing, ya know. Like," she snorted in wonder, "she doesn't even know she's broken."

Now he understood. "It's a defense mechanism, my dear, called *survival*. You do what you have to do with what you have and make the best of it. I admire her for that. She's raised a good, well-balanced daughter, provided for her, and remains full of life, when some would just become bitter and resentful."

"I call her success a God thing," Annie countered. "Her faith has pulled us through some rough times. It's just that Mom deals better with the trials than she does with blessings sometimes. Like—" She groped for the right words. "Like, except for dishes and cleaning," she said with a tinge of regret, "it's hard to do stuff for her. She wants to do all the giving, know what I mean?"

"So you're saying it won't be easy to take care of her, huh?"

"Did I mention stubborn?" Annie asked.

"No, but I'm getting the picture. Time with loved ones is more appreciated than any material gifts."

"From Mom's lips to yours."

The little tract he'd gotten at the airport popped up in Blaine's mind, the thing about getting up early, sitting up late—always working to provide for his family, when all they'd wanted was *him*. Had he made work his escape from the unhappy home it was responsible for? Had the tool he used to build it been the same one that brought it down?

God? Got any answers?

Or was that his answer? Caroline had built her house with faith in her toolbox. He hadn't. He'd resented the trials, yet wanted the blessings. Somewhere along the way, he'd gotten the wrong idea that they were free, like salvation.

"You are wiser than your years, Annie Spencer," Blaine said in earnest. "I'm glad to have you on my side."

"So it's a go then? You want to date my mom?"

"If I can pull it off." Dating was good. Hard for a guy who recognized a good deal and grabbed it off the table before anyone else had the chance, but good. "And I need to talk to Karen—" Blaine hadn't finished before Annie broke away and tapped Karen on the shoulder with more boldness than she'd ever exhibited to date.

"Mind if we cut in?" Without waiting for an answer, she edged John away from Karen.

He chuckled to himself. At least one of them was decisive.

"What's gotten into her?" Karen complained as Blaine claimed her for a partner.

"I think the love bugs are out."

"Annie and John?" Karen's head pivoted around. "But he's *my* date."

"Your *date?*"

She quickly backtracked. "What I mean is that he likes *me,* not her. I mean, she's his friend and all . . ."

"And you are . . . ?"

"Dad." Karen glared at him in exasperation. "I *am* sixteen. I am not a little girl. Is it so beyond you that a boy like John could be interested in me?"

"Not at all. But you are my little girl. When you are sixty-six, you will still be my little girl. And I will still want to protect you, as I do now."

"Protect me. You want me in a convent."

"No, I want you to be hap—"

"Then leave me—"

"—py and safe."

"—alone."

"But maybe I'm going about it the wrong way."

"What?"

For the first time in ages, Blaine had Karen's complete attention. "I said, maybe I'm too protective in some ways and not enough in others." He sighed. "If you'd come with a manual like a car, I'd know exactly what to do, but you didn't. So I'm just trying the best I know how. Obviously, I'm a failure, but that doesn't mean I don't love you more than anything on earth."

Karen's rebellion softened. "I know you do, Daddy. You just don't understand women."

"Show me any man who does," Blaine lamented. "Which is why I've appreciated Caroline's input on this trip."

"She is so cool. I mean, she doesn't let us get away with everything, but she doesn't stroke out on the little things like you do."

Stroke out? The exaggeration pricked at him, but now was not the time to debate the issue.

"A man isn't meant to raise a little girl alone." Blaine let the words sink in, watching for his daughter's reaction. "All I know is how a guy feels when he sees someone as pretty as you, and it spooks me to know some guy might be feeling that way about my daughter. A woman knows how her daughter will react or what's going through her head. I guess every girl needs a woman's input to keep her father in line."

Karen gave him a pointed look. "Like Miz C?"

"Maybe."

Karen's squeal drew the attention of those nearby. "I think you should be dancing with *her,* not me." Reaching up, she straightened his tie with a motherly tug. "And I think you've just made me one of the happiest girls in the world."

CHAPTER 17

"You older guys get some rest." Clad in a new swimsuit, Annie gave Caroline a bear hug and turned to see if Blaine was ready to go to the pool.

Older guys. Caroline held her tongue but exchanged a glance with Blaine. At Annie's age, she'd have said the same thing.

"Enjoy," she called out, leaning against the door.

After dinner and playing Prince Charming with her and the girls on the dance floor, Blaine turned to walk the girls toward the pool area in the moonlit pass between the guest villas. It had warmed her heart to watch Annie's awkward nervousness give way to confidence and laughter under Blaine's practiced lead. And when Caroline was in his arms, more than her heart was warmed.

A dreamy sigh turned into a yawn, giving her second thoughts about Annie's comment. Okay, maybe she *was* an "older guy." Since the bus would leave early for a tour of some nearby caverns tomorrow morning, she'd best take advantage of the unoccupied bathroom and quiet. A few curlers in her hair tonight, she thought, retreating to the bathroom, would save the curling iron versus blow-dryer competition for the vanity's single electric socket in the morning, while a mint mask would do wonders for the bags beneath her eyes.

Before Caroline could make it to the bathroom, the phone rang.

"Buenas noches," she answered.

"It's me, you shoulder-baring hussy," Dana teased from the other end.

"Got caught, didn't ya?" It served her buddy right, trying to embarrass Caroline in front of her escort.

"He was clueless," Dana insisted. "But look, if I come over, will you let me borrow your shell necklace for tomorrow? I'm trying to get things in order while the guys are at the pool."

"Sure." Caroline turned to the closet where her zippered jewelry bag hung, and took out the piece. "I have it right here. Come on over."

"I'll be there in a few minutes," her friend answered, hanging up with a click.

Just enough time to get comfy, Caroline thought, shedding her dress for her nightshirt. At the tiled sink, she gave her face a critical examination. Was that age or fatigue sagging beneath her eyes? With the tips of her fingers, she tried lifting the skin, and sighed.

"Sweetie, only a skilled scalpel could help these babies," she said to her reflection.

Part of her wanted to age gracefully, but a more rebellious nature preferred to fight tooth and nail—or facelift and tummy tuck. Since she was afraid of needles and her purse trembled at the prospect of a surgeon's bill, Caroline opted for better living through chemistry—the mint green mask she smeared on her face and foam curlers for her perm-shocked locks.

Annie's and Karen's clothes were scattered around the room, so while the mask dried and *lifted,* Caroline straightened up. "I can pick up the panties," she sang, "toss 'em into the drawer." Jamming the discarded underwear into the designated dirty clothes hamper in the closet, she turned and kicked the closet door closed. "Till this mom can wash 'em," she ground out, hands on swinging hips, "so they can wear 'em some more, 'cause I'm a woman, a W—O—M—"

A sharp knock on the entry door cut Caroline off. Grabbing up the necklace and skipping childlike to the door, she cracked it open. "Here you go, dear—"

It wasn't Dana Gearhardt standing in the hallway, but Blaine Madison. In one arm he held a bottle of some sort and in the other, a rose.

But he couldn't possibly be standing here, she reasoned, because he was at the pool.

Oh yes, he is, her senses insisted, *in the gorgeous flesh.*

Unable to close her gaping mouth, Caroline inhaled again, her last breath still waiting release.

"I knew you didn't do mornings, but in case you hadn't noticed, it's a beautiful starlit evening." He smiled.

My, what a wonderful smile he has . . .

"And I'd hate to waste it alone on the rooftop."

Which was a miracle, considering he was gazing upon Cinderella in after-midnight disarray. Squash indeed.

His smile faded at her continued stupor, and concern dominated his expression. "Are you all right, Caroline?"

All right? She had pink foam in her hair, green gunk on her face, and she was gaping like a large-mouth bass with lockjaw.

"Maybe I should go," he said, uncertain.

Go? Let Prince Charming go?

Caroline shoved a restraining hand through the crack, shaking her head. "Yes! No, no, no!" At least the babble tripped the brake release on her tongue. "I mean, yes, go away, but come back in five minutes." *Five minutes?* "Make that fifteen."

Without waiting for his reply, she slammed the door and shrank against it. Fifteen minutes. Tearing rollers from her hair and letting them fall where they may, she rushed to the bathroom.

One step blurring into the next, she slapped on makeup, blew dry the damp hair she'd just rolled, styled it with frantic fingers, and tugged her dress back on. She was breathless and on the verge of heart failure, but she was at least presentable.

"Coming," she called out in response to his knock. Shoving one shoe on, she hobbled with the other in her hand across the tiled floor to the door, scattering handwoven area rugs in her wake.

"Why, Blaine," she gasped as she tangled with the door and a rumpled mat. "What a surprise."

"Milady . . ." With a cavalier air, he took the shoe from her hand and replaced it with the rose.

Dumbfounded, enchanted, or both, Caroline stood speechless as he knelt and eased the practical pump onto her foot as if it were a glass slipper.

"I'd have sent for a carriage, but maneuvering the steps to the rooftop patio could be tricky."

Caroline laughed outright. This couldn't possibly be happening to a Sunday school teacher, nursery school administrator, and mother of a sixteen-year-old. Yet, it was.

"You are full of surprises. I thought you were going to stay with the girls and their dads at the pool."

"And waste a night like this without my *señora?*"

His purr of *my señora* ran Caroline straight through, tickling more than her fancy. Butterflies took flight from sensation, making her giddy as . . . as a sixteen-year-old. So who needed a face-lift when one walked on air?

• • •

Boy, had he blown it. He had asked Dana to call her room to make certain that Caroline would be there when he came. It never crossed his mind that she'd do whatever it was that she'd done to herself before he could get back from the pool. But like all the speed bumps they'd hit on the trip, the lady seemed to take it in good stride and recover like a trouper.

He glanced at the way the moonlight toyed with the red-gold highlights of her hair. A very lovely trouper, he amended, his gaze drawn to her shoulders. Ivory and silken, they almost beckoned his lips with a voice of their own. He could imagine how they'd feel to the nuzzle of his cheek, how the light jasmine scent she wore would tantalize his nostrils with images that evoked feelings he'd shut out for years. Inevitably, Ellie had made him regret those feelings, demon alcohol twisting something right between a man and a woman into ammunition to destroy the feelings he'd once vowed to keep forever.

But this was Caroline, high on her love of life, not her attempt to escape it.

"Blaine." Caroline's breathless exclamation as they emerged from the stairwell to the roof snuffed out the harsh recollection. The knot in his stomach eased. "What *have* you done?"

The four words that once rang with admonition sounded in delight. Pulling away from him, she rushed like a child to the tree on Christmas morning to where two glasses of sangria sat next to a three-wick candle surrounded by roses. The candle and flowers were Annie's idea. On a side table by the love seat sat a hotel ice bucket keeping the bottle cold.

"I can't take full credit for this. The girls helped."

Caroline turned. The rose she twirled beneath her nose stopped. "The girls?"

"They seem to be in favor of this romance." Blaine handed her one of the glasses. "I'm inclined to agree with them. What do you think?"

"Romance."

Blaine held his breath. Usually he could read a client like a book, but Caroline's echo cried neither yea nor nay.

Finally, the corner of her mouth turned upward in welcome absolution. "I think we've all been moon-struck," she demurred, sniffing the sangria.

"It's nonalcoholic," he said.

"If I were any higher, I'd need wings."

Blaine chuckled as she sipped the sangria. But he was not about to let her escape with that irrepressible humor of hers. "I'm trying to be serious, Caroline." He took her glass and set it down. Business first, then . . . what-ever transpired as a result. "You haven't answered my question. What do you think . . . about *us?*"

Her shoulders were as soft as he'd imagined to the palm of his hands. He waited, his breath lodged in his chest.

Caroline closed her eyes. "I think I'm dreaming." Opening them, she delved into his gaze with her own. "On the one hand, I think you are too good to be true."

Wariness nipped at Blaine's voice. "And on the other?"

She stepped closer to him. "It's been so long since I've felt like this and . . ." She moistened her lips. "And I'm a little afraid because of it."

Relief flooded through him. "My thoughts exactly." Blaine kissed her, tentatively at first.

When she didn't run, he set about assuring her with all he knew that this magic kindling between them was real, not the result of a fickle moon. The sway of her body against his fired reactions that threatened to consume him. He wanted this woman, not just in body, but in heart and spirit.

One step at a time. Reluctantly Blaine heeded reason, pulling away. He'd planned on courtship, not the ravishment that beat double-time in his veins. "Would you like to dance?" he asked, huskiness infecting his voice.

Caroline leaned back in his arms, a dazed expression on her face. "But there's no music."

With a grin, he rested his forehead against hers. "Sure there is." He kissed her on the tip of the nose. "It's in here," he said, pressing her hands against the beating of his heart. "Hear it?"

With a sigh, she laid her head against his chest. Blaine tucked her arms around his neck and began to lead her to the primal music.

"Yes," she whispered into the lapel of his jacket. "I hear it."

One—*beat,* two-*beat,* three—*beat,* four-*beat.*

Over and over, step by step, beat by beat, they moved

to the order of the heart, sharing the moment, the moon, and surrounding hillsides that twinkled as though inhabited by fairies. Blaine nuzzled Caroline's hair, his left brain giving way to sensations bombarding the overactive right. They filled him with a conviction that had no scientific basis whatsoever. It couldn't be measured or quantified. It either was or it wasn't. In this case, it was love—or the closest thing to it that he'd known in years.

CHAPTER 18

"So, did Dad say anything about Caroline when he turned in last night?" Karen asked as the tour group followed a path between papaya trees to a bridge at the Grutas de Cacahuamilpa in the early morning sunlight.

"I don't think your dad likes me enough to confide that kind of thing." John Chandler looked up at the top of the tall steep steps leading to the cavern entrance where a guide awaited. The first group, including the girls' parents, had already gone in. Because the girls had lingered at the jewelry counter in the snack shop, John, Karen, and Annie wound up with Kurt, Wally, and Wally's parents.

Or maybe it was by design, John thought. It was kind of cute, the way Karen and Annie had taken up the Cupid role where their parents were concerned. It reminded him of how his little sister had been all for love and happily-ever-after too. Thankfully, for Penny's sake, it had worked out. Their stepdad didn't have a little girl, and who couldn't love John's baby sister? On the contrary, John was the spare part of the family.

"He did kind of hum this morning while shaving," he ventured in an attempt to lift the disappointment on Karen's face. "Usually he stalks around in silence—like an assassin with his eye on a vic." He grinned. "Me."

Karen gave him a chiding look. "Don't be silly. If he hated you that much, he'd have sent you packing."

John shrugged. "Maybe he hated upsetting you more than putting up with me."

Karen gave him the elbow. "Not!"

"Hey, you're lucky to have a dad who loves you so much," Annie reminded her from a few steps behind them.

"So you think Miz C and Mr. Madison are really an item?" Kurt steadied Annie as she leaned against the railing to snap a picture.

Annie snorted. "If Mom's voice hadn't been normal when she came in last night, I'd have sworn she'd been sniffing helium."

"Yeah." Karen chuckled. "She tried to act like there was nothing in the works, but she was practically floating . . . and everything was funny."

"You're *both* lucky. Let it go at that." John didn't mean to be curt. But what had begun as a lark, spending time with these goody-goody people, struck a chord of envy that was tightening about his throat like a garrote. Besides, he'd outgrown wishing things were different. They weren't. They'd never be. And who wanted to take over his old man's insurance office anyway? His stepbrother could have it. John just wished it was his stepfather's company footing the loss of the stolen stamp.

Walking into the caverns gave him the sense of being swallowed by the earth. John never ceased to be impressed by the *Star Wars*–like setting. The concrete staircase wound down and down past huge, craggy formations through some twenty caverns, many as big as a football stadium. Despite the balmy temperature of the cavern, Karen huddled close to him. John obliged her, slipping his arm around her shoulders, but annoyance grated at his nerves.

She was too young to be involved with him, much less with Jorge Rocha. If that ponytail of hers swatted him one more time in the mouth, he would be sorely pressed not to snap at it.

"It *does* look like a red-eyed wolf," she marveled at one of the natural pictures carved in relief by crags and swirls in the rock walls.

Ahead, the tour guide did a trick with two flashlights that made rock silhouettes look like a man and woman moving closer and closer until they appeared to kiss.

"It's my mom and your dad," Annie snickered nearby.

"Then who's the old hag sneaking up on them with a club?" Kurt countered, indicating the shadow of what appeared to be just that—a crone with a raised club.

"Nobody we can't take out with another flashlight, right?" Karen looked at John as though he could conjure the light right there.

John was noncommittal. "I guess."

"These caverns were once used by banditos," the guide informed the tourists, "as a hideout and place to stash their loot. They knew their way around like rabbits in their rabbit holes."

"You mean *warrens?*" Wally's scholarly scowl was wasted on the young female guide.

"If you wish, *señor,*" she answered, as if to say she really couldn't care less.

Kurt elbowed his pal, teasing, "If you wish, *señor.*"

With a huff of boredom, Karen grabbed John's arm and dragged him out of the mainstream of visitors. "Let's get away from these children." She pointed to a dimly lit niche in the rock. "Take my picture over here."

Assuming a Hollywood pose for the camera, she smiled. The flash went off with John's push of the button.

"Now let me get you."

"Let's not let the group get too far ahead."

"Indeed, that would be a bad idea, no, señor?"

The hair on John's neck lifted, raked by the cold invisible finger of recognition. He knew that voice even before he saw the face of Jorge Rocha's henchman, the same guy who'd beat the greedy college student to a pulp. Argon was taller and thinner than his boss, with a ragged scar across his face from forehead to cheek. John wondered how the eye it skipped over had been spared.

"John?" Innocent as she was, Karen recognized a thug when she saw one—or maybe it was Argon's overpowering cologne that ran her off. She hurried to John's side for protection, sending his thoughts into a furious spin.

Argon ran with the pack, too cowardly to take anyone on alone . . . which meant he was most likely here to deliver a message.

"Don't be frightened, *señorita.* I work here and do not wish for you and your friend to get lost. You are not to leave your group."

"Right." Karen tugged on John's arm. "Let's go."

"Young people should keep in touch with their families, no, *señor?*"

So that was it. John had not touched base with Rocha since the day at the pyramids, and El Jefe was getting nervous.

"They might think that you have run off or gotten lost."

Like he was crazy enough to make the same mistake as the last kid who double-crossed Rocha?

John nodded. Javier must have OD'd on carbs and forgotten to let his uncle know what had happened. "Yeah," he said. "We'd better catch up. When I get my cell phone charged, I'll even call home."

"John, the tour's almost out of sight," Karen said.

John lifted his hand at Argon. "Keep up the good work, buddy. Sorry we dallied."

By the time he and Karen caught up with the tail end of the tour, John ventured a look over his shoulder. Instead of moving along toward the exit with the crowd, the illustrious Argon was heading in the wrong direction, the idiot. Still, John's heart scampered over itself from the encounter. Even idiots were dangerous.

Caroline sat on a bench near the snack stand and rubbed the back of her heel. It wasn't blistered yet. To save further abrasion from the sandal strap, she put a Band-Aid on it.

"I can't believe you wore sandals," Dana remarked. "The brochure recommended sneakers for all the tours."

"What price, beauty," Caroline grumbled.

The yellow daisy on her black sandals had been a perfect match to the one on her black and yellow cropped pant set. Contrary to her practical nature, she'd tried for a feminine look as opposed to the sensible but klutzy pyramid-climber ensemble. But after all that walking down into the belly of the earth and climbing back out, she looked as though she'd just finaled in the Olympics—sweating, limping, and grinning through the pain.

"Besides, I didn't get to read the brochure last night like some people. Otherwise I'd have worn sneakers and left this sweater behind." She tugged at the garment tied to her waist. "I thought all caves were cool."

"If you had gone out and missed Blaine last night, I'd have personally wrung your neck."

Caroline cut her friend a sidewise glance. "You *could* have warned me about this Cupid conspiracy."

When Caroline had returned to the room last night, the girls interrogated her until she pulled rank on them, insisting on lights out and quiet. In truth, she could have played coy at their questions in a pajama party. Instead, she'd replayed the scenes with Blaine over and over in her mind—their conversation, the dancing, the romance—until sleep claimed her with the memory of his goodnight kiss outside the door.

She should have guessed the girls would be spying. But for the latch catching when she finally opened the door to her room, both would be sporting black eyes. As it was, they sprawled backwards, dissolving into squeals of embarrassed laughter. Surely Blaine heard the commotion, but he retreated like a gentleman to his room, rather than amplify Caroline's embarrassment with his presence.

"Blaine is the only one that matters." At Caroline's scowl, Dana held up her hand as if taking an oath. "No one else that I know of. Of course, Randy knows about it, but refuses to weigh in one way or the other. But even those who don't know that you two are involved think you should be."

Involved. The word bounced off the walls of Caroline's mind like the echoes in the caverns. Reason seesawed back and forth between excitement and caution. Part of her wanted to fly on the wings of love. Blaine wanted to take care of her—and of Annie. When her daughter told her how he'd asked her permission to court her mother, Caroline's heart had melted. And when he'd awakened a side of her she'd thought beyond revival with his touch, his kiss, so had the rest of her.

Yet another side wanted to run on the feet of fear. He wanted to take care of her. Did that mean putting her in a box where she lost her identity again? Would he break Annie's heart? And could the woman he'd awakened in Caroline bear rejection again when someone younger and smarter turned his head?

"I see you found the Band-Aids," Blaine said, interrupting the mental fray with his return from the snack bar. "I wouldn't be surprised if there wasn't a kitchen sink in that bag somewhere."

"Mothers invented the Boy Scout motto," Dana told him. "Be prepared."

Blaine handed over one of the iced lemonades he and Randy purchased from the vendor.

"Delicious," Caroline pronounced after taking a sip. "This is the real thing—"

"Mom!" Annie snapped a picture before approaching the bench with her entourage in tow.

Great, Caroline thought. Now her what-the-cat-dragged-out-of-the-cave look was preserved for posterity. *Thank You, God, that Annie wasn't around when Blaine showed up last night. I have enough to atone for without bludgeoning my child to death with a disposable camera.*

She pulled an exaggerated grimace. "Gee, we missed you guys."

"I hope you didn't try to get any pictures in the caverns," Blaine said. "There's no way to capture something that impressive on film."

"We know." Annie grinned at him, nothing short of

adoration in her gaze. "Buy the postcards. What is it with you? Have you got a postcard franchise or something?"

Blaine winced, digging into a bag from the souvenir shop. "I've been found out." He produced a book. "I guess I can return this book with professionally done pictures about the caves."

"Oh, man." Annie took the book and opened it. "I was looking at this earlier, but it would break my pocketbook. It'd be great for Mom's school."

"That's what I was thinking."

"Are you going to tell them about that creep in the cavern?" Kurt asked, peering over Annie's shoulder at the book.

"What creep?" Caroline asked.

"You are such a big mouth," Karen admonished him.

"It was nothing really," John spoke up. "Karen and I stopped to take a picture, and some guy who worked for the place came out of the shadows and told us to catch up with the others."

Blaine pounced. "Couldn't you take a picture without leaving the group?"

Karen jumped in on the defense. "Not without a dozen other people in it, Daddy."

"Yeah, they weren't that far behind," Kurt said, earning surprised looks from Karen and John. He heaved a big shrug. "So sue me. I went back to check on you two and saw him. He didn't look like a tour guide to me."

"Me neither," Karen agreed. "This guy wore a suit,

and his aftershave stunk to high heaven."

"What made you think he worked for the place?" Blaine asked John.

John threw up his arms. "Look, I don't know, man. He told us to catch up with the others, and we did. I wasn't going to stand there and argue with him."

"And it was my fault, Daddy," Karen said, coming to John's defense. "I wanted to sit on the rail and pose by one of the big rocks, so I made John wait till the others moved on." She gave Kurt a scathing look. "I wasn't going to say anything about it."

Blaine studied John. "Do you think we should report this guy?"

John held the man's gaze. "I don't think it was a big deal, but do whatever you think. It doesn't matter to me."

Caroline spoke up. "Maybe you should report him," she said. "Can't hurt, and might help." At least it would take the paternal heat off John.

CHAPTER 19

"Acapulco or bust."

The excitement of the students resounded in the cheer as Bill pulled away from the restaurant-souvenir shop where they'd stopped for lunch. With history out of the way, only fun and adventure awaited for the next two days.

"So what did Hector say?" Caroline asked Blaine,

once the vehicle was underway. "About the guy in the cavern."

"He informed the manager, and a couple of security officers were sent to sweep the caverns, although the likelihood of finding someone who doesn't want to be found is small. They didn't seem terribly concerned, since no one was hurt and the guy did offer good advice."

Caroline leaned against the bus seat. "Well, at least they know about him."

"Maybe a little scare will make my daughter have more respect for the rules." He whistled a breath of exasperation.

"Hey, rebellion isn't just limited to teens," Caroline protested. "I read in my devotional this morning about a hotel that sat on the edge of a river. They posted a sign that said 'No fishing from the rooms,' but everyone was doing it. Then one employee suggested to the exasperated manager that they take the sign down. He did, and the fishing stopped!"

"A 'lead me not into temptation' rule, huh?"

"I guess people never thought of it until they saw the sign." Caroline frowned. "I'm sure there's a message in there for us as parents . . . like, concentrate on dos rather than don'ts?" Her thought process brightened. "It's basically a standard educational tool that accents the positive."

Blaine shook his head in wonder. "How do you do that?"

The mental light went out. "Do what?"

"Make connections like that. I'd never have compared a fishing sign to working with kids."

"That's because you are left-brained, or linear in thought. Being a scatterbrain, I find the pieces off the beaten path." Caroline grinned.

"Scattered or not, it's a gift." Blaine put his hand over hers and squeezed it.

The compliment made her squirm . . . or was it the kindling of interest in the gaze Blaine locked with hers. He wanted to kiss her . . . and he did. Not with his lips, but with his look. The memory of his kiss the night before played upon her lips as though it were the real thing.

"Mom?" Annie peeked through the crack between the seats in front of them. "Are you going to the beach with us this afternoon?"

Caroline's heart sighed as the moment disintegrated. "Where?"

"The beach," her daughter prompted. "You know, swimsuits, water, sand?"

The word *swimsuit* washed the last away like a bucket of ice water. Blaine hadn't seen her in unforgiving spandex. She could wear a T-shirt. After all, the tropical sun was vicious on skin like hers.

"I'm thinking about it," Caroline answered truthfully. Although if this relationship were to go anywhere, her baby-stretched, middle-aged belly was part of the package. And, with the aid of sunscreen, she did enjoy the sun-bathed beach and the rush of ocean. Besides, it was what she came for, wasn't it?

• • •

Four hours later Caroline's belly did a flip-flop, just as it had on the steep downward ride into Acapulco. Blaine walked out of the high rise Cabana Azul in swim trunks and a matching open front shirt. She watched as he grabbed a towel from the stack provided by the beachfront hotel, then searched the crowded strip of sand for Caroline and the girls. He'd remained behind to make a few business calls, insisting the ladies go reserve a patch of beach for him to join them later.

Lord, I know You have a reason for men aging so well, while we females go to potbelly, but I'd like to go on record as saying it's just not fair.

Not that she was overweight, she consoled herself, sucking in her abs for all they were worth and waving as he spotted them on the crowded beach.

"Have you tried the water?" he said.

Ignoring the protesting cramp beneath her rib cage, Caroline looked at him as if he'd lost his mind. "What, and get my hair wet before going out tonight?"

"You're one of those dry bathing beauties, eh?" he teased.

"Hey, you've seen the lengths I go to for beauty," she reminded him with a droll twist of her lips. "Besides," she added, "we decided we wouldn't have time for all of us to wash our hair and dry it before going to see the cliff diving."

He squinted at the water, blinding with the glare of the late afternoon sun. Even his crow's feet looked good, Caroline marveled silently.

"Well, I think I'll take a dip and let the sun dry me afterward. Anyone care to join me?"

The girls declined with a sleepy "Nah" from Karen and shake of the ponytail from Annie, whose nose was buried in a book.

"Where's John?" Blaine asked.

"He left to hook up with his tour group," Karen answered with a downturn of her lips. "Said he might see us later, if they're going to the cliff diving."

Oblivious to his daughter's melancholy, Blaine gave Caroline a head-to-toe-and-back look that almost made her lose the breath she held. "Sure you won't change your mind?"

Caroline nodded. Exhaling as he trotted off toward the water, she dropped to the beach towel with a groan.

Annie glanced up from her book. "Are you okay?"

She rubbed her right side under the rib cage. "Yes," she said, not nearly as certain as she sounded. This was yet one more good reason why courtship was usually assigned to the young.

Facedown, Caroline unfastened the back of her one-piece suit and tugged the straps off her shoulders. Already protected by the lotion Annie had rubbed on her in the room, she gathered up a lump of sand beneath the towel for a pillow and relaxed on the warm beach. It brought back memories of her youth—napping on the beach, to the massage of the sun's fingers and the lullaby of rhythmic surf and hawking cries of the gulls. Surely it didn't get any better than this—this side of heaven.

How long she dozed, or exactly how the slab of ice water that broke over her sun-heated skin got to the tropics eluded her. The water engulfing Caroline's ears sounded like amplified seashells, muting the distraction around her. Time slowed to an underwater crawl. The startled shrieks of the girls scrambling next to her reinforced her instinct to jump up and do the same, but just as quick to register was the fact that her swimsuit was unfastened. There it was. Expose herself and breathe, or drown in modesty.

Caroline chose the latter. Just when her initial startled gasp, now locked and aching in her lungs threatened to give out, the wave mercifully receded. Swimsuit gathered to her front, she struggled to her knees, at the same time trying to see through the hair plastered over her face if anyone was watching her.

"Where's my top?" Karen, a soaked towel clutched to her chest in like modesty, crawled around on the wet sand.

"My book!" Annie wailed.

Similar dismay echoed around them in Spanish and English. Caroline struggled to her feet, tugging and fastening as her fumbling fingers would allow, when Kurt trotted up from the receding water's edge, the top to Karen's suit in his hand.

Annie giggled at her scarlet friend. "That's why I wear a one-piece."

"I don't understand it," Caroline puzzled aloud. "The tide wasn't anywhere near reaching us when I laid down." She watched the water come in again, inching onto the beach several feet short of them as before.

Wally walked up, drying his glasses, book tucked under his arm. "They call 'em rogue waves. Every once in a while a big one will come all the way up on the beach." He pointed to the beachside snack bar in front of the hotel. "Almost went up to the Cabana Shack." He beat the sand from his soaked sci-fi novel. "Got my book too," he commiserated with Annie.

"I'm going to the ladies' bath house to put this on," Karen announced, disgusted with all of Acapulco at the moment. "I might as well go rafting, now that I'm already wet."

Blaine's voice echoed from behind Caroline. "Looks like you three got it good." Bending over, he picked up the lump of water-soaked towel he'd left behind. "Want me to exchange yours for a dry one?"

"That would be lovely," Caroline answered with an involuntary shudder. "I thought the water was warm down here."

"It is," Wally spoke up. "But even at eighty-something degrees, your body temperature is 98.6. Factor in the sun's heat to that, and the difference is enough make it feel like ice water, even if it isn't."

Blaine chuckled. "Exactly what I was going to say, Wally." He gathered all the remaining wet towels. "Anyone up for a Cocabananaberry cocktail?"

"Me," Annie called out. She'd been wanting to try the frozen concoction of coconut and strawberry.

"What about you, boys?"

Kurt and Wally gave Blaine a simultaneous nod.

"Caroline?" Blaine asked.

Caroline tore her gaze from her shadow on the sand—that of a female with a lopsided Mohawk or a severely deformed head. Brushing one's locks away from the face with one's fingers always worked for the bombshells in the movies, but for her, it just bombed. "I think I'll head back to the room and get a shower before the girls take over . . . maybe even take a nap before dinner. A *dry* nap," she added with a crooked grin.

"I'll walk you to the towel stand and get you a dry towel."

Preempting protest, Blaine put his arm about her waist and ushered her toward the hotel. At the towel cart, he dumped the wet ones and took up a fresh one.

"This is fresh from the dryer," he told her, wrapping it around her and holding her within the circle of his arms the way she used to do Annie, when her little daughter would come shivering and blue-lipped out of the Atlantic at home. "This ought to warm you up." He rubbed her back with brisk strokes, coaxing her against him.

Caroline laid her cheek against his chest, a purr of pleasure in her throat. It wasn't the dryer-fresh towel or the buffing that warmed her. She put the blame on Blaine.

John Chandler lifted his shoulders in a hapless shrug. "It wasn't my fault, man," he told Javier Rocha. "You were there when the lady didn't come down from the pyramid. Did you expect me to tick off the girl by leaving her friend's mom stranded?"

His dark-haired roommate shook his head. "I don't know, man. *Tío* Jorge is really steamed."

John paced back and forth in the bargain version of the hotel where the bus had dropped the Edenton tour group earlier. How could Rocha think he'd pull a double cross after the things John had seen in the organization? He wiped perspiration-damp palms on his slacks. Was it nerves, or had the air conditioner gone on the blink?

"I kept my eye on the girl with the stamp. That's what's important. I can't help it if my cell phone went dead. My charger was on the bus with you."

"You could have called collect." Javier tore open a bag of pizza-flavored pretzels and shoved a handful in his mouth.

John cut him a sharp look. "And you could have explained about the pyramid rescue deal and my missing the bus. What, was there a sale on pizzeria rolls to distract you?"

The jibe rolled off the easygoing Javier like water off a duck. "I told him, man, but you know how my uncle is. He trusts no one after . . ." He didn't need to finish. Javier had seen the beating too. "Anyway, you could have called from the orphanage. Surely there are phones there." He offered John the bag of treats.

John pushed them away. His head hurt, and he felt a little nauseated. "Easy for you to say, *amigo*. You weren't traveling with a group of religious strangers, dependent on them for your food and lodging." It simply hadn't occurred to John to call collect. It should have, but it didn't. He plopped down on the bed, looking at the phone as if it might bite. "So is he going to call or not?"

Javier gave a short humorless laugh. "Oh, Jorge will call . . . as sure as the rooster rises in the east."

"What's the hype all about any—"

The phone rang as though on cue. John picked it up.

"Hola?"

"Where have you been, *chico?*"

John felt a cold sweat begin to form on his forehead. He'd heard that tone before. It was loaded with disappointment—packing consequence. But everything was cool. All he had to do was convince Rocha. That he was here was a good start.

"With the goods, where else?" At least his voice was steady, even if his nerves weren't. He waited for the silence to break at the other end of the line. It became intolerable.

"I'm sure Javier told you what happened at the pyramids, why I missed the bus. I knew I could catch a ride with the little courier. Just as well, too, since their tour broke from the usual route."

"You have talked to no one?" Rocha said.

"No one," John assured him. "Not even Argon." He scowled at the out-of-the-blue question. "Why would you even ask that?"

"Because we have a mole in our midst . . . on one of the buses, according to my source."

The pulse in John's head ceased to pound, then

resumed with gathered power. “You mean an informer?” He fished the aspirin tin out of his pocket and motioned for Javier to get him some water. “Well, if there is an informer, he would have been on Javier’s bus. There’s no one on the tour but kids and their parents. I doubt the feds would put kids on something like this.”

“You doubt my source?”

“Hey, I’m just thinking out loud here. I guess it could be the driver or the guide.” With enough relatives to populate a small country, it was no surprise when John found out that Rocha had a brother-in-law in the criminal investigation department in the *Servicio Postal.* He’d be privy to knowledge of ongoing investigations.

But who was the plant? John groaned inwardly. It figured that something would go wrong on his last gig.

“I want you to pull the goods. We’ll deliver them when this problem is taken care of.”

“Take back the letter?” Dubious, John blew breath through his lips. What reason could he come up with to tell Karen? That he found something he wanted to add to it? His thoughts raced ahead through the throbbing fog assaulting his brain. At least it would be a relief to *un*-involve Karen and her family.

“Tonight, if possible,” Jorge said on the other end of the line. “We can put it away until this investigation is over. Your *mother* can wait for her card, no?”

John didn’t want to know to whom the card was really going. The less he knew, the better chance he had of making a clean break from all this. “Right. I’ll give the girl a call and tell her I need to put something else in the card."

"Then you and Javier return to Mexico City on the next bus with it. *Entiende?*"

"Got it. See you tomorrow."

"Eyes are watching you."

John grimaced. "I have no doubt." He hung up the telephone.

"Well?"

"There's a plant in the tour group, watching us. We need to pull the item and secret it away until the heat blows over," John explained to his friend.

"So we are not in trouble?" Javier looked relieved.

John exhaled, as though to rid himself of worry, but it still felt as if a cinder block lay wedged in his chest. "No, not yet."

He gave his buddy a friendly clap on the arm. "Piece of cake, *hermano,*" he declared, not nearly as certain as he wished. "Piece of cake."

"Speaking of cake—" Javier handed him the glass of water. "I could scarf up some pizza. How about you?"

John downed the aspirin, refusing to let the picture his friend conjured take shape in his mind. Aspirin was bad enough going down, much less the opposite.

CHAPTER 20

Shades of brilliant pinks, oranges, and yellows colored the western horizon when they arrived at La Perla.

The restaurant was located in the Mirador, a hotel that cascaded, terrace by terrace, down a steep hillside directly across from the famous cliffs of Quebrada. On the way over, Hector explained how the divers trained from childhood, sons following in their fathers' footsteps.

"Pay special attention to the water below before the sun sets," Hector advised them. "The tide at the foot of the cliff rushes in with such force that it can fluctuate anywhere from eight or so feet to sixty in depth with each wave. This makes the timing of the dives critical."

A wry smile played on Caroline's lips. Like as not, it was one of those sixty-footers that had taken everyone by surprise on the beach that afternoon. In the end, it proved advantageous. For the first time on the trip, she had uninterrupted time to do her hair and dress. If she did say so herself, she looked and felt as elegant and sophisticated in her flowing wash-and-wear pantsuit as the sequin-sheathed and statuesque woman climbing out of a black limousine at the hotel entrance. Caroline even had a sequin or two at the center of the pale pink and white flowers on her shawl jacket.

After Blaine purchased and pinned a fresh hibiscus from the lobby flower shop on her lapel, Caroline mimicked a model spin.

"Why, thank you, kind sir," she proffered, not caring that the entire Edenton group watched. How could they miss the fireworks going off in her heart?

"Mom," Annie said from somewhere in another

dimension, "what is that lump on the back of your slacks?"

Lump? Disconcerted, Caroline glanced over her shoulder at her calf. Just below the bend in her knee, the soft material of her slacks clung to a fistful of something.

"There is something there," Blaine observed, bemused.

What? A pair of panties from laundry day past? Caroline stared at the lump as if to make it disappear. If she retreated to the ladies room, would the culprit shake out? Or maybe she should just give the onlookers an early show and dive off the balcony into an eight-foot swell.

Vexed, Annie dropped to her knees and ran her hand up Caroline's pant leg.

"Got it," her daughter announced, producing a dryer-shriveled pair of pantyhose with the flourish of a magician.

"Way to go, Miz C!" Kurt's clap led to a round of general applause.

Caroline couldn't decide which youngster she wanted to strangle with hose the most—the boy or Annie. "Never let it be said that I'm not prepared." She tried tucking the stowaway into a tiny evening bag that barely held a folding brush, lipstick, and tissues until Blaine came to her rescue.

"Allow me, Cinderella," he teased, tucking the wad of stocking into his coat pocket.

"What can I say?" she remarked as the headwaiter

motioned for them to follow him. "It stores better than a glass slipper."

It boggled her mind that a man like Blaine Madison didn't run with all speed in the opposite direction instead of beating the maître d' to Caroline's chair.

"Milady."

Her dignity somewhat restored, Caroline allowed him to seat her at a table for six, located at the balcony rail overlooking the cliffs.

"This is *so* cool," Annie observed as a busboy hastily removed the extra settings. She wasn't talking about the boy or the breathtaking view of the cliffs or the panoramic spectacle of sunset on the glittering waters of Acapulco Bay. She embraced Blaine and Caroline with her gaze, then turned to her friend. "Did you know your dad was so romantic?"

Karen shrugged. "I never thought about it." She studied her father as though seeing him for the first time. "He's not bad for an older man, I guess."

Blaine winced. "Thanks . . . I think."

"What do you think, Miz C?" Karen was serious. No smile tugged at her mouth. Her dark eyes searched Caroline's face, expectant.

Nothing like being put on the spot.

"I think that is between Caroline and me," Blaine interceded.

Relief washed over her. "Exactly." She cast a grateful glance in his direction before mischief gained rein. "So far, he's scored a ten on the Prince Charming scale, but beyond that—" She paused, grinning, as the girls moved forward on their seats in anticipation. "You'll have to stay tuned for the next episode."

Their anticipation collapsed with a simultaneous groan.

"Bet if it was John and me, you'd want to know all the details," Karen grumbled.

"Age has its privileges." Blaine opened his menu, effectively ending the topic.

The fierce crash of the surf below drew Caroline's attention from the list of foods. They practically had a box seat, affording an unobstructed view of the steep, jagged cliffs where the dives took place. It was incredible that no one in the sixty years of the tradition had ever been killed.

"Would you care to share a Chateaubriand for two?"

For two. Caroline schooled her face toward thoughtful, rather than grinning in Cheshire cat delight. Two was a lovely number when Blaine was part of it.

"Wow, Dad," Karen teased. "You even make the food sound romantic."

"We could order two and make it a family affair if you girls are game," he suggested.

Annie frowned. "What is it?"

"It's a special cut of beef, with a minced stuffing of onion, celery . . ." Blaine paused. "Herbs and other stuff. Quite delicious."

"And a welcome break from something with tomato and chiles." Caroline closed her menu. "Chateaubriand sounds delightful. You order for me. I think that rogue wave did a literal brainwash on me this afternoon."

Order for me? The challenge surfaced amid the other reactions Blaine aroused in her. She'd sworn once that she'd never let a man lead her around like a possession without will or want of her own. Yet here she was giving the decision away. Except that Blaine *asked* her to share. Frank would have ordered for them without considering her opinion.

Father, Blaine is too perfect. The only fault I've seen is his falling from faith over the death of his wife . . . and that could happen to anyone. But for Your grace, it might have happened to me. And he seems to be reaching for You again. Help me see what is wrong with this picture before I'm hopelessly lost . . . If there is anything wrong, she added hopefully.

"Excuse me." A woman's gruff voice interrupted the hum of indecision over the menu at the table. "Are those two seats taken?"

Drawn from her angst-filled prayer, Caroline glanced at the two empty seats at the end of the table and back to the imposing stranger. "I . . . I don't think so."

At least six feet tall, with ample frame, the older lady looked as though she could hold her own on a football scrimmage line. She gave them a bright lipsticked smile. "Then would you mind if my sister and I join you?"

Blaine rose. "Absolutely not. The more lovely ladies, the merrier." He glanced past the tall, broad figure of a woman in search of her companion.

"I'm Eloise Hayman," she said, extending a ring-bedecked hand. She had one for every finger. "I'll go get my sister. She's in a wheelchair, as she twisted her ankle just before we left on this trip."

"May I help?" Blaine offered.

The older woman reached over and gave his smooth-shaven cheek a cajoling pinch. "Now aren't you just a prince?" She winked past him at Caroline. "Handsome as one too. If I were a few years younger, you'd have some competition, sweetie."

"What was *that?*" Karen exclaimed after Eloise led Blaine in the flowing wake of her royal purple knee-length tunic and palazzo trousers.

Caroline laughed. "I guess it's an Eloise Hayman."

A few minutes later, Blaine wheeled a woman as petite as Eloise was imposing up to the end of the table. It stretched the imagination to consider that the two might have emerged from the same gene pool, but once they were seated and everyone had ordered, the resemblance became obvious. Both had a zeal for life that was infectious.

"We're on a seniors' trip," Eloise told them, "but Reenie and I went on the booze cruise in the harbor this afternoon and got back too late for the early show with those old fuddy-duddies." She snorted. "If some of them don't eat early, they get sick, you know."

"Now, Weesie," Irene chided. "They can't help it if they have sugar."

"Maybe so," her sister said, "but some are just as set in their ways as their arthritic joints, diabetes or no."

"Eloise was a physical therapist," Irene informed the group. "A health nut."

"A life nut, Weesie. There's a difference."

Hardly having spoken since placing the dinner order, Blaine leaned over with a discreet whisper for Caroline's ear alone. "I think the show has started early."

Irene Barker was a retired nurse. Since the death of her husband, she and Eloise, who had never married, had traveled with senior groups all over the world.

"Life is too short, girlies," Eloise told Annie and Karen, who were completely taken by the pair. "A body's got to grab life now, before it gets too old to catch it."

Caroline could well imagine the thoughts running through their minds. If they thought Blaine was an "older man," they must think of Eloise and Irene as ancient.

"So how was the booze cruise?" Karen's dark eyes twinkled in anticipation.

"Nice enough, I suppose."

"If you're a masochist," Irene added.

Eloise turned to her. "Now, Reenie, you said yourself you thought you'd split your sides laughing. The games and sights were fun."

Irene jerked an accusing finger toward her sister. "Easy for her to say. She got to salsa with the men. I didn't." She turned to Karen. "Frankly, dear, the music was too loud, the company too rowdy, and the swells made the boat lurch from side to side like a carnival ride."

"All you had to do was turn down your hearing aid, Reenie," Eloise pointed out. "She's just put out because she couldn't dance the way she usually does."

"Well, it is hard being confined to a hard bench seat while everyone else is having fun," Irene pouted, placing a hand on Caroline's arm. "Honey, I could hold my own on a dance floor with the best of them . . . and will do again, soon as this ankle heals." Irene's eyes twinkled, bracketed by lines etched with laughter over the years.

"Anyway," Eloise went on, "we got to see houses of some rich folks like Julio Gladius—"

"Iglesias," Irene corrected.

"Yeah, him." Eloise never broke verbal stride. "And the water was gorgeous. Just because it was a booze cruise didn't mean you had to drink, mind you. To each his own, I say, though I don't touch the stuff myself. Makes me sluggish."

It was hard to imagine anything sluggish about Eloise. Caroline imagined the lady as having one speed—full steam ahead.

And so the conversation continued, never slowing, even when dinner was served. Where one sister left off to munch, the other picked up. They'd been everywhere and tried everything. On the agenda for this trip were parasailing and a day tour to an island beach for horseback riding and fishing.

"Horses!" Annie gave Caroline a pleading look. "Oh, Mom, can we go? I love horses. It's so romantic, riding on the beach."

"Yeah," Karen added. "You and my dad couldn't help but fall in love then."

Eloise cocked her head like a watchdog that picked up a strange sound. "You mean you aren't married?" Her gruff words fell somewhere between accusation and surprise. "But you look so natural together."

Caroline felt heat rise from the tips of her toes to the hair follicles on the crown of her head.

Irene put a delicate hand to her cheek. "My word, Weesie, we haven't given these dear people a chance to say yea or nay for nothing, save their given names." She gave Blaine and Caroline an apologetic look. "We get carried away sometimes. Weesie and I do love to talk."

"Not a problem," Blaine insisted. "We've been fascinated."

By the time dessert was served, the sisters had exchanged addresses with Caroline. On hearing that Caroline ran a day care center, Eloise insisted on sending to the children a burro piñata that she'd won in a drawing.

"What would I do with the bloomin' thing?" she blustered when Caroline tried to refuse. "I'll pay the postage to get it off my hands."

"No need. If you insist on giving it away, it will fit into my spare case." God worked in strange ways. Caroline had reconciled herself to doing without a piñata after giving so much of her change and paper money away. Mexican money didn't look real, so it seemed to go faster . . . and the people needed it more than her kids needed piñatas. "Thanks so much."

"You can thank me with a wedding invitation."

"A what?"

The big woman took Caroline's hand. "Sweetie, if you aren't married to this handsome fella here, you ought to be."

An outbreak of applause saved Caroline from having to reply. Below on the viewing platform, a torch-lit parade parted the thick sea of onlookers.

"Maybe we should listen to our elders," Blaine whispered in her ear.

Despite his impish expression, Caroline missed the first men diving into the water below the cliffs. By the time her shock thawed, they were swimming toward the opposite cliff.

CHAPTER 21

Was that a proposal?

The surf on the ragged rocks below mirrored the sudden churn of delicious beef she'd shared with Blaine at dinner . . . *for two*. Toy-sized at the distance, the dark, sun-bronzed swimmers heaved themselves up on a craggy ledge.

Did she even want a proposal? Blaine was probably just playing along with their guests, she told herself, focusing on the four scaling the cliff side like human spiders. In a distant dimension of the present, Annie, Karen, and the two sisters rated the divers on a hunk scale of one to ten.

"Scrawny, but brawny," Eloise declared in defense of her score.

Enchanted by the lively senior duo, Annie giggled. "You are *so* funny."

But what if Blaine was serious? Was she ready for that? She'd only known the man five days. But then the passage of time didn't exactly ensure love everlasting. She'd dated Frank all through high school, and look at the disaster that turned out to be.

Once they reached the top of the cliff, the men prayed and crossed themselves at the shrine of the Lady of Guadalupe, silencing the crowd with their reverence. In order to see more clearly, Blaine scooted closer. With one set of senses, Caroline noted that the divers had taken positions farther down the cliff side, while another set registered Blaine's nearness. His body heat, alternately soothing and arousing, mixed Caroline's thoughts with blades of confusion.

Across the rocky, narrow channel, a single diver saluted the crowd and leapt into thin air.

Her heart did a simultaneous flip with the man before he plunged into the thrashing surf below. Was she willing to take such an emotional plunge?

Cameras clicked and flashed. Applause erupted from the onlookers, but it was just background noise to the quandary brewing in Caroline's mind. Divers two and three now saluted the crowd.

Besides, she wouldn't be leaping alone. There was Annie to consider. Sure, her daughter was charmed by Blaine, but Caroline knew all too well that courtship and marriage were two different matters. Annie was in love with love.

The two athletes flew off the jagged rock in a choreographed air ballet and struck the water below at the same time.

What if she and Annie didn't bob to the surface like the men below when the tide overwhelmed them? Caroline had survived one marriage on the rocks. Dare she risk two?

The narrator—over speakers placed strategically throughout the crowd—called for silence. Everyone's attention now focused on the last man, who stood at the highest peak. The lights went out, casting the cliff side in dramatic darkness. Not only had the sun sneaked down during dinner, but it had dragged the last remnants of light below the horizon with it. Tall, wiry, and straight-backed, the diver was a silhouette against the evening sky.

"Omigosh, look." Annie pointed below where the previous divers lit newspapers. They lined the rocks below with the makeshift torches, creating a primitive ring of fire to guide their colleague to the fluctuating pool.

"Good thing they prayed first," Karen quipped to no one in particular.

Good thing they prayed first. The remark robbed the wind from the sails of Caroline's doubt. She let out the breath she'd inadvertently held and, with it, the gathering anxiety.

If or when the time came for her to make such a dive, all she had to do was pray first. Until then, she needed to follow Eloise and Irene's philosophy. Grab life while she could still catch it. And she'd come to Mexico to grab. Turning from the table to fold her arms on the adjacent balcony rail, Caroline rested her chin on them to watch the last man. Like him, she was in God's hands.

With a final salute, he launched from the highest peak, plummeting like a hawk after prey, ever lower and lower. The crowd erupted in thunderous applause at his seamless entry through the ring of fire and rock into the sea. Smiling, Caroline joined them.

On returning from the diving exhibition, Blaine pocketed the receipt for the family snorkeling adventure he'd booked for the morning and made his way from the tour office to the Cabana Azul. One of the two excursions the girls wanted was better than none, he thought, although they'd be disappointed. The excursion to a private island for fishing and horseback riding was sold out. End of story.

A mingle of cigarette smoke, perfume, and salt sea air assailed his nostrils as Blaine searched for his little group. Guests relaxed on the rattan furniture, which was arranged in cozy clusters throughout the spacious open-air room. He found Caroline beyond a screen of a large fanning palm plant saying good night to the two sisters, who, it turned out, were staying at the same hotel.

Karen and Annie had reunited with John and his friend, taking seats across the room as far as possible from the adults. Like a bad penny, that boy kept showing up, Blaine thought, dropping down on a tropical-print love seat next to Caroline.

"What a pair," she observed a few minutes later when the ladies took their leave.

Eloise parted the crowded lobby like the Red Sea with her booming voice and her sister's wheelchair.

"When I grow up, I want to be just like them . . . living life to its fullest. I don't want to miss anything."

She leaned her head against the arm Blaine had slipped behind her and gave him a look that made him forget everything but the woman behind the many dimensions of her gaze. Who needed a night sky when all the stars in the universe twinkled there? He wanted to spirit her away and kiss the sweetness of her smile, hold her soft body, show her just what she was missing . . . what they both were missing.

A squeal from across the room braked the passion that was gaining momentum in his blood. Karen had launched a playful attack on John, and in response he had pinned her against the couch and was tickling her. Blaine glared in the teens' direction, a cross between a groan and a growl vibrating through his lips. No man should be torn between kissing a captivating woman and protecting his daughter from another male with the same hormones stampeding his brain. Not at the same time.

"Time to go to bed." Caroline's tired purr and feline stretch turned up Blaine's frustration another notch. "We have to be at the dock at eight, right?"

His throat went dry as a desert wanderer's, the water

just beyond his reach. He cleared away the dust and frustration. "That's the plan," he answered. Not *his* plan, but the plan nonetheless.

The following morning, Karen awoke in a major tizzy. With the drapes thrown back to bathe the hotel room in the morning light reflecting off the bay, she dug through the bags of souvenirs that Caroline had packed in the spare cases. "I can't find it."

"It's got to be there somewhere," Annie assured her.

Caroline tugged on a big gauze overshirt that matched her swimsuit. "Find what, honey? What are you looking for?"

Staring at the pile of purchases in exasperation, Karen put her hands on her hips. "A stupid card . . . I . . . I had a card for John, and I've lost it."

At that moment, a sharp knock sounded on the connecting door. "You ladies almost ready?"

Caroline pulled it open. "Sure, come on in."

"I missed you on the beach this morning." Blaine leaned against the doorjamb, head cocked. He'd tried to talk her into joining him for a morning jog on the beach, to no avail.

"As someone somewhere once said, my idea of exercise is a brisk sit."

"You missed a beautiful sunrise."

"I'll buy a postcard." She turned her attention from his vexed face to where the girls stuffed, rustled, and zipped the booty-to-date in the bags.

"Honey," she said to Karen, "I'm sure we can buy

another one in the hotel gift shop."

"Another what?" her father asked.

"Karen misplaced a card she got for John," Caroline explained.

Blaine's face darkened for a split second, but he mastered his disdain. "We have to get going now. She can get it later."

"Yeah," Annie consoled her friend. "We don't have to have it until tonight, and it's not like it has to be that very one, right?"

Karen shrugged in reluctant resignation. "I guess not."

A ping of suspicion surfaced on Caroline's motherly radar, but she quickly dismissed it. *It was probably personal,* she thought, as the girls ran ahead to ring for the elevator.

"How about a compromise?"

Caroline gave Blaine a blank look. "A who?"

He put his arm around her and coaxed her into the elevator like a carnival hawker about to fleece an unsuspecting country girl. "A compromise," he repeated. "Join me for a *walk* on the beach tomorrow morning."

She pretended to contemplate the offer on the way down to the lobby. "Okay," she said when the doors rolled open, "but I'm warning you—"

"I know." He held the doors back until the others were off. "You don't do mornings." Turning, he gave her a peck on the cheek. "We'll have to work on that."

CHAPTER 22

"Hey, it's Manny!" Annie sped up ahead of Blaine and Caroline on the pier.

Waiting in line to board a huge catamaran, a Mohawk-coiffed young man in baggy swim trunks turned upon hearing his name and waved at the approaching girls. Blaine didn't recognize the mythical creatures tattooed on Manny's arms, but the hair and studs lining his eyebrows and ears were unmistakable. It was another of the boys from the Mexico City disco, the one who'd danced a couple of numbers with Annie.

"Yo, dude," he said when Annie reintroduced him, raising his hand for a high five at the same time Blaine extended his for a handshake. Somewhere in between, they brushed palms. "You ever been snorkeling, Miz C?"

Caroline shook her head. The cute bob of hair she'd pulled back in a band moved with it, too short to swing of its own volition. The reddish gold wisps of curls that had escaped made a soft fringe around her hairline.

Like a rebellious halo for an earth angel, Blaine mused, resisting the urge to touch one.

Angels. Blaine's ramblings staggered to a halt. He didn't think in terms of angels or spiritual things, but just being around Caroline made it impossible to avoid such notions. Had God answered his unspoken heart's desires? His mother always said God knew our needs better than we did. If asked prior to this trip, Blaine would have answered that he was doing just fine; Karen was a problem, but all teens were supposed to be. Sure, a woman might understand his daughter better, but in the end, he was in control. That was enough for him.

Until Caroline. Sweet Caroline. He woke up to the song playing in his mind. He couldn't wait for "the girls" to begin stirring in the room next to him. He listened for her laughter, her voice as she alternated between mother and girlfriend. This morning, he'd forgotten to call the office to be certain that Alice had sent off the Toronto contract that he'd faxed her after reading through it once more. All he could think of was this incredible woman. She was smart, funny, attractive, and had a heart bigger than she was. She was . . . *the answer to an unspoken prayer?*

Unable to help himself, Blaine curled his arm around her as they walked across the narrow, rope-railed gangway onto the catamaran. It didn't hurt his feelings when the bench where the kids sat filled, forcing him and Caroline to squeeze into a narrow corner of the pontoon with their backs to the higher platform deck. It was as though she'd been made to fit under the protective crook of his arm.

The crew tossed the lines. Engines growling, the catamaran eased out of the slip. From a built-in compartment in the pontoon, a perky young woman in the same red tee and white shorts as the crew prepared sodas and punch for the guests. Satisfied to drink in Caroline's nearness, Blaine declined his. With his head resting against the rise of the seat back, he closed his eyes and inhaled the fruity scent of her shampoo and the salt air whipping his hair around his head.

So what are you waiting for? Blaine's senses came to full alert. He'd heard that voice before, that conviction that it was time to make a move. It never failed him. He had expanded the family business beyond his father's dreams listening to it.

"You know—" Caroline raised her voice above the din of the engine and passenger chatter, turning her face up to him. "I wish I could stay here in this moment forever. Paradise can't be any more beautiful than this."

She spoke, of course, of the sun-splashed clear water and the curve of sandy beach dotted with exotic green. Or maybe the bleached whites and pastels of the tiled-roofed hotels and casas that lazily climbed the verdant hillside. Or the sky where little puffs of angel-white clouds drifted on a sea of blue, and circling gulls allowed for their human counterparts suspended by colorful parachutes.

"Me too," Blaine shouted back. Except that the paradise he spoke of was in his arms.

What are you waiting for?

He leaned in close and cleared his voice of the huskiness that filled it. "It could, you know."

She cocked her head with a puzzled expression. "Where do I sign up?"

Riding on a pontoon boat with a group of strangers and their offspring was hardly the most romantic setting, but if Blaine didn't say what was on his mind, he'd burst.

"At the Edenton courthouse."

"Huh?"

Obviously their minds were not on the same track. And he didn't even have a ring.

"We can start with a marriage license."

Caroline wrinkled her nose—the most kissable nose he'd ever seen—and cupped a hand to her ear. "A carriage *what?*"

He gave in and brushed its tip with his lips, working his way to her ear. "Marry me."

She screamed and karate-slapped his neck. Startled by the hysterical nature of the reply, Blaine felt an urgency to assuage it. "It's okay, you don't have to ans—"

Shoving out of his arms, Caroline danced with some footwork that would turn a boxer green with envy, her ear-shattering "Blaine!" seeming to drown out the engine.

As the boat coasted into neutral, a crew member inserted himself between Blaine and the accusative finger Caroline aimed at him. "Is everything okay here?"

"Dad, what did you do?" Accusation mingled with disbelief reflected in his daughter's voice. From the other twenty or so passengers, just the first prevailed.

Embarrassment scorched Blaine's neck and pumped hot blood through his temples. Even if he could unlock the teeth-aching clench of his jaw, what could he say?

He felt as though the anchor a crewman tossed over the side had his tongue attached. His brain too, for that matter.

"Mom?" Annie stumbled across the rocking deck to embrace Caroline, who now shook her head in a fervent denial and started scanning the deck around his feet.

"I asked Caroline to marry me—"

"Spider!" Caroline's squeak of a voice mingled with Blaine's disconcerted reply.

Blaine flinched, his eardrums blasted by Karen's and Annie's double shriek, and jumped to his feet, examining and brushing first one shoulder and then the other in bewilderment. "Where?"

Jerking her head up from her scrutiny of his feet, she gave him a startled look. "You asked me *what?*"

Annie tugged on her arm. "Mom, what did you say?"

"Please say yes, Miz C."

"I want a sister and a dad."

"You'd be a great mom."

"He's handsome."

"Annie can be your maid of honor, and I can be a bridesmaid."

As shock-wide as Caroline's eyes were, the brightness pooling there made them look even bigger. "Me?"

"No, her." With a laconic grin, Blaine pointed over Caroline's shoulder to a large woman who peered at him between the wide brim of a sun hat and the top of wraparound sunglasses, as if trying to decide whether or not to clobber him with the quart-sized bottle of sunblock in her hand.

Caroline afforded the half-slathered tourist a darting glance before returning tear-brimmed attention to Blaine. Palms clasped to her face in shock, she bit her lower lip to steady the chin that had begun to tremble.

"Say yes, Mom."

"Say yes, Miz C."

"Say yes," someone nearby shouted, starting a chant that grew louder and louder. "Say yes. Say yes. Say yes . . ."

Encouraged by the support, Blaine shook his loose-fitting shirt. "Look, spider free." With a single step, he closed the distance between him and the freckle-faced woman of his dreams.

"Say yes," he said, his plea gruff with the surge of love he felt for her. He wanted to protect her from all the spiders and threats of the world. Ever so gently he coaxed her hands from her face and kissed the knuckles on each one, never once releasing her from the electric meld of their gazes.

He had his answer, though not a word had been spoken. He saw it dancing among the thousands of green jewels that made up Caroline's eyes. At her slow-motion nod, the onlookers erupted in hoots, whistles, and cheers, but Blaine heard nothing more than the voice of his heart urging him to kiss her.

"Blame it on the moon or the sky or the sea," he said, the deep timbre of his words vibrating against her chest, "but I've fallen head over heart for you, Caroline Spencer. And when I see something I want . . . I move on it."

He didn't just want her. He *needed* her. He cupped her face between his hands. "I need you, Caroline. Just say the word."

No wonder he was so successful, Caroline thought. Who could say no to this kind of negotiation? *God, speak now before my heart overtakes my head. Help me see the downside of this.*

"Mom, puh-leeze," Annie cajoled.

I want a sister and a dad.

You'd be a great mom.

I need you, Caroline.

"Say yes. Say yes. Say . . ."

Caroline's heart swelled with the replay of each word in her mind. Perhaps God had already spoken.

Impatient, Annie gouged the "Yes" that teetered on Caroline's lips off with an elbow jab.

Caroline framed Blaine's clean-shaven jaw with her fingertips. "Oh yes, yes, yes, yes, *yes!*"

"No!" she averred an hour later as Blaine tried to coax her into diving around some rocks. "Honey, it's just not working." She stretched on the warm bed of sand. "I am perfectly content to watch you and the girls swallowing the ocean one dip at a time."

Diving was another fancied profession Caroline could cross off her list. She preferred jobs where she could see and breathe. About the time she focused on the underwater glory, her mask fogged or leaked. And she had a mental block about breathing through her nose. After prying the mask off her face for the third time, she threw in the snorkel.

"I'm perfectly happy to look at your photos," she said. The tour included an underwater throwaway camera for each guest. She'd have to deal with the pictures of her underwater, looking like a drowning blow toad, later.

"But you're missing some beautiful stuff," he countered.

No, she wasn't. She gave him a quick head-to-toe, envious of the water running in rivulets down the trim, sun-bronzed lines of his torso and legs. Strong, firm legs . . . warrior legs. He'd be a knockout in a toga.

Caroline gave herself a mental slap. One itty-bitty proposal and she'd gone from moonstruck to manstruck. *But just for this man, God.*

"If God wanted me to swim underwater, He'd have given me gills." She wriggled her nose. "Instead, He made me a beach bunny."

Blaine's gaze narrowed with accusation. "You *bunnied* me. That's not playing fair."

The same rogue force that gave his lips a devilish tilt fanned the pilot light that just being with Blaine lit under her senses.

"So, are you guys coming or not?" Karen called out from the natural jetty of rock protruding into the water, where she, Annie, and their tattooed and riveted friend had been swimming.

With a wave at his daughter, Blaine dropped to his knees on the sand. "Just remember, you took off the gloves with that twitchy thing you did with your nose, not me."

"What do you mean?" Caroline's pulse quickened. She glanced around the quiet cay. Except for a thoroughly oblivious couple further down the beach, most of the tourists were in the water. A few hundred yards away, the catamaran swayed and dipped with the tide, its staff divided between the craft and the water. Then there were the impatient girls out on the rocks. "Our daughters are watching you."

Blaine gave her a look that would melt butter. "Then they'll have to get used to this, won't they?" He pulled Caroline's sun-warmed body against his cold, wet one, and showered her with hungry little kisses.

"Blaine!" The shiver from without doused the quiver from within. Caroline dissolved into laughter. "You are freezing me."

"Serves you right," he growled, continuing to nibble at her neck. "Mmm . . . salty."

Caroline collapsed beneath his weight against the sandy bed. "And you're getting me all sandy."

How could she alternately freeze and burn?

"I like my women with grit." He doggy-licked her temple and then jerked away, trying to spit off the sand that stuck to his tongue. "Okay," he said, raking it with his teeth afterward to be certain it was all gone. "Maybe not quite this literally."

Caroline laughed at the face he made. "What on earth has gotten into you? You're acting like a kid." And it was infectious. For all her grousing, Caroline had to admit, the boy in Blaine was as endearing as the man—and got away with so much more.

Still holding her in his icy grip, he backed away. Sheer mischief stirred the golden flecks in the dark russet of his eyes. "You, sweet Caroline." He paused, glancing to where Karen and Annie pretended they weren't watching. "You're under my skin, in my blood . . . and if you don't come back into the water with us, I'm going to sing to you."

Down the beach, a group of snorkelers straggled out of the water, their finned feet smacking the wet sand.

"You wouldn't." While she wasn't sure she was up to being center stage again, her heart danced in her chest.

"I would."

Climbing to his knees, he placed a hand over his heart and cleared his throat with a deep cough. "Oh, whoa, whoa . . ." he crooned in a not unpleasant baritone, "Sweet Car—"

Caroline sealed her name on his lips with her hand.

"Okay, okay," she giggled. "You win." She replaced her hand with a quick kiss. "Now that you've gotten me all sandy, I have to wash off anyway."

Blaine helped her to her feet.

"Now help me into this mess," she grumbled, pointing to her discarded snorkel, mask, and fins.

After rinsing her equipment off, Blaine knelt and lifted her foot to help her on with a fin as big as a turkey platter.

"This is a pitiful substitute for a glass slipper."

She was caught up in a wonderful but warped fairy

tale. *Okay,* she thought, heaving a sigh of surrender, *so what if it is warped?* She stood on one foot like a love-dazed flamingo. It was worth every bizarre moment.

CHAPTER 23

Banditos in Acapulco was in a newer building than the one in Mexico City. While decorated with the same bandit motif, there was a long sleek runway in this one that shot out into the dance floor, practically dividing it in half. There the more flamboyant of the crowd could display their style—or lack of it. At the moment, it was filled with the early set, those too young to purchase alcoholic beverages.

Every frayed nerve in John Chandler's body wished it were later. His stomach burned and his head already ached, despite two aspirin and an antacid. A salt-rimmed shot of tequila could hardly make them worse, he reasoned, walking over to the latticed and fake-vine entrance from the dance room to the foyer. And it might brace the brittle edge upon which he teetered.

Karen Madison and her group were due at the early show. He twirled the live rose he'd purchased for her. That last night at La Quebrada, she seemed to buy his excuse that he wanted to write something more in the card.

"Sure, no problem." Dark eyes bright, she'd shrugged off the subject, unaware that it would come down on her—and him—like a giant hammer if anything went wrong.

John rubbed sweaty palms on his khaki designer slacks. What was that saying about crossing bridges when one got to them? Of course, whoever came up with that didn't have a thug like Argon stalking him to make certain he crossed. And Rocha's organization was no closer to finding out who the undercover fed was.

Hector. John breathed a sigh of relief as he saw the Edenton tour guide enter the foyer of the club at the head of the group. Karen and her "family" followed. At least Annie, Miz C, and Mr. M felt like a family to him. They were closer than his had ever been. He wished his mom had found someone like Blaine Madison.

Madison was a fair-minded man, successful and honest. Sure, he didn't really like John, but only because he wanted to protect his daughter. John could understand that. Blaine was who John wanted to be, but John had blown it by wanting too much too fast. If he could do it over, he'd wash dishes at Sanborn's or do whatever it took to work his way through school, rather than steal it. Because boiled down, that's what his involvement with Rocha amounted to.

"Hey there!" Looking like a dark-haired teen Barbie, Karen Madison waved with one hand while the bouncer stamped her other with the Banditos mask.

Too late for second chances, both for him and, because of him, for her. He'd have killed anyone who'd set his little sister up like this. John met Karen halfway and gave her a hug.

"This is for you." John handed her the red rose.

One would have thought it was a dozen the way she squealed.

"Hey, take it easy. It's nothing. A beautiful flower for a beautiful girl." And that's all she was, a girl. A kid. If only there'd been someone older that night in Mexico City—

Karen stood on tiptoe and kissed him on the cheek. "It's the thought that counts."

Beyond them, Blaine Madison watched him like a hawk. John waved at him and Miz C.

"Aren't they cute? You'll never guess," Karen said.

"Guess what?"

"Dad asked Miz C to marry him, and she said yes!"

John winced with Karen's enthused hug, forcing his grimace to a smile. "That's fantastic."

Sheesh, he had to get over this funk. First guilt, now envy. Given his druthers, he'd get the card and leave, but the time and place had to be more discreet than opening hour in the well-lit foyer.

"That's awesome, girl." He ushered her over to the table where the family was being seated.

"Hi, John," Annie said with a sunshine smile.

Did she know about the card? He'd asked Karen to keep it between them, but girls that age tended to be chatty. "I understand congratulations are in order," he said, extending his hand to Blaine Madison. "Mind if I kiss the bride-to-be?"

"You don't usually ask for permission to distribute your kisses, but be my guest."

Uh-oh. Mad dad alert.

"Dad," Karen protested.

"It's okay, Karen. Be glad you have a dad that cares." John turned to Blaine. "For that I apologize, Mr. M. I'm not used to meeting girls accompanied by their parents . . . especially such cool ones."

"She *is* young," he replied, giving John a pointed look.

"I'm sixteen," Karen declared, full of indignation.

John didn't want to start the evening with a standoff. "And as long as I'm around, you have nothing to worry about. I'll look out for her like I would my kid sister." His words left a sour taste in his mouth. "You have my word." A filthy, dirty one. "I wish you every happiness, Miz C."

"Thank you, John," Caroline replied, accepting his brush on the cheek with a blush. "I'm still pinching myself."

"Well, better you than Mr. M." John gave her a roguish wink. "At least for now."

Around them, the lights overhead went out for a second and then came back on.

"The light show is starting," Karen said, dragging John down to her chair. "Sit down. I'll share with you."

With a hapless glance at the parents, John reached behind and grabbed an empty chair from a nearby table.

He'd seen the show dozens of times in the company of his various marks. While pictures flashed and changed on the giant screen behind the DJ's pit, laser lights coordinated to the rock music flashing about the room like electronic fireworks. With the card on his mind, he hardly paid attention, but next to him, Karen and Annie marveled with adolescent gasps of delight. They made him feel old.

Glancing around the room, John spied Javier near the dance runway with some of the teens from the tour group he and his roommate had traveled with. His gaze met with Javier's, the latter casting a pointed glance toward the bar. Following his look, John felt his pulse stumble.

Argon. He was dressed in jeans and a black Banditos T-shirt instead of his customary tailored suit, but it was the same man who'd confronted him at the caverns. Argon lifted his glass.

Rocha really was nervous, to have a watchdog around. But everything was cool, John convinced himself. With a nod at the thug, he turned back to the show that now filled the air with a finale of laser blasts and fog. Soon he'd have the card, pass it on to Argon, and the heat would be off, at least off John. Taking in a brace of air, he nearly choked on the artificial fog. He soothed his throat with a sip of soda.

"*Y ahora.* And now . . ." the DJ shouted. Behind him, the Banditos mask and roses flashed on the screen overlooking the fog-screened dance floor, while laser lights swept in all directions at once. His Wizard of Oz–like shout came across the speakers bigger than life. *"Baila, baila, baila!"*

From four sides, the traditional opening number

blasted the dance floor, still awash with the fake fog from the finale.

John tapped Karen on the shoulder. "You heard the man. Let's dance." Turning to Blaine and Miz C, he shouted across the table. "Care to join us?"

Karen's dad shook his head. "Maybe after our eardrums recover."

Miz C gave him an elbow jab and laughed. "You go on, kids. We'll just sit back and enjoy."

Blaine whispered something in her ear, making her smile even wider.

Is that what love looks like? John wondered. "Hey." He turned away, tapping Annie on the shoulder and pointing across the room to Javier's table. "I think I see that guy you met at Banditos in the city."

Annie's face brightened almost as much as her mom's. "It *is* Manny," she exclaimed. "He said he'd be here tonight."

Good, he thought, ushering Karen out to the dance floor. Enough mushy family sentiment. Annie was out of the way. The parents were accounted for. All he needed was a slow dance.

Four numbers later, winded, Karen fell into his arms. "At last," she mumbled against the damp silk of his shirt. "Umm, you smell good."

"So do you." *So just ask her.* "Did you bring the card?"

Her hesitation made his heart skip. "Not exactly."

Now his lungs froze. "What do you mean, not exactly?"

She pulled away. “We looked everywhere for it—”

It was getting worse. *“We?”*

“Miz C, Annie, and me,” she said, as if he were a dullard. “We checked all the packages. It just wasn't there.”

“I can't believe it.” No, he didn't want to believe it. It was over. Over for him. Over for her. Maybe over for—

“So I got you another one, just like it,” Karen announced, as though that were the answer to the world's problems. “It's in my Banditos bag.”

He held her off by the arms. “Are you sure you looked everywhere? Absolutely certain?” Remembering Argon's watchful eye, he pulled Karen back to him and gave her a kiss on the top of the head, as if she'd given him good news, but his mind was a black wash of panic.

“We took all our bags apart. It just wasn't there. But the one I got is just like it.” She paused. “I mean, it's a mother's birthday card. It's not like I looked at the other. It was sealed.”

And for a reason. John's brain volleyed balls of panic against his temples until he felt a bit nauseated. If the authorities didn't get him for this, the thugs would.

He schooled his features against the dread running cold in his veins. “I had money in that card.” Talk about understatement.

Karen's wide-eyed innocence gave way to dismay. “Omigosh, I'm *so* sorry. How much? I'll pay you back.”

John coaxed her head against him and whirled her

around, away from the view from the bar. If Argon saw her upset, he'd become suspicious. John had to play it as if all were going according to plan. "Forget it. It wasn't enough to get upset over. I'm overreacting. I'll bet your card is just as special."

He felt her relax in his arms with relief. "It says wonderful things, you know, like moms like to hear."

He'd take the card and slip out the back before Argon or Javier realized what was going on.

John pressed the blood from his lips. Rocha would kill him, nephew's friend or not.

The music faded.

"Tell you what," he said to Karen. "Would you give me the card, and I'll get it ready to mail in the bathroom where the light's better." He glanced to where Javier was talking to a chick with dark hair down to her waist. He always was a sucker for long hair.

"Sure, no problem. Need a pen?"

He caught Javier's eye and gave him a discreet signal to follow him. "What?"

"I said, do you need a pen, silly." Karen gave him a playful punch. "Where are you tonight?"

John shrugged and gave her a beguiling smile. "Pretty girls make me dizzy."

It always worked. Indignation melting into a giggle, she grabbed his hand and dragged him back to the table. Javier had already split for the men's room. All John had to do was get the card, fill his friend in, and split.

"I know your mom will love this card," Karen said,

oblivious to the dangerous gaze that followed her from the bar.

It wasn't as if he had a choice, John argued against the growing guilt gnawing at him. He was already taking a risk by letting Javier in on what was happening. He couldn't save everyone.

CHAPTER 24

Leaving the loud music at Banditos early would have been a relief to Caroline, if Karen weren't so upset. John had excused himself to go to the men's room and not returned. Perhaps it was a mother's eye, but he hadn't looked well to Caroline. So when Karen asked Blaine to check on the young man, Caroline concurred. John was nowhere to be found.

"He was mad," the girl sniffed as she donned her swimsuit for an evening dip in the hotel pool.

Annie, who had made arrangements with the studded Manny to join them later, tried consoling her friend. "Look, if a guy is going to act like a jerk over something as simple as a card—"

"But it had money in it!"

You shouldn't have taken the card in the first place, money or no. You knew the rules. Caroline checked the admonishment. "Did you offer to repay it?"

"Yes, and he said it wasn't worth worrying over. It was like a twenty or something." Wearing her heartbreak on her face, Karen looked at Caroline, hungry for some sage or comforting advice.

She had none, at least none that would make a difference. Caroline crossed the room and pulled the distraught child into her embrace. "He's right about that, sweetie. But it's easier said than done."

"And on the bright side, you wouldn't have seen him after we left anyway," Annie pointed out. "You've lost two hours at the club tonight and maybe a couple of hours tomorrow. No biggie."

Karen shot Annie a grudging look. "You have Manny."

"And you have *all* of us." Caroline gave her a kiss on the forehead.

"And Kurt and Wally," Annie called from the hotel balcony. Leaning over, she waved. "Hey, down there."

Alarm shot Caroline's voice. "Annie, be careful."

Her daughter turned, reentering the room. "Mom, the rail is a concrete wall."

"Great, Kurt and Wall-eye," Karen mumbled, tugging a T-shirt over her head.

"Aren't you going to change, Mom?" Annie asked.

Caroline picked up her carryall bag. "I'm equally satisfied to watch the moon and stars over the ocean with a Cocabananaberry fruit thingy."

"It's a bay, Mom."

Caroline gave her condescending offspring a light cuff on the head. "Well, someone needs to let the water know that. It nearly drowned me our first day here."

When the elevator doors opened, the two elderly sisters they'd met at La Quebrada were inside. Dressed to the nines in spangles and sparkles, Eloise gave Caroline a big hug.

"A little birdie told us that you and that handsome Blaine have made it official."

Caroline's face flushed warm. "He asked me this morning."

"So your friend said," Irene told her. She frowned. "Now, what was her name?"

"Gearhardt, Reenie," her sister answered. "And she was just as tickled as we are for you. I think you've got yourself a good 'un."

Caroline tugged Karen under her arm and Annie under the other. "*Three* good 'uns." The way Dana had carried on when Caroline told her about the bizarre proposal, it was a wonder it hadn't made the world news network.

The door opened at the busy lobby. Annie held the elevator until Eloise could wheel Irene off.

"So where are you two off to?" Caroline asked.

"We're headed for a nightclub tour." Irene held up two tickets, her gaze as bright as the chandelier overhead.

"Going to paint the town," her sister chimed in.

"Paint the town?" Annie quirked her brow at Eloise.

The elder sister laughed so that her padded shoulders cast darts of light in all directions. "We're gonna get down," she explained with a mischievous wiggle, "and have a blast."

"That is way cool," Annie said.

"Yeah, you look awesome," Karen agreed.

She was trying to be cheerful, but Caroline's heart ached for the youngster. Granted, it was child's play at this point, but Caroline knew the pain of abandonment firsthand—of having the man she thought was too good to be true turn out to be false.

"And there's our bus," Eloise announced, pointing to the curb beyond the lobby entrance, where a huge diesel-belching vehicle had pulled up. She gave Annie a wink. "Tomorrow we fish and ride horses on the beach."

"Then we go home and collapse," Irene sighed as her sister wheeled her toward the bus.

"It'd be neat if we got on the same plane," Annie observed as the vivacious duo headed out.

"At least we'd get to *hear* about the riding and fishing." With a disappointed shrug, Karen let the idea of the private island tour they'd tried to book go as if it were the hope of the world . . . next to John.

Caroline corralled Karen with her arm as they headed down the corridor leading to the pool deck. "Hey, grass hasn't exactly been growing under your feet. We've not stopped a minute, except to grab a few hours of shut-eye, since the night before we left."

"Buenas noches, señora and señoritas." Blaine stood up when Caroline and company entered the pool compound. "I was about to come looking for you."

Caroline wrinkled her nose at him. "Girl talk."

He kissed it. "I have a round of Cocabananaberries on order."

Slipping his arm around Caroline's waist, he led her

to a pair of chaises. On a table next to them, hotel towels were piled in disarray amid the miscellaneous belongings of the boys in the water.

"Yo, dude!"

Caroline winced as Annie called out to the young man with the wet, wilted Mohawk. With a running start, she dived into the water and bobbed up in the opposite end of the pool like a sea sprite—who spoke like one of the guys. Mom was definitely going to have to spend more time working on her daughter's feminine side.

"Karen, catch." Kurt tossed a foam disc to the girl, and the game was on.

Once Caroline was seated and the skirt of her sundress neatly tucked about her, Blaine shoved his chaise against hers and settled there. Undaunted by the armrests that separated them, he covered her forearm and hand with his. His electric warmth spread from skin to skin, nerve to nerve, soothing and stirring at the same time. Just his nearness made her feel alive, safe, and protected—things she'd not felt in ages.

"I got it!" Karen shouted from the shallow end of the pool.

Kurt intercepted the disc and got a prompt ducking. With accompanying screams and giggles, the two scrambled for the disk.

Caroline smiled. With three-to-two odds, chances were good the night might be salvaged for the girls after all. As for her . . .

She stole a sidewise glance at her companion, who watched the horseplay with a paternal eye. His square jaw relaxed when Kurt emerged victorious and struggled out of Karen's reach.

As for Caroline, the one-to-one odds were just right.

The man wasn't right in the head, Caroline thought. Or maybe she was still dreaming—with a phone stuck to her ear.

"Come on, sleepyhead," Blaine cajoled on the other end. "You can walk, and I'll jog circles around you. You promised."

"It sounded good in the moonlight." Caroline squinted at the clock radio. Six o'clock. What happened to a day of rest and packing before tomorrow's departure?

"Some time alone. Just you and me. Then a private breakfast on the restaurant balcony overlooking the bay."

That wasn't fair. "As I said, it sounded good in the moonlight."

He chuckled. "I'll be waiting outside your door in five minutes."

Caroline stifled a yawn. "Okay, but I'm warning you, I really don't do mornings."

At the closing click of the connection, her eyes flew open. Five minutes? What, did he think he was talking to another man? A woman needed at least thirty to get rid of the raccoon eyes.

Blaine gave her ten. She opened the door at his gentle knock and took the note he'd written to remind the sleeping girls of their whereabouts and that they were to have breakfast with the Gearhardts as arranged the night before. Leaving the paper on the vanity, Caroline slipped out into the hall.

"What you see is what you get," she said, raising her hands as though to deny any responsibility for her disheveled state. "Ten minutes' worth."

"You look like a million dollars."

"Worn, wrinkled, and not all there?" she quipped as he bent over to kiss her. His smile melded against her lips. Had she brushed her teeth? *Lord, tell me I brushed my teeth.*

"Mmm," he said, drawing a breath away. "Sweeter than wine."

"Old or new?" Her wisecrack practically touched his mouth. *Heavenly Father, when he looks at me like that, I don't feel the least bit angelic.*

"I'm going to have to teach you to accept compliments, sweet Caroline." His voice was husky.

Somewhere inside Caroline, little curls of delight wound even tighter. The wall at her back left no room for escape, but who wanted to? Her breath quickened. Their noses touched.

The elevator bell rang.

Blaine broke away from her like a boxer at the gong, but the long, lingering gaze he gave her more than made up for the withdrawal of his body heat. He obviously liked what he saw, but as they rode the elevator down, Caroline wondered if they were looking at the same woman.

The one in the mirror was stripped of makeup—at

least the raccoon eyes were gone—and sported a wild, half-cocked ponytail gathered into a yellow scrunchy. Her new Mexico T-shirt all but covered her shorts. Caroline turned slightly to see if the back was as bad as the front. No, it was worse. Something hung out the back leg of her jogging shorts. She groaned inwardly on recognizing the tail of her nightshirt peeking out from underneath. Caroline would have sworn she'd removed it. How could she get her Wonder support on under two shirts and not notice?

Discreetly, she tried tucking it back in the leg of her shorts, while Blaine held the elevator for an Asian couple. Naturally, he looked like he'd just stepped out of a sportswear catalog. He'd even shaved.

Maybe to keep her from getting whisker burn. It wouldn't do for the mother of one of the students to sport a telltale rash around the lips.

Caroline gave herself a mental slap, but a devil of a smile would not leave her lips.

An hour later she was still smiling as she walked barefoot along the waterfront while Blaine jogged back and forth in circles around her. Since no container was on hand, the seashells that had caught her eye filled her *huaraches*.

"What's that about?" Blaine asked, tracing the tilt of her lips with his finger. "I didn't think you did mornings."

"I'm having second thoughts," she demurred, running her hand lightly over his damp chest.

"On jogging?" he teased. His gaze devoured her as if

she were a goddess, not the middle-aged mom of a teenager. But then, he hardly looked the father of one either. He looked like . . . like a man hungry for the woman in his arms.

"I love you, Caroline." His hoarse whisper took the very breath of the surf away, drying the beach as it dried her mouth.

She moistened her lips. "Me too." No, that wasn't right. "I mean—"

Unable to think, Caroline acted. Rising on tiptoe, she kissed him, transformed into a beautiful, vibrant woman without inhibition by the sun-streaked sky and glittering water. The cry of the gulls gave an urgency to the give and take of their lips, of the hands that alternately embraced and caressed. They dropped to their knees, and all the tender moments shared between them mounted like kindling to an all-consuming flame of sensation and emotion . . .

And water. A solid wall of it slammed into the two of them, bowling them over like duckpins. Gasping and sputtering, Caroline scrambled like a blind crab on the sand, uncertain if she was headed for dry land or water. Suddenly, a pair of strong arms hauled her out of the fierce clutch of the receding wave and to her feet.

"Wha—" The sharp press of Blaine's arm against her abdomen forced the remainder of her water-filled gasp out.

"Easy, sweet." Dragging her beyond the reach of the rogue wave, he brought her upright, turning her to face him. "Are you okay?"

He was soaked to the skin, like her, and covered with sand. Rivulets of water caressed his jaw where her hand had been only moments before. Just like an old Hollywood movie except—

"This wasn't in the script," she coughed. At his bewildered look, she explained, tugging up her shorts before the weight of the water soaking them pulled them to her knees. "I saw this in a movie, and it didn't turn out like this. Lancaster and Kerr never wound up bottom over teacups."

Blaine's beautiful, deep laugh filled the air. Grabbing her up, he swung her around until he nearly lost his balance in the sand.

"I love you, Caroline Spencer. I love this woman!" he shouted, drawing Caroline's attention to the pool attendant on the other side of the decorative concrete wall. "Isn't she beautiful?"

The image Caroline had seen in the elevator flashed through her mind. Now soaked and sand-covered? She looked at Blaine with incredulity, an old adage striking her with equal wonder. Love really *was* blind.

Whether the pool boy understood or not, he nodded, his white smile glinting in stark contrast to his tropical brown skin and crop of raven black hair.

"How about a quick shower and breakfast, sweet Caroline?"

Sweet Caroline. Music to her ears. Caroline nodded. "Sounds good to me. Let me fetch my shoes."

As miraculous as the love she'd found, her *huaraches* had been tossed by the rogue wave onto what was now dry beach, but the shells were scattered everywhere.

"You can't take them with you anyway," Blaine consoled her, playing Prince Charming as he helped her on with her slippers after they'd both rinsed off under the beachfront shower.

Swathed in oversized beach towels, they ambled arm in arm into the hotel. Some of the guests were lining up for one of the bus tours as they entered the elevator. Offloading guests met Caroline and Blaine with knowing smiles. Did the glow she felt inside show that much—or did they just look ridiculous?

Caroline glanced at her mirror image. Maybe a little of both, she decided, too happy to care. At the door to her room, she unzipped the pocket of her shorts and got out her key. She could well imagine what the girls would say.

"Meet you in half an hour?" Blaine said as the green light signaled it was okay to open it.

"Sure." Since love was blind, that was plenty of time. "Unless the girls hog the shower," she said over her shoulder.

He kissed her smile and pushed the door further open. "What the—"

Caroline turned to see what had shocked him and caught her breath. The room was a wreck. Suitcases were tossed around, souvenirs dumped from their bags, clothes strewn everywhere.

Alarm pummeled Caroline's voice as she started inside. "Annie? Karen?"

Blaine grabbed her arm. "Wait."

He stepped past her and glanced through the open door of the bathroom. Seeing no one, he moved farther into the room, stepping over the scattered items. Caroline held her breath. *Dear God, let the girls be safe.*

Opening the door to the adjoining room, Blaine dashed inside. A moment later he was back, face blanched. "Mine's been tossed too."

"Where are the girls?" Caroline hardly recognized her voice—or Blaine's.

"Gone."

CHAPTER 25

"*Señora,* think," Hector Rodriguez urged. "Did anyone give you or the girls anything to take back to the States?"

"What about that guy John?" Manny suggested. "Or one of his friends."

At least in dry clothes, if not freshly showered, Caroline sat on the edge of the bed staring at the upside-down lettering on her T-shirt that read "Relax! God's in Charge," as though expecting some divine answer to the question. But nothing surfaced from the disbelief spin-drying her brain.

Hector Fuentes was with the World Customs Organization, and the Mohawk "kid," who'd taken an interest in Annie, was actually Manuel Santos, a United States postal inspector. Agents under Manny's Mexican counterpart, a short mustachioed gentleman by the name of

José Caro, searched the hotel rooms from top to bottom for clues as to what happened to the girls.

"It wouldn't have to be big," Hector said.

Postal inspectors. A light came on in the dark confusion of Caroline's brain. "There was a card." She glanced sideways at Blaine's chiseled countenance. They'd both been walking, talking statues since their return to the hotel.

"Tell us about the card," Hector prompted.

"John Chandler gave Karen a birthday card to post in the States to his mother."

Blaine swore. "She knew better than that." He referred to Karen, but the piercing look he gave Caroline left no doubt that he meant her too.

"He asked for it back, but Karen lost it. It . . . it had twenty dollars in it."

"Karen lost it?" Manny repeated.

Caroline nodded. "So we bought another one yesterday and gave it to John last night at the disco."

"Then he split before I knew it," the younger agent lamented. "I sent Caro's men to Chandler's hotel and stuck with the girls."

Caroline couldn't believe Manny was an undercover agent, much less that he was almost thirty. Nothing was what it seemed, and what *was* real, she wished with all her heart was not.

"Señora." Hector handed her a worn newspaper and pointed out the headlines. "As you can see, it was not twenty dollars in that card, but $50,000 or more."

Caroline read enough to see that a priceless stamp

collection had been stolen in Mexico City. She handed the paper to Blaine. This couldn't be happening. She'd read about horror stories involving tourists and contraband, but Karen and Annie weren't just good kids; they were chaperoned by their parents.

"Why didn't you say something about the card?" Blaine shoved the paper back at Hector, but his accusing glare was for Caroline. He raked his fingers through his salt-stiffened hair and stared at the ceiling as if begging for a patience that wouldn't come. "How could you be so thoughtless?"

"It was just a birthday card for his mother. He said he didn't trust the Mexican postal service to get it there on time. I thought it was sweet."

"I knew there was something wrong about that kid. But you," Blaine derided, "you had to see the good in everyone." He pivoted, like a loaded gun with no viable target, aiming some of the blame at Hector. "And where were you when all this was going down?"

Caroline refused to let him see the hurt, how his derision shattered her. She remained as she was, hoping her stare was as cold as she felt inside. She was determined not to take it again. Not from Frank or from any man . . . even Blaine. There was nothing to be gained by starting a shouting match on who could have done what when. What was done was done. It was time to pray for God to reveal anything she might have overlooked and for guidance now.

"Waiting for them to make a move," the inspector replied, a far cry from the happy-go-lucky tour guide he'd pretended to be. "We knew he'd pass the goods along, but not when."

"We'd hoped to intercept it at customs," Manny informed them. "Find out who gave the goods to the girls and get the address so that agents stateside could catch Rocha's accomplice there."

"But you can be sure Jorge Rocha is at the center of this," Inspector Caro said from the adjacent doorway.

"If you know who is behind this, then why not arrest him?"

"Because we need witnesses, *señor,*" Caro replied, immune to Blaine's accusing tone. "He has slipped through our fingers many times."

"So why aren't you combing the streets, looking for the girls?"

"Or the beach," Caroline added. After an inventory, she'd found the girls had taken their swimsuits—wherever they were.

"I have officers investigating their disappearance as we speak. We are checking all the tour services and the beach." Caro gave Caroline a sympathetic look. "It is a good sign that there was no evidence of struggle."

How could they tell? she wondered, taking in the disarray of the room.

"They took time to change clothes—"

"Or had changed and were going to join us on the beach when the room was invaded," Blaine inserted, deflating Caroline's hope.

Despite his wildfire of accusation, Caroline felt the same pain and panic that grazed Blaine's face.

"And the maid did not hear anything unusual," the inspector pointed out, unaffected in the line of Blaine's fire. "There is no blood on the scene."

Blood. The mention of the word curdled in Caroline's stomach. She closed her eyes. *God help us,* she prayed for the umpteenth time.

"Caroline! We just heard." Dana rushed by the guard at the door to where Caroline sat on the bed and hugged her.

Randy was right behind her. "Blaine," he said, seizing the man's hand in a stiff handshake. "What can we do?"

"Is it kidnappers?" Dana asked, searching the faces of the investigators. She stopped at Manny, incredulity breaking on her face. "*You're* a cop?"

He made a grimace of a smile. "I look young for my age."

Little by little, Dana and Randy were filled in. John and Javier Rocha were suspected couriers for a contraband organization under a thug named Jorge Rocha. No, Jorge didn't bother with drugs. He dealt with black-market collectibles. John and Javier evaded crossing the border with the goods by cajoling naive young women to do the job for them. Their game fell apart when Karen evidently lost the package with a valuable collector's stamp in it. Now, Karen and Annie were missing.

"But we have no sign that the girls' disappearance has anything to do with the stamp," Caro pointed out. "At least, not yet."

"Still, they wouldn't have gone anywhere without

telling us," Caroline insisted. "I know my Annie."

"And I know my Karen," Blaine said. "She's unpredictable, rebellious . . ." He exhaled heavily, giving up the rest of his assessment. "I don't know what to do with her." Razor-sharp emotion tore at his voice. "I don't know what to do, period."

Caroline resisted the urge to put a reassuring hand on his arm, but she needed to say what was on the T-shirt she'd grabbed in the frenzy to dress. "Relax. God's in charge. All we can do now is pray for God's speed."

Blaine shoved his hands into the pockets of the slacks he'd hastily donned in the time it took the authorities to respond to his alert. "You pray," he challenged. "I'm going out on the streets to see if they went off on their own."

"We have men on the str—" the Mexican inspector started.

"It beats just sitting here, waiting." Blaine pivoted toward the door without a glance at Caroline.

Randy fell in beside him. "I'll go with you, buddy. Two sets of eyes are better than one."

If Blaine wouldn't accept God's help, at least he had a godly man with him in Randy, Caroline thought, staring at the door long after it closed behind them.

The manager brought breakfast for two to Caroline as well as a fruit and cheese tray for the detectives. "We are all at the hotel praying for your *chiquitas,*" the manager told them in heavily accented English.

For where two or three are gathered together in my

name, there am I in the midst of them. St. Matthew's words flowed in mental concert with the man's assurance. Caroline felt the peace blanketing her despair.

As the word spread, others from the Edenton group continued to come, in twos and threes. The inspectors determined that the other families had no more idea where the girls had gone than Caroline and Blaine. The Butlers, Señora Marron with Rick Scalia and his mom, Mrs. Atkins and Eddie, and the Petermans with Kurt and Wally. Caroline's hope was battered as one after the other claimed to have no idea of Karen and Annie's whereabouts.

After the questioning by the inspectors, Señora Marron led them in fervent prayer that the girls would be safe, wherever they were, and that they would return to Blaine and Caroline soon.

"In the name of the Father, the Son, and the Holy Spirit—"

The charged silence in the room broke with a strangled sob. Kurt turned into his mother's shoulder with ragged tears.

Reverting to day care-mom mode without second thought, Caroline went to the distraught boy and squeezed his arm gently as she'd done since he was a toddler. "Everything is going to be fine, Kurt. I believe in God's promise. There is an explanation for all of this."

"But it—" He sniffed. "It's my fault."

For a split second, the collective heartbeat in the room stopped. Finally Dana held her son away from her.

"Kurt, what are you talking about?"

"Do you know anything about the girls?" Manny asked, interrupting the call on his cell phone.

Kurt shook his head. "No, I don't know where they are . . . honest," he added at the inquisitive tilt of his mom's head.

Caroline's suspended breath gave way with a dying flicker of anticipation.

"But I know where the card is," the boy said.

"What?" said Manny.

"Where?" Hector asked at the same time.

Kurt cleared his throat, and blinked the irritation from his eyes. "In the mail."

"I think you'd better explain more than that, young man." Dana Gearhardt narrowed her gaze at him. "Every little detail, please."

Kurt cut a sidewise glance at Wally, launching Mrs. Peterman into inquisition mode as well.

"Wally!" She pinched her son's upper arm. "Just what do you have to do with this?"

Round-eyed, Wally rubbed the offended spot. "Nothing. I just helped Kurt get the card from Karen's stuff and mail it."

"Where did you mail it?" Hector asked.

"Cuernavaca," Kurt told them. "Remember, I asked where the post office was?"

"That was three days ago," Hector figured aloud, turning to José Caro. "It's probably still in the Mexican system somewhere."

"From the beginning, boys." Manny pulled out two

chairs from the table by the window and motioned for the youngsters to take a seat.

It was bizarre watching the studded, tattooed, and fire-engine-red-haired young man interrogate Kurt and Wally. But then, there had been Blaine's marriage proposal in front of a goggled and finned audience. The whole trip had been surreal. Maybe if Caroline pinched herself, she'd wake up and find it was all a dream.

Kurt had witnessed John giving Karen the card and heard his spiel about poor postal service and wanting his mom to get it on time for her birthday. Suspicion, tinged with a dislike of his competition, prompted him to intervene. The morning they left for Cuernavaca, he and Wally lifted the card while helping load the luggage, then mailed it in the colonial town.

"Why didn't you tell us?" Dana asked when Kurt finished.

"I'm no snitch. Besides, me and Wally talked it over. If we just mailed it, there wouldn't be any problem with customs at the airport—just in case there was something weird in it."

"But we didn't think there was," Wally put in hastily. "We thought it was just a dumb card."

Kurt sighed, shaking his head. "We just didn't want anybody to get caught with something they shouldn't have had—even if it was just a dumb card."

"Any chance you remember the address?" The skepticism in Hector's voice betrayed his hope, or lack of it.

Kurt shook his head.

"But we have it," Wally spoke up, drawing all the

attention to him. "You remember," he told Kurt. "We decided to send it priority so the post office wouldn't lose a mom's birthday card." He glanced at Dana and Caroline as though checking to see if that brought them any grace. "Anyway, they gave us a receipt with the address and all on it. It's got to be in one of the souvenir bags."

"We need that receipt, guys," Hector informed them.

Wally and Kurt left to search their bags.

"So maybe Rocha doesn't know the card is missing . . . just that his courier is." Manny toyed with one of the studs in his ear, lost in speculation.

"Which probably means that he's focusing on John Chandler, not the girls," the young man said, going on to explain. "If I were Chandler and had flubbed the deal, I'd split, leaving Rocha clueless . . . which is what it appears he and his roommate did."

"Okay, so the couriers split. So what about this?" Hector countered, taking in the messy room with a sweep of his arm. "Why would Rocha's men search the room?"

Manny wasn't certain. "Maybe he caught John or Javier and knows the card is missing. He'd send someone to double-check their story before he slit their throats. Or maybe he's just covering his bases, determining where the card isn't. Rocha leaves nothing to chance."

"Maybe," Hector acknowledged. "Or maybe he's getting rid of all the loose ends."

"But the girls know nothing about Rocha or the stamp

. . . just a greeting card," Caroline spoke up, her beating heart on her sleeve.

Manny shrugged, "Man, I can't put my finger on it, but I throw in with Caro." He glanced at the unmade beds where the girls had shed their sleep shirts. "Missing swimsuits tell me Rocha has nothing to do with the girls' disappearance. The fact that two teenage girls are so unpredictable falls in their favor."

"Annie might have been swayed by Karen," Caroline conceded. "It just isn't like her not to leave a note."

But all things were possible. Again Caroline focused through her tears at the upside-down slogan on her T-shirt. Clenching the cotton-knit promise in her fists, she just knew Manny was right.

Four hours of stopping at every shop and café along the beachside boulevard and showing the photo strip of pictures that Karen and Annie had taken in a vending booth pounded Blaine's anger into exhausted frustration. No one had seen his daughter. He and Randy were just going over plowed ground.

"Oh, sí," clerk after vendor told them. "I see her picture with the *policía* before you."

The situation was out of his control. He was out of control. The minute he'd launched his attack on Caroline, he'd wanted to take it back. But the trigger had been tripped, and the relay of his exploding nerves wouldn't stop. How could she just sit there so calmly when her world was falling apart?

Relax. God's in charge. Blaine pushed the uninvited

message out of his mind.

If he'd flown into Ellie like that, she'd have taken up the gauntlet and beat him to a pulp with it, pointing out everything he'd done wrong from the day they'd met. But Caroline hadn't. Sweet Caroline. Frightened Caroline. Calm Caroline.

"Here we go," Randy said, returning with two espressos from a sidewalk cafe. "Black as sin."

Blaine took the offered cup. "Did you have to use that word?" At Randy's quizzical expression, he explained. "I'm feeling guilty right now . . . the way I spoke to Caroline. The way I—what is that word the kids use—*dissed* her faith."

"You were under incredible stress."

"So was she, but she had that blasted T-shirt."

"No, Caroline has the faith of a saint and defends it like a pit bull. It shows in everything she does . . . or wears," he added with a slight smile. "Let's take a load off our feet."

Blaine walked after him to one of the empty bistro tables. A myriad of scenes flashed through his mind. The day at the pyramids when Caroline explained how God hung the first clock in the moon and stars. The way she comforted Karen—and him—at Guadalupe. He'd felt closer to God that day than he could ever remember, as though God had sent this angel to comfort him and his daughter, to put to rest the pain Ellie's death had left behind.

And he'd had the nerve to call her naive. Maybe she saw more clearly through those rose-colored glasses than he did with twenty-twenty vision.

"Aren't you going to sit down?" his companion asked.

Blaine obeyed, consumed in thought.

"He *is* in charge, you know. It doesn't always seem like it, but there's a reason for everything. What goes bad, God turns to good. I've seen it happen time and again." Randy blew the steam from the coffee, giving Blaine time to digest his words.

"But how do you *know* that?" Blaine asked. "That it wasn't coincidence."

"You have to know God . . . personally. Being able to recite Scripture alone doesn't do it. Going to church every Sunday doesn't do it. It's the one-on-one relationship that matters." There was that hint of a smile again. "You walk and talk with Him just as a child does an imaginary friend. Except God isn't imaginary." Randy's confidence gave way to wonder. "I know it sounds weird, but truth is stranger than science or fiction."

The way this trip had come about and evolved, Blaine couldn't argue that. "How do you know it's God sending you a message and not just what you want?"

"That's where studying the Word comes in. If your answer is in keeping with the guide He gave us, then it's Him."

"Yes, but what about all the interpretations? One group believes one thing, another something else."

"Key word is *study.* God will reveal His meaning for

you. I'm always finding something new in passages I've read time and again." Randy snorted as though he still found it hard to believe.

But he did believe. There was no doubt in Blaine's mind about that. Like Caroline, Randy lived his faith, not in flamboyance, just plain day-to-day living. He'd rallied to Blaine's side like a comrade in arms . . . like another messenger from above.

"If you don't mind, I'd like to pray."

A blade wedged in Blaine's throat, cutting on all sides. Unable to speak, he nodded his assent.

"Heavenly Father, give Blaine and Caroline and the girls strength and courage in this hour of need. Give the police wisdom and speed in bringing justice to those who deserve it. And deliver our children safe into the arms of their parents. In Jesus' name . . ."

Blaine couldn't have said it better himself. Fact was, he couldn't assemble his wits enough to say it at all. Yet, the heaviness in his chest seemed to ease, as if lifted by an unseen hand, and the mention of the name *Jesus* freed his voice enough for an "Amen."

Conviction took the reins of his shattered thought process. The trip was no coincidence. These godly people were not here by chance. God saw Blaine's need and sent him earth angels. Surely, He *was* in charge.

CHAPTER 26

"Hold the elevator."

Impatient to return to Caroline, to lay his heart at her feet for forgiveness, Blaine pushed the hold button and peered around the elevator door to see what the holdup was. Eloise was laboring to get Irene's wheelchair into the cubicle before she missed the ride.

"Here, let me help," Randy offered, stepping out and taking over.

"I'm out of puff," the elder sister exclaimed, leaning against the rail next to Blaine. "Too much nightlife."

"And the brake was half on," Randy observed, remedying the situation.

"Well, that just takes the cake." Irene twisted in the chair, addressing her sister. "And neither one of us with enough sense to get a cab and come home," she chuckled. "But we had a grand time."

"I'm glad your girls could use our tickets to the island, though," Eloise said. "I don't think Reenie and I—"

Blaine zeroed in on the word *girls*. "You know where the girls are?"

"Why, yes. They went on the private island tour in our place. I called them first thing this morning so the tickets wouldn't go to waste. Didn't they tell you?" Irene frowned. "I insisted that they ask you first."

"Yes, Reenie did insist," Eloise told them. "I heard her."

Free tickets and no parents—what scatterbrained teenager could resist?

Armies of anger and relief vied for the field of Blaine's mind.

He'd wring their necks.

Thank You, God.

Reenie read the answer in his silence. "Oh, my. I am so sorry."

"You must be frantic," Eloise said.

Relief, reinforced by gratitude, won. The victory practically lifted Blaine off his feet. "Frantic, yes. Sorry?" He grabbed Eloise in a bear hug. "I love you."

"Oh my," she tittered. "That was worth the fifty bucks apiece."

"Praise the Lord," Randy cheered from the corner.

Blaine straightened from planting a loud kiss on Irene's cheek. He felt the same grateful joy he saw on Randy's face. Even when he went to church, Blaine wasn't the demonstrative type, but he couldn't help himself. "Amen, brother," he whispered, broken by the grace filling his heart. "Amen."

God *was* in charge.

He had to tell Caroline. The moment the elevator door opened, he raced down the corridor and into the hotel room. It had been restored to some semblance of order—suitcases packed, beds made. Inspectors Caro and Santos were gone. Hector sat at the table on a cell phone. Dana and Caroline stood beyond the sliding glass door on the balcony.

Caroline turned and ran inside. Like him, she still

hadn't showered from their dunking—that seemed like yesterday—but even with her naturally curly hair frizzed, face without makeup, and clothes rumpled, he'd never seen her so lovely.

"They know where the card is!" she told him, breathless.

"I know where the girls are!" he said at the same time.

They froze just short of each other.

She thawed first. "The girls? You found them?" Blaine caught her up as she bolted into his arms. "Where? Where are they?"

"Horseback riding and fishing on that private island tour Eloise and Irene told us about."

"How do you know?" Hector's voice bounced off the private sphere of elation enveloping Blaine and Caroline.

Blaine loved her. He needed her. He needed her God. "I'm so sorry."

"How do you know, Mr. Madison?" Hector repeated.

"You were upset," Caroline answered. The forgiveness shining in her eyes was a balm to his guilt-ravaged conscience.

"We met two ladies in the elevator," Randy explained to the inspector. "They said they gave the girls their tickets this morning."

Caroline frowned suddenly. "Annie would have left a note . . . and if she didn't—"

"Perhaps the burglar found the note," Hector reasoned. "In which case . . ."

"My babies are still in danger?" Caroline's face blanched.

First they were safe. Now they weren't. Blaine steeled himself against the merry-go-round of emotions. "Then we're going to the island . . . now."

A quick phone call from Hector, and two boats manned with police waited at the waterfront. From his expression, Caroline knew that neither he nor Manny Santos, who followed in the second craft, wanted Caroline or Blaine to go along, but one look at the bulldog set of Blaine's chin killed any objection.

Grateful not to be left behind to worry and wonder, Caroline held on to the rail of the lead craft, the wind whipping the loose tendrils of her hair about her face in the salt-water spray as she clung to the rail, knuckles white. A few feet away, Blaine stood, braced against wind and water as though daring it—or anything—to get in his way. If only Karen could see him now, she'd know just how much he loved her. She'd never doubt again. And Annie—

An invisible knife slashed at Caroline's throat. *God, keep them safe. God keep them safe,* she prayed over and over, leaving it to the Holy Spirit to embellish.

Ahead, the island's gentle green hills with patches of salted gray rock and a fringe of white sand rose against a canvas of azure sky and crystal blue sea. Gradually, the brightly colored dots on the island beach took the shape of fishermen at the water's edge. Some were kicked back in lounge chairs with attached rod-holders, while their more avid counterparts stood, attentive to the tension of the lines strung from their reels. Behind them, tropical trees shaded a market of thatched-roof stalls before climbing up the hilly terrain.

It wasn't a large place, but it could take forever to search. Squinting, Caroline made out some movement on the clear patches of rock further upland. Like toy horses carrying dolls, she thought. Hopefully, her living dolls.

Instead of beaching the boat directly, the helmsman veered off and circled counterclockwise around the island. A cluster of paddleboats manned by swim-suited tourists forced him to shift down to a slow drift toward the dock where a ferry shuttle was moored. By the time their craft tied up, curiosity seekers had gravitated toward the landing.

Blaine climbed onto the salt-treated decking and turned, extending his hand to Caroline. "Come on, sweet Caroline."

She answered with a strained smile. They were both trying hard not to come unglued. As Blaine pulled her up, she took comfort in his firm grip, equating its effect to the invisible hand that reassured her spirit—warm, loving, able.

Once she had her footing, she linked her arm in his. "Let's go find those little prodigals."

"I think the prodigals have found you," Hector said from the edge of the pier.

He pointed to an approaching paddleboat where two gangly teens worked the pedals for all they were worth, cutting through the flotilla of their elders.

"Mom!"

"Dad!"

Caroline rushed with Blaine for the spot of beach where the girls were headed.

Happy as clams, *safe and sound* little clams, the pair alternately waved and paddled until they reached the beach, where Caroline, Blaine, and company waited.

"What's going on?" Annie asked as an island staff member took the craft.

"Yeah," Karen said, taking in their uniformed company. "What's with the police escort?"

"What's with leaving the hotel and not telling anyone where you were going?" Despite the reprimand in her tone, Caroline grabbed Annie, wet swimsuit and all, and hugged her as though to never let go again.

"We did," her daughter protested against her shoulder.

"We did," Karen reiterated at her father's skeptical look. "I wrote it on the back of Miz C's note and put it on the bathroom counter. Honest, dad."

"I believe you, baby." With that, Blaine pulled Karen to him, pressing her head against him. "I just thank God you're safe."

"Why wouldn't I be?" she asked, squirming away with a bewildered expression.

"Have you girls noticed anyone on the island watching you?" Hector intervened.

"Like, I wish," Karen snorted.

Annie pulled a face. "There's nobody but old people

here, except for the boys running the paddleboat pier."

If the situation had been any other, Caroline might have laughed at the attitude of grave injustice in the girls' replies. "What did you two expect on a seniors' tour?"

Instead of answering, Annie looked past her, the derision on her thinned lips transforming to a delighted smile. "Manny, what brings you here?"

"He's an undercover agent for the U.S. Postal Service," Caroline announced.

"Omigosh." Annie gave Karen a startled look. "The postal service?"

"It's the card. I didn't mean to lose it." For once, Karen could not get close enough to her father. "Am I under arrest?" she said in a small voice.

"No, but you're one lucky little girl," Manny answered. "You both are."

"You're a cop?" Annie was still unconvinced.

Grinning, Manny dug his badge out of his baggy jeans and flashed it.

"How old are you?" she asked.

"By your standards, over the hill," he replied before turning to Karen. "Remember the guy you saw in the caves? You haven't seen him or anyone weird around here, have you?"

"No, just old people."

With her brow knit, Karen reminded Caroline of her father when he was vexed.

"Is it illegal to mail a Mexican birthday card for

somebody in the States?" Karen asked, thoroughly confused.

"Were there drugs in it?" Annie asked, just as bewildered. "Is John a drug smuggler?"

Karen's gaze widened. "And he was getting me to move his stash?"

Hector interrupted the adolescents' increasingly excited interrogation. "Why don't we move this back to the boats?" he said to Manny. "I'll question the girls, and you take the other crew and search the island, just in case."

Manny high-fived him. "You got it, man." Turning, he gave Annie a wink. "Babe, if I really was who I pretended to be, your momma would have to watch me like a hawk."

"I already was," Caroline informed him. "Blaine, too."

Back at the hotel, Hector ordered dinner for everyone delivered to the room, instead of joining the other Edenton travelers on a preplanned farewell dinner cruise. Having had enough of Mexican cuisine, those remaining behind munched Chinese carry-out, while Hector questioned the girls for any other hints they might have to help the investigation.

"So I got John in trouble by losing the card?" Karen's lips had thinned to a bloodless line with the weight of her disregard for the rules.

"And yourselves," Blaine pointed out. "We were frantic."

Karen squeezed her father's hand. "I am *so* sorry, Daddy. I didn't think—"

"No, you didn't." While his tone was stern, the hug he gave her was eloquent. "But we all make mistakes that we're sorry for."

He chanced a glance at Caroline, her wince of a smile small consolation for the guilt he still felt at blowing up at her.

Manny Santos arrived.

"We found no one suspicious on the island," he told them, his face a mirror of disappointment. "But Inspector Caro has agreed to station men in the hotel just in case Rocha sends someone back to visit." He picked up a cold egg roll and unwrapped it. "But chances are much better that he's got all his thugs looking for his nephew and John Chandler, since the search here was a bust."

"So you think the girls are out of danger?" Blaine asked. It was too simple a conclusion to what had been a complex conspiracy.

Manny shrugged. "Anything is possible with Rocha, but with Chandler and Javier Rocha on the run, the odds are Jorge Rocha will think they decided to cut out on their own with the card. We're the only ones who know the card was mailed."

"But they could kill John for a card he doesn't have, right?" Karen asked, concerned.

Blaine gave his daughter an incredulous look. "Don't tell me you are still smitten by that manipulating jerk? Don't you know how close you were to being involved in contraband smuggling and possibly being murdered in the process?"

She gave him a *You are so overreacting* look. It settled like a lit match to the keg of tumultuous emotions bottled up inside. But before he could explode, Caroline pulled the fuse.

"It's hard to separate the crook from the charm of first love, isn't it, sweetie?"

Maybe it was a woman thing, he thought, noting the kindling of feminine understanding between the two. As far as Blaine was concerned, Chandler had been a conniving, silver-tongued devil from the start.

"Maybe John got snookered in with the bad guys like we did," Annie observed. "Only he can't get out."

"I can't believe these women," Blaine exclaimed, looking to Hector and Manny for support.

"You gotta pay to play, man." Manny shoved the remains of the egg roll into his mouth.

"Just hope we find him before the bad guys do," Hector said.

Later, after the agents left them to Inspector Caro's guards, Blaine held back as Caroline and the girls offered a prayer for John to be found safe and alive. Personally, Blaine wanted to snap the kid's neck with his bare hands. Instead, Blaine prayed that it was really over—that his family was safe.

Lord, just deliver us home to Pennsylvania tomorrow, as far away from Jorge Rocha and his likes as possible. And thank You, Father, for Caroline.

Leaving the girls to their beauty ritual, which involved the splashing and smearing of every pricey product known to womankind, Blaine followed the woman of his heart out on the balcony afterward. Instinct told him not all was well.

"What's wrong, Caroline?"

It was a balmy night, but she rubbed her arms as though chilled. "I was just looking at the moon and thinking." She hesitated. "About us."

Blaine had hoped her discomfiture was about Rocha, not him. "I thought you'd accepted my apology." He turned her so that he could see her face in the moonlight. Her eyes were bright . . . too bright. *God, I can't lose her now.*

"Tell me what you want me to say . . . what you want me to do. Caroline, I love you. I know I hurt you, but I was crazy with the idea of losing my daughter."

She smiled. "I know. It's just . . ."

"Just what? Tell me. I'll fix it."

She shook her head. "No, it's something I have to fix myself. I have to give it over to God." Pulling away from him, she faced the tropical panorama of the bay, buffered by white sand and the hotels. "It's just that when you blew up at me, it was like a dart from the past." She sighed. "All the insecurities my ex-husband nurtured in me came flooding back . . . how stupid and inadequate he made me feel."

"Dear God, I am so sorry." Blaine buried his face in the cradle of her neck and shoulder.

"I know you are." She ran her fingers up the side of

his cheek, leaning her head against his. "And I forgive you. Your reaction was perfectly understandable. Perfectly forgivable. The imperfection is with me and my own insecurities."

"Caroline." Blaine pulled her around, looking down into her tear-pooled gaze. "Sweet Caroline." Her cheeks were hot and moist to his touch, confirming what he knew. She'd been crying before he joined her. He'd made her cry.

God, give me the words.

"You are a blessing, sent straight from heaven to bring this dead heart back to life. No," Blaine stumbled. "This dead *soul*. This is going to sound corny and canned, but, sweet Caroline, I was so lost. Lost in work, lost in fatherhood. Lost in life, lost in faith . . . until I met you. You found me, Caroline. You made me see with the laughter in your eyes, the love in your heart . . . and above all—" Blaine's voice broke—"the light in your soul. Because of you and your wisdom so far beyond mine, God is real to me now." He pointed to the starlit sky above them.

"He hung the moon and those stars for man to mark time and place by, to live and love by." He moistened his lips, but his mouth was as dehydrated of water as his life had been of the living water before Caroline. "Live and love with me, Caroline, for the rest of our lifetime."

Blaine held his breath as she cupped his jaw with her hands. Her chin trembling, she rose on tiptoe and gave him his answer—with a kiss.

CHAPTER 27

The chaos of departure matched that of the embarking eight days before. Sleep had come in scant bits and pieces, despite the guards posted outside. High on the love of the most wonderful man in the world, Caroline forgot to put in a wake-up call, so after she finally succumbed to exhaustion in the wee hours of the morning, she overslept. Fortunately, she'd showered the night before.

Now Karen commandeered Blaine's shower, while Annie bathed in Caroline's. Freshly shaven and dressed, but showing the strain of too much excitement and too little rest, Blaine held down the lid to Caroline's Pullman so she could zip it.

"Heaven help the customs official who opens this up." Her droll comment prodded a smile from her somber companion.

"What's in those bags?" he asked, pointing to the gaping top of a fake straw bag with *Mexico* emblazoned on it.

"More souvenirs," she replied.

With a sigh she surveyed the cases covering the unmade beds. Each person had two cases plus a few packages. "I guess we'd better call and see if the bell captain can send up a forklift."

"I'll call," Blaine offered. "You put a rush on the girls."

Half an hour later, the teens were dressed and putting the final touches on their hair. Caroline sat at the bistro table on the balcony reading her morning devotional in a weary stupor.

Not by might nor by power, but by My Spirit.

Ain't that the truth, she mused, gazing unseeing beyond the little booklet at the beach coming to life below. The helplessness she'd felt yesterday still made her tremble, but God had intervened in so many ways.

"Peso for your thoughts." Blaine leaned over her shoulder from behind and kissed her cheek.

Caroline pointed to the highlighted verse. "Today's horoscope . . . although it really suits yesterday better."

"Wow," Blaine said after reading it. "I see what you mean. God was working overtime for us this time yesterday. What if the girls had been in the room when the thugs ransacked it?"

"What if they'd found the girls on the island before we did?" It never ceased to amaze Caroline how incredible the Word was. "See why I call it my horoscope? There's always something that applies to something either I, or someone I know, is going through. Like it knows before it goes to print," she said with a mysterious wiggle of her eyebrows. She gave herself a little thump on the forehead. "Duh, that's why it's *living*."

When Blaine remained silent, Caroline looked up to see him lost in thought. "Peso for *your* thoughts."

"I was just remembering . . . at the airport luggage claim, on my way to catch your plane, this lady gave me a pink slip of paper. Like something from a fortune cookie," he explained. "It was a Bible verse that basically warned me that all my work was in vain without faith. My house was falling apart, no matter how much time I put on it."

Caroline remembered the high-strung, troubled man Blaine had been when they first met—such a contrast to the faith-seeking, compassionate, and passionate soul of last night. Was it only days ago? So much had changed. "Maybe that lady was an angel . . . an earth angel put in that place at that time just for you."

Blaine scowled, not quite comfortable with that train of thought. "Does that mean those two batty sisters are angels, too? I mean, they certainly saved our girls."

What a joy it was to see mischief light in his gaze. "Could be." Caroline chuckled. "I understand angels come in all shapes and sizes."

"Then we've been traveling with a band of them." A glaze formed over his eyes for a moment before he blinked it away. "I don't know what I'd have done yesterday without Randy. He's quite—"

A knock sounded on the door, followed by an accented "Bellman."

"I'll get it," Karen announced, shoving her hairbrush in her knapsack.

Instantly on guard, Blaine cut her off. "No, *I'll* get it."

"There are guards out there, Dad," Karen protested, relegating Blaine back to stupid-dad status.

Yes, life was returning to normal, Caroline thought, closing her devotional and heading inside to put it away.

Cautiously Blaine opened the door as far as the chain allowed and peered out.

"You call for the luggage cart, *señor?*"

"Yes, *gracias*."

Caroline expelled the breath she'd inadvertently held.

Blaine took the chain off and stepped back to allow the uniformed man into the room. But instead of bringing in the brass luggage cart, the bellman stepped aside, allowing a second man into the room before Blaine had a chance to react. Like a sinister magician, the second man suddenly brandished a pistol with some kind of attachment on the end and leveled it at Blaine.

"Easy, *señor,*" he warned Blaine. "Keep your heads and no one will be hurt."

"Omigosh!" Karen backed against the wall as if she'd seen a ghost. "It's the man from the cave!"

"You have a good memory, *señorita,*" the assassin acknowledged. "Perhaps you will also remember where your boyfriend is?"

"He . . . I haven't seen John since he ditched me at the club the night before last." Karen gave her father a plaintive look.

Blaine could hardly do anything at gunpoint, save the half-surrender, half-caution display of his raised hands.

The masquerading bellman brought a brass luggage cart inside, letting the door drift shut behind him. "All clear, Argon."

Despite his weapon, the young man in the uniform didn't appear nearly as threatening as the man he called Argon. Caroline had never seen an assassin, but this guy fit her image of one. His narrow face was scarred, with a large hooked nose—probably broken in some mob brawl—and the ointment plastering his black hair in place most likely contributed to the psoriasis flaking on his part.

"Look, *amigos,* your card or stamp or whatever it was is gone," Blaine said.

The malicious glint in the gunman's eye made Caroline's blood run cold. Would he shoot them for bad news?

"*Señorita,* put the hair dryer down."

All attention shifted to Annie, who in her frozen state held the running dryer like a pistol in her hand. "Mom?"

If the situation weren't so dire, it might have been funny. "Turn it off and do as he says, Annie," Caroline assured her with a calm she hardly felt.

Annie snatched the cord from the wall socket and tossed the dryer onto the bed like a hot potato.

"What happened to the guards?" Blaine asked, as Caroline coaxed her daughter behind her.

"In the supply closet, sleeping off the coffee I brought them earlier," the uniformed accomplice informed them. The manner in which he glanced at Argon for approval was akin to worship.

Maybe he really was a bellman—a greedy kid who'd been paid off by this Argon.

Caroline summoned her nerve. "Well, you've wasted time and risk for nothing, since we don't have the card. The kids had second thoughts about taking it across the border and put it in the mail in Cuernavaca."

The devil with catching whoever was on the receiving end of the mail route. All Caroline wanted was to get these guys out of here.

"As she said, you're wasting your time here," Blaine chimed in. He started to reach for Karen, but Argon stopped him.

"Stay where you are, *señor.*"

"Daddy?" Karen's terrified look as Argon grabbed her arm with his free hand tore at Caroline's heart.

Blaine looked as though he'd been kicked in the belly. "Why? You already know she doesn't have the card . . . or stamp . . . or whatever it was."

"*Señor,* don't make me shoot you in front of your little girl." The gunman held the gun steady at Blaine's chest.

Caroline's mouth went dry. For one half of a heart-beat, she thought it was over. She tried reading the Mexican's swarthy face. The deep lines furrowing his face relaxed. One corner of his pencil-thin lips twitched, a precipitous sign of what? Reprieve?

Argon made it a short one. "Put the girl in the trunk, Ricki."

Trunk? For the first time, Caroline noticed an aluminum case on the luggage cart, the kind that media equipment was often transported in. Or a child . . .

"Omigosh," Karen sobbed, coming to the same sick conclusion. "I c . . . can't get in there."

"It's okay, baby, I'm not going to let anything happen to you." Blaine stood glued to the spot, but the steel in his voice left no doubt in Caroline's mind that Karen was leaving over his dead body.

Dear God in heaven, please . . . do something.

"Why?" Caroline cried out. "Why do you need her? Why can't you just go?"

"My boss, he picks up all his bases." The assassin's convoluted metaphor would have been funny in any other setting. "And she will be our insurance until the goods reach the right person, no?"

Even if Argon did spare them, the chance they'd ever see Karen alive again was at best remote.

"Now, *señor,*" Argon continued, "I suggest that your next step be backward, toward the balcony with the lady and the other girl. Otherwise, I will have to shoot all of you. It matters not to me."

It really didn't. Caroline could see the man had no emotion in his black gaze. She exchanged a furtive glance with Blaine. His look spoke volumes of love and desperation, volumes that she returned with understanding. The decision was his.

Blaine contemplated the gun, every muscle in his body coiling tighter, awaiting his decision. Surely God hadn't given him a second chance with his daughter for it all to end like this. He had Caroline and Annie to think about as well. He was close enough to kick the gun from Argon's hand—if he still had the sureness of his old football days.

Not by might nor by power, but by My Spirit.

His thoughts tumbled to a halt at the challenge. Was

Caroline's devotion about letting go and trusting the Holy Spirit meant for today . . . for this? He rebelled at the idea of acquiescing to Argon's demand, of turning his daughter over to the gun-wielding demon before him.

Or was this God's demand? Professing faith was one thing. Putting it where his mouth was, where his loved ones' lives were, was another. The split-second decision took an eternity to make in Blaine's mind.

Dragging his first foot backward was like moving the Quebrada cliffs, but somehow he did it. Then the second. And another backward, and another . . . until he felt Caroline's hand on his shoulder.

God, I claim Your Word, he prayed as Karen pulled away from bellman's grasp with a terrified "Nooo!" and ducked through the open bathroom door.

The sound of it slamming against the porcelain of the tub inside erupted in gonglike thunder. Ever so briefly, Blaine thought a gun had gone off in it. Head pivoting, so apparently did Argon. But it was neither the bathroom door, nor a gun. It was the slam of the hallway door striking the luggage cart. The cart careened into the gunman.

Caroline's astonished "John!" penetrated the adrenaline rush in Blaine's ear as he tackled the distracted thug.

CHAPTER 28

A far cry from the clean-cut college boy he'd been when Caroline last saw him, a disheveled and unshaven John Chandler plowed over the gunman—and Blaine—with the luggage cart just inside the door. Caroline hunkered over Annie with her body, cringing as the gun went off. It splintered the nightstand and flew from Argon's hand toward the pile of jackets, carry-ons, and cases by the bed.

There was no time to think, just act. Caroline pushed her daughter toward the safety of Blaine's room. "Go, Annie. Get help."

With Annie out of harm's way, Caroline grabbed the teetering luggage cart as Blaine and Argon, half under it, scrambled to their feet. The cart toppled over on the bed, taking Caroline with it. Argon lunged for the mountain of luggage and bags where the weapon had disappeared, but Blaine grabbed him, hauling him back. Cursing, the assassin reached inside his jacket.

Caroline saw the flash of metal reflecting the bright light cast in through the balcony doors. "Blaine, he has a knife!"

Holding off the luggage rack with one hand, she slung a pillow, missing Argon and striking Blaine full in the face. Not quite her intent, but it did take the brunt of the knife's slash intended for him.

John reeled backward from the bathroom into the

closet, followed by the bellman.

As John struggled to his feet, Karen leapt on the bellman's back, beating his face with a still-spurting bottle of mousse. John dropped his adversary with a kick to the groin, followed by a sucker punch with the iron from the rack inside the closet.

"Caroline, get the gu—" Blaine fell into the other room, locked in a death dance with his armed opponent.

The gun. Caroline crawled over the pile of suitcases, tossing jackets right and left. It was like finding a needle in a haystack. As she moved aside her souvenir bag, a heavy package slid out, landing on her foot. Blinking away the stars of pain, she focused on the plastic bag containing the heavy granite dish she'd purchased at the pyramids. Taking up the weapon of chance, she rushed into the adjoining room. Argon straddled Blaine, the knife he wielded suspended over Blaine's throat. His face red with blood rush and strain, Blaine held it at bay . . . just.

Now or never, Lord.

Feeling a sudden kindred spirit with David as he let his stone fly at Goliath, Caroline swung for all she was worth. The thud as the dish struck Argon on the back of the head made her wince. The thug rolled to the side with the blow, landing on his back like a swatted fly. The knife fell on the carpet by his hand. Blaine scrambled to retrieve it and hauled himself upright on the side of the bed with labored breath.

"The gun?"

Caroline exhaled. "No time to look for it." She held

up the cudgel still swinging in its plastic sling. At Blaine's befuddled look, she produced the granite dish he'd teased her about. "My jewelry dish."

"The bellman?"

"Karen blinded him with mousse and John clobbered him with the steam iron."

Blaine's wary expression gave way to relief. "You call the police. I'll look for the gun, just in case."

The door to the room burst open. *"Policía!"*

Armed police spilled inside, with Hector Rodriguez at the lead. A simultaneous echo followed in the adjoining room.

Startled by the sudden invasion, Karen shrieked, "Daddy!"

Leaving Caroline glued to the spot in the connecting doorway, Blaine rushed to where his daughter stood frozen in terror next to a wounded John Chandler. "It's okay, baby," he said, drawing her to him. "It's all over."

The officers swarmed over the rooms, taking charge. Annie was allowed in after the unconscious thugs were cuffed and medics were called.

She ran straight into Caroline's arms. "Mom, are you okay?"

"I'm fine, sweetie." In spite of her assurance, she was grateful for the support of the doorjamb at her back. "And proud of you. You kept your head."

"All of you did." Blaine gave her a taut smile. "You don't mess with my girls."

Manny Santos dragged the ashen John Chandler to his feet from his sitting position on the floor.

"Do you have to cuff him?" Karen protested.

"He's a criminal, just like the others," the Mohawk kid told her.

The bloody towel that John had clutched to his chest fell away, revealing the hilt of a knife protruding from his shoulder.

"Daddy, do something."

"You heard the man, baby."

Blaine held Karen back so that Manny could help the boy over to the bed. Caroline and Annie rushed to clear it of jackets and a carry-on case.

"Just stay here till the medics arrive," Santos told him. "Don't try to remove it."

"Daddy, please, say something."

Blaine's jaw looked about to pop from the battle waging on his face. Caroline empathized. If John hadn't endangered them in the first place, he wouldn't have needed to rescue them.

But he didn't have to come back. He could have just run away.

Reluctantly Blaine must have come to the same conclusion. "If John hadn't shown up, we wouldn't have stood a chance. They'd have taken Karen."

"He's still a thief among thieves, if not the actual one who stole the stamp," Hector reminded them. He moved to the foot of the bed, crossing his arms. "So why *did* you come back, Chandler? We expected you to be in the States by now."

"Rocha would have found me, no matter where I went," John told him. "Besides . . . I found out I had a conscience." His eyes sunken with pain and fatigue, the young man sought out Blaine. "Maybe it was hanging out with all these religious folks, but I couldn't leave your daughter to Rocha's assassin, so I tailed Argon."

He grabbed his lower lip with his teeth to bite back the resulting pain of his half laugh. "That was the last place they'd look for me."

Had their kindness to John saved them all? Caroline's heart quickened with affirmation. All things were possible.

"Where's Javier Rocha?" Manny asked, more concerned with the justice on this side of heaven than on the other.

Weakening, John closed his eyes. "In South America by now, I imagine. He headed straight for the airport and the first plane south."

The medics arrived, preempting further questions. Argon and the bellman were promptly carried out, while John was being stabilized. Gathered in a family cluster within the scope of Blaine's protective arms, Caroline and the girls watched. The medics left the knife in place, instead administering IV meds. As soon as they finished, John was moved to a gurney. Manny cuffed the wrist without the needle to the rail, securing the prisoner.

"I'll go with him to the hospital," he told Hector. "You can finish up here."

Karen drew away from her father. "Daddy, you have to do something to help him. You know all kinds of people."

"They're just doing their job, kid," John said, resigned to his fate.

"Daddy, we owe him," Karen protested.

"For jeopardizing your life . . . and ours?" Cynical as he sounded, Caroline could see that Blaine was torn.

"But he didn't know it was going to work like this. He said so. He told me he was sorry."

"Save it, Karen. Your dad is right. I conned you." John looked past her at Blaine. "If anything, I owe your dad . . . and the others."

Seeing surprise claim Blaine's face, he went on. "You reminded me that I had a conscience, man . . . and that all things are possible, even for a screwup like me. If I at least try to do the right thing."

Gooseflesh pebbled Caroline's arms. "What was it we read just moments ago, about things being accomplished not by might but by the Holy Spirit?" she asked no one in particular. Moved by all that transpired for their good, despite their helplessness, she squeezed John's cuffed hand.

"Sweetie, you believe it. All things *are* possible with God. He loves you as much now as He ever did . . . and so do we."

"Well, that's good, Miz C," Manny Santos remarked with a sardonic smile, "because he's gonna need all the love God can give him in the hospitality of a Mexican calaboose."

"But he's an American." Karen tugged on Blaine's sleeve. "They can't keep him here, can they?"

Forgiveness didn't come as naturally to Blaine as it

evidently did to Caroline. He wanted to see the boy who'd courted Karen's heart and endangered her life strung up on the nearest tree. That the process didn't work that way was becoming less of a factor than that blasted Scripture. Was John really moved by the Holy Spirit or because he figured to use his nobility to his favor? He could be conning them even now. Why should Blaine give him a second chance?

"We can and *will* keep this man in our prison," Inspector Caro announced as he entered the room. Reaching the gurney, he pulled aside the towels stanching the boy's wound. "Once he is treated, transport him to the prison," he ordered one of his men.

"Shouldn't he stay in the hospital?" Caroline asked as the medic replaced them. "I don't mean to insult you, but is it clean in the prison?"

"Prison or a pig sty, *señora,* what does it matter to the likes of this one?"

"Would you want *your* son in there, wounded like this?"

Caroline squared her shoulders, reminding Blaine of a mother hen, ruffling her feathers to protect one of her chicks. He might not feel the same way toward John that she did, but Blaine had to admire her spunk—and the faith at its root. What had he done to deserve her?

To deserve a second chance . . .

The lightning clarity of the thought left no doubt in Blaine's mind as to the source. God corralled him with the help of strangers, giving him a second chance at love and family. No way could Blaine do less.

"You said you needed a witness, Inspector," he reminded the official. "It would do you well to see that this young man is treated and protected like a national treasure, if you want to put Rocha's gang away."

Caro snorted. "He is just a—how do you say—a pawn."

"A pawn who undoubtedly knows names, places—"

"I saw Rocha and Argon beat one of the student couriers not long after I got involved. He'd taken some stolen jewelry for his own profit." The young man lowered his head. "I don't know what happened to him." His chin quivered with emotion under Caro's skeptical appraisal. "So help me God, I had no idea they'd do that kind of thing until then. I thought they were just petty thugs . . . jokes." He swallowed, his words beginning to slur as he went on. "By then it was too late to get out."

"That ought to give us a little more bargaining power," Manny Santos observed.

"He gives you Rocha and his thugs," he said to Caro, "and you let him face trial and imprisonment in the States. We both get our man."

One of the medics interrupted. "*Perdonamé,* Inspector, but we need to get this man to the hospital. He is losing much blood."

"I'll give my superiors a call," Manny assured Caroline as Caro gave the nod to move John out. "Till then, I'll stick to him like glue."

"Promise?" Karen called after him.

Manny gave her a thumbs-up and followed the speeding cart out of the room.

Blaine would bet that the promise was more for the feather in Manny's Mohawk than heartfelt motivation to keeping John's hide out of a Mexican jail, but it was welcome, either way.

"I'll make a few calls myself," Blaine said, as much to himself as to the others. He knew the undersecretary to the president from the urban renewal project. And wasn't Aquino's brother-in-law some kind of wheel in the police hierarchy?

Karen threw her arms around his waist, winding him with her hug. "Thank you, Daddy. I knew you could help."

"We will need you and your family to delay your departure until tomorrow in order that we may take depositions," Hector said, before Blaine could revel in his reinstatement as Best Dad in the World. "At the government's expense, of course."

"Can't we just phone them in?" Caroline objected. She leaned into the shoulder Blaine offered her.

"I'd feel a lot safer if we went home until you had Rocha and his men in custody," Blaine told the agent. "If we have to, we can come back, but I see no reason they can't be taken via a video conference, since both countries are working together and we have the technology."

"Yeah, I want to go home," Annie said, dropping onto the bed in despair.

Karen plopped next to her, arms crossed. "Me too."

Hector held up his hands in surrender. "Okay, peoples, who am I to blame you? I will talk to my boss, but

I think we can work it out." He turned to the men who'd been taking pictures and collecting evidence.

"Do you have everything that you need?" he asked. At their nod, he produced a wide grin. "Bueno. Then let's went."

Feeling as though he were on his last leg, Blaine followed them to the door and let them out. As he turned away, he came face-to-face with Caroline. She looked up at him, her eyes sparkling wet with emotion.

"What?" Had he overlooked something, worse, hurt her inadvertently?

Her chin trembled. "I love you, Blaine Madison."

The words filled him. If she made him feel any taller, he'd have to stoop to stand.

The irony wasn't lost on him. He'd started this trip feeling small, insignificant to those who mattered most. Then he'd met Caroline . . . *Sweet Caroline.*

"I love you too, Sweet Caroline."

Words weren't enough to thank this woman in his arms for all she meant to him. Nor was the love he planted on her lips. Or the gratitude with which he coveted them. She'd given him back his daughter with her wise counsel. Her love and laughter smoothed the raised and ragged scars left on his heart by Ellie's loss, while her delight and faith in her God filled the dark void of Blaine's soul with His light.

The first time Adam held Eve in his arms, he could have known no more joy nor want than that coursing through Blaine's veins at this moment. Surely the first man was equally torn between the spiritual urge to worship and the primal urge to ravish this warm, soft, and yielding creature in his arms.

"Sheesh, Dad, give her a chance to catch her breath."

"Yeah, come up for air, you two."

Blaine caressed Caroline's mouth once more, then backed away with a sigh.

She gazed up at him, mischief twinkling in her eyes. "Did you hear anything?"

Blaine smiled. "Come to think of it, no." Miraculously, the room had cleared and they were alone . . . together. He pressed his forehead to hers. "Now, where were we?"

"Paradise," she sighed, the ethereal green of her gaze inviting him back to that private place where only they existed, man and woman, made by God's love for the purpose of love.

Only a fool would resist . . . and Blaine was no fool.

EPILOGUE

Red and white poinsettias adorned the Edenton church and hall for a Christmas wedding. In the candle glow, supplemented by overhead lighting, friends and family focused on the ivory linen-draped head table, bedecked in red and green floral arrangements. Even the two sisters from La Quebrada had come out from their home in Idaho.

"Never miss the chance to share in the joy of friends," Eloise told Caroline when she called to accept Caroline and Blaine's invitation. Free of the wheelchair now, Irene held her own with her sister as they made their way down the small reception line, each one extracting the promise of a dance from Blaine and his brother.

After a dinner of home-cooked food provided by the ladies auxiliary, Mark Madison rose at the wedding party's table for the traditional best man's toast to the bride and groom. Tall, handsome, with rakish sun-bleached hair curling at the starched collar of a made-to-order tuxedo, he lifted a glass of sparkling cider.

"My brother said that his bride was the other half of his heartbeat. And if you have spent even a minute with Caroline," he said, "you'll know why."

He gave Caroline a look that bordered on flirtatious, but then, having been around Blaine's brother on more than one occasion, she knew that Mark looked at all women that way, regardless of age or marital status. Annie was completely in love with her charming uncle, and the sisters from Idaho were well on their way to the same infatuation.

Caroline whispered through her smile to the man at her side—her lifemate and lovemate. "Did you really say that?"

A camera flashed, blinding her.

"No," Blaine said, "but I *wish* I had." His candor was just as heartwarming. "Mark is the silver-tongued devil of the family." He breathed in her ear before pressing his cheek to hers for another blinding photo. "He inherited the gift of gab. I got the responsibility."

"And an equal share of mischief," she said, slapping

his hand under the table.

The girls had wanted a formal wedding. The church ladies wanted to go all out for Caroline in thanks for all the showers and wedding receptions she'd helped to plan. All Caroline and Blaine wanted was each other . . . but neither had the heart to elope and disappoint the multitudes. So they'd waited and planned the holiday wedding, giving them time to tie up loose ends and make arrangements to go away in advance.

Thanks to their depositions and John's testimony, Jorge Rocha and his henchmen were behind bars. John was serving a sentence in a United States federal penitentiary, for which he'd be eligible for parole in five years if all went well. He corresponded regularly with Caroline and Blaine, who helped him enroll in an online engineering school with the offer of a job, if he earned his degree.

"May the love and happiness you share," Mark continued, "grow ever more. Although . . ."

Caroline felt Blaine stiffen at his brother's pause. Although it didn't show that Mark had been drinking, they both had smelled the liquor on his breath when he arrived at the church. Not that Caroline had ever heard the charmer say anything crossing the line of harmless mischief.

Mark lifted his glass higher. "These are the first newlyweds I've ever known to return on their honeymoon to where they met and fell in love . . . for the purpose of adopting a child."

It was true. Neither Caroline, nor Blaine, had been

able to put the little Mexican boy out of their minds. Within a week, Berto was to become Alberto Marin Madison. His "I make thees" had become a slogan in the Spencer and Madison households. The church had even combined a wedding and toddler shower.

When Blaine and Randy traveled to Mexicalli to purchase the hacienda for the orphanage—another of God's miracles—Blaine gave the little boy a cell phone. The family had been talking with him, à la help from Father Menasco, on unlimited minutes ever since.

Which was another blessing, since the priest couldn't stop talking about the expansion project Blaine was working on. The owner, convinced that the rumor of the place being haunted would limit his chance to sell, all but donated it to the orphanage as a tax write-off. All they had to do now was raise the money for the renovation that Madison Corporation was designing gratis.

"What can I say?" Mark teased, shaking his head. "In one fell swoop, I have a new niece and a soon-to-be nephew. The bride and groom's cup, and their house, runneth over. To Blaine and Caroline, best of life, love, and happiness."

A chorus of approval and applause erupted at the toast's end. "Here, here!"

"Amen!"

"God bless!"

Blaine seized the moment to shower a few wishes of his own upon Caroline's lips. Although silent, Caroline heard them with every fiber of her being. A multitude of invisible caresses stirred the suppressed longings of the woman within, calling them to arms for the promise of the night at hand.

"Gee, you'd think our big brother was in love or something." The voice of Blaine's sister, Jeanne, drifted up the table from where she sat with Neta Madison.

Caroline reluctantly came down from the euphoria of her husband's affection as he pulled away to answer. "You better believe it, Squirt."

"If he isn't, it's too late now," Caroline told her.

From a family of two to a family of five. It still boggled Caroline's mind.

"Mom, Miz Dana is waving at you. I think it's time to cut the cake. Mom?"

Clad in green velvet, Annie looked like a snow princess as Caroline's maid of honor with the white fur headband and muff in lieu of flowers.

Next to her, in red, an animated Karen turned from chatting with her grandmother. "Yeah, *Mom*." A broad grin spread across her face. "I can call you that now, since you're official."

"You'd better."

Annie and Karen had stood up with Caroline and Blaine for the small candlelit ceremony, while Dana assumed the role of wedding planner. She'd coordinated the wedding and the reception—a priceless friend in more ways than one.

"I guess we'd better cut the cake," Blaine said, as their knife-waving friend caught his eye. "Before she cuts herself."

As he pulled back Caroline's chair, she realized for